Salutation Road

Salma Ibrahim is a novelist, short-story writer and marketing manager at UNICEF. Her debut novel, *Salutation Road*, while still in development, won the London Writers Award in 2019 and was a runner-up at the Future Worlds Prize in 2021. She lives in Greenwich, London, and has also spent a lot of time the Middle East and East Africa.

Salutation Road

Salma Ibrahim

First published 2025 by Mantle
an imprint of Pan Macmillan
The Smithson, 6 Briset Street, London EC1M 5NR
EU representative: Macmillan Publishers Ireland Ltd, 1st Floor,
The Liffey Trust Centre, 117–126 Sheriff Street Upper,
Dublin 1, D01 YC43
Associated companies throughout the world
www.panmacmillan.com

ISBN 978-1-0350-4434-4

Copyright © Salma Ibrahim 2025

The right of Salma Ibrahim to be identified as the
author of this work has been asserted by her in accordance
with the Copyright, Designs and Patents Act 1988.

All rights reserved. No part of this publication may be reproduced,
stored in a retrieval system, or transmitted, in any form, or by any means
(electronic, mechanical, photocopying, recording or otherwise)
without the prior written permission of the publisher.

Pan Macmillan does not have any control over, or any responsibility for,
any author or third-party websites referred to in or on this book.

1 3 5 7 9 8 6 4 2

A CIP catalogue record for this book is available from the British Library.

Illustrations © Sinead Hayward

Typeset in Fairfield by Jouve (UK), Milton Keynes
Printed and bound by CPI Group (UK) Ltd, Croydon, CR0 4YY

This book is sold subject to the condition that it shall not, by way of
trade or otherwise, be lent, hired out, or otherwise circulated without
the publisher's prior consent in any form of binding or cover other than
that in which it is published and without a similar condition including
this condition being imposed on the subsequent purchaser.

Visit **www.panmacmillan.com** to read more about all our books
and to buy them. You will also find features, author interviews and
news of any author events, and you can sign up for e-newsletters
so that you're always first to hear about our new releases.

To Hooyo and Aabo

Part I

'A cat in her home has the teeth of a lion.'

Chapter One

*'The teeth and the tongue are close neighbours,
and yet they sometimes bite each other.'*

The Greenwich Peninsula is shaped like an earlobe. 'It looks like an earlobe!' I once shouted out in class, to which my teacher replied blankly, 'Not quite.'

As a child, I discovered that this was where time stopped moving, right on Salutation Road. I used to imagine myself digging that dangling piece of land away from the rest of London, bit by bit, so that the Thames would swell up around it and we could be on our own little island. Many years later, as an adult, I savoured every walk home down the quiet, winding path and cloaked myself in solitude. In this static part of the city where no one lives and nothing grows, I walk away each time believing that life will stay this way for ever. I see the same strangers pass by on their way home from the Underground station before eventually acknowledging that they mean a little bit more to me than nothing. The same stray cat shows her quiet appreciation by blinking slowly. The rain holds back until I finish my walk. On this patch of land, I can walk out of one life and into another. Who I am and what I have been through doesn't matter. I'm just a girl passing through, and this place is like another country, another person's story far from here.

Nostalgia. It washes over me on these walks down Salutation Road. Over and over, painfully and tenderly. Sometimes it's a stabbing sensation lasting only for a second. Memories of my early life in London have become steeped in a purple haze, always in a particular lavender hue. In these memories, our house is filled with people, some of whom have passed on now. My father is often in them, so they must be pre-2005. He spins a silver globe to quiz us on every capital city in the world, and I am still too young to feel like I should be somewhere else. There's time to talk – really *talk* – and dream out loud. Frankincense burns on the mantelpiece, but it's too early to know what that scent will do to us in the end.

Nostalgia is the future telling the past that things will be OK, and the past rubbing up against it to say that they will never quite be the same. Sometimes it's a specific scent from a perfume or a person long forgotten. *Hey!* Sometimes it's a voice saying things like, *Remember. It wasn't all so bad. Some of it was beautiful* . . . I get so tired of remembering and deciphering things about the past that I don't understand, but I can't shut them all away. They're too big. The memories are like the pieces of broken furniture hanging out of abandoned skips on Salutation Road – they'll never fit.

It dawns on me that most of my youth has been spent in a repetitive cycle of work and survival. Yet I am strangely attached to this simple existence. I have a little bit of money that I am wishfully saving to do something unspecified – whatever it is, it had better be life-changing. Aside from that, I've got four pounds left in my main account. My desires are simple and tomorrow doesn't exist yet. I get myself a hot chocolate and continue my walk.

*

My brother, Hooyo and I left the apartment in a state this morning. There's a plate of leftover toast on the side, a pot of cold black tea atop the stove and a constellation of seven ajwa date pips dispersed around the glass kitchen table. My brother's schoolbooks and a carrier bag containing his dirty PE kit are spread out on the floor. The stillness of the apartment is unsettling. The home sounds that normally go unnoticed are now startlingly loud. The freezer buzzes loudly at random intervals, water rushes through the pipes and the voices of neighbours are as clear as if we were all in the same room.

I change out of my work clothes into a light blue cotton baati with white daisies and a hoodie. It's one of the oldest in my collection, but still as soft as the day my aunt sent it to me in a case full of clothes from Somalia. It billows in the breeze coming in from the open window and takes on its own delicate shape. Spent and cold, I tuck myself under my bed covers to rest for a while. Just behind the wall, near my headboard, my neighbours are ringing in the weekend with Donna Summer's 'Hot Stuff' and the barking of their new puppy. They are a young couple who bake bread and cakes from their kitchen and sell them at the Sunday market. They share their dessert with us on Christmas, and we always return the favour with a Tupperware box filled with xalwad on Eid.

'Siraa-aad.' My mum's voice floats into my room.

'Hooyo?' I step out into the hallway, where I find her taking off her coat. She grips the radiator as she slides off her shoes, still catching her breath from the long climb upstairs.

Something is off about her this evening. I follow her to her bedroom, where she opens the wobbly doors of her wardrobe and tears off her hijab. Her hair is a riot of dried curls.

'Is Ahmed home?' she asks. I shake my head. She rifles

through the neatly folded clothes, her agitation growing as she struggles to find something to change into. I hand her a baati from the side of her bed.

'This boy. This *boy*.' My mum usually starts her rants off in English and switches to Somali as her irritation intensifies.

'He's probably studying at the library,' I reason. We both know that isn't very likely. Ahmed is different now. He's probably roaming the blocks across the river with those boys from the year above. He stopped using the camera we bought for his birthday to try to find him a worthwhile distraction and he hardly touches his schoolbooks. He comes home just after dawn in rebellion against years of being told where not to go and who not to befriend. Every other week there is a report of a teenage Somali boy going missing or murdered. With these new friends, we can't quite work out what Ahmed is escaping or what he's running towards.

'He's ignoring my calls,' says Hooyo. 'Call him and tell him to come home *right now*. It's not safe outside. I saw it with my own eyes today.'

'Why? What's going on?'

'A man stopped me on the way home. Somali, but not someone we know. He asked me a few strange questions. I've never seen him before.'

'Questions?' I'm already on edge. 'About what?'

My mum looks genuinely disturbed. 'He asked me how long I've been here and if I need help getting back.'

'Back here? Why would he ask you that?'

'I just ignored him, of course. I think he was unwell.'

'What on earth did he mean by that? He didn't ask you anything else?'

'All he said as he walked off was *be careful*. Not in a

threatening way, but as though he was warning me about something . . .'

'He's most likely not well. Please don't talk to strangers around here, Hooyo. Next time, just walk away.'

She changes the subject. 'Make sure you call Ahmed, will you? I got a message from his teacher about his recent marks. This child will embarrass me to *death*.' She shakes her head slowly and slides into her light pink flannel dressing gown. It's a frayed old thing she bought from a market stall in Lewisham one distant winter. She struggles to let old pieces of clothing go, especially this one. She insists on wrapping herself in it every evening. The sight of it fills my chest with sadness.

'Ahmed's going to be fine,' I huff. 'He'll grow out of it.' I attempt to call him a few times, give up, and then begin to refold the clothes that she has piled up on her bed.

Hooyo asks me to pass her handbag from where it hangs on the bedroom doorknob. She pulls out an envelope from its outer pocket that has already been ripped open.

'Read this,' she commands, flicking her nails against the letter before handing it to me. 'Tell me what they mean by this? What do they actually mean this time? Didn't I tell them I'm back to work for good?' She starts to whisper things under her breath that I can't make sense of; prayers and lamentations mix into each other.

The letter is from her manager at the hospital. He says that all the sick leave she has taken has been putting a lot of strain on them, and that they can't afford to keep her on any more. In their words, they've come to the difficult decision to 'let her go'. I stop reading and fold it back into the envelope, my breath stuck in my throat.

'That's it. No more work,' she declares. 'No more work, no more, no more . . .' She's now half laughing, half turning her words into a strange little melody as she straightens her bedsheets to lie down. Her hair splays out around the pillow. I follow the strands up to their silvery roots. Her lips are rouged and dry, a helplessness lingering on them. How strange it is that only when she feels vulnerable does she doubt her understanding of the English language.

My mother lies in her bed, in the place where the contours of her body have created an impression over the years. For the past few weeks, she has complained of some kind of fatigue that she finds difficult to describe. She sometimes says that her mind feels numb and that it is hard to think. Often, she complains of an ache that spreads around her body and settles in her back. In all cases, she refuses to see a doctor. She is fine, she reassures me, she just wants sleep and silence. She simply puts on that dressing gown and disappears into her cocoon.

She draws up her knees into a foetal position. I have never seen her this way before. Despite feeling worried, I remember how my mum always says there has to be *kheyr*, goodness, in difficult times. The only reason she ever felt compelled to work so much was to fulfil the wishes of relatives who took advantage of her good heart. Part of me feels honoured by the knowledge that I now have to step up and take care of everyone. But a bigger part of me is afraid. She half nods and closes her eyes, as though she can read my mind.

I open the windows to let in the syrupy night air as she turns away to face the wall. Too many evenings have played out the same way. I ask her if she wants to eat dinner and she meekly refuses, but I ignore her and plate up some pasta or rice with a side of cut-up bananas and bisbaas sauce. It's always one large plate for the both of us on her bedroom carpet and a bowl of warm water for her to wash her hands.

When I come back to the bedroom with the food, she is

sitting bolt upright on the floor. 'Sirad, I was thinking about something,' she says, taking hold of my slim left wrist. Our arms are almost identical in shape and length, and even our complexion is the same coppery brown. I remember how relatives joked that Hooyo had given birth to a copy of herself. 'One day, Ahmed won't want to come back home.'

'What makes you say that?' I ask.

'It's inevitable. He's just like your father. He has his whole face and soon he will act just like him too.'

I close my eyes for a second and try to remember how my father's face looked. His thick moustache and large oval eyes. Ahmed doesn't have a moustache yet, but he has our father's eyes. 'But what does that have to do with anything he's done?'

'If you grow up and live long enough, you'll realize things always repeat themselves, just in different ways.'

I laugh it off and we finish our food in silence.

'I'm going to bring your medicine.' I say, after we finish.

'I don't want it any more. Keep that away from me.'

'But if you don't, you—'

'Sirad. *Please.*'

I relent and turn her bedroom light off as I leave.

I sit on the sofa in the middle of the dark living room, illuminated only by the light of the TV. The past few weeks have felt as though life is rising around me like a flood.

Tucked into the side of the sofa are a pile of unopened envelopes, glowing white. I already know what is in them as I rip open the seams one by one, deciding which ones I can put off for a little longer. I think of my cousin Osob who, at twenty-three like me, has never seen a bill and probably never will.

Outstanding payments, available balance, arrears, urgent notice. My stomach drops. I have no idea how my zero-hour advertising sales job will even begin to cover this. We are two months on from the Brexit referendum, and the general mood of the country is uncertainty and fear. I'm suddenly seized with the same emotions, as if they are diseases that were going to reach me sooner or later.

Tucked further down the sofa cushions, as though it has slipped there, is a small brown envelope. To my surprise, the address is handwritten, and so is 'For Sirad' in spindly handwriting. A minimal blue stamp embellishes the corner with a motto: *For light and truth*. I open this one carefully and stare at it, not yet reading what it has to say. The writing is barely legible but self-assured.

Dear Sirad Ali,

We hope you are as well as you can be. Rest assured that wherever you are, this message was meant to find you. You have been selected.

We are a small group of scientists from a London university which we cannot name. We are fascinated by technology and the topic of migration and find ourselves excitingly positioned at the intersection of both. While curating an exhibition on artificial intelligence and travel, we have found ourselves tackling some complex and unexpected questions. For so long, society has looked to technology to make our lives easier, but what if it could also make our lives more meaningful? What if it allowed us to be better people? With Brexit on the horizon and in the aftermath of the referendum, the I-word is on everyone's lips: immigration. The environment is startlingly more tense than ever before. We feel a sense of duty to do something more useful with our knowledge and resources, something that will heal our society.

We invite you on a special journey – a journey to cross over into a parallel realm for a day. A journey to somewhere both familiar and completely new. With your help, we want to use science in a way it has never been used before.

UNCLASSIFIED is a unique project that allows third-culture young people like you to experience their roots in an alternate lifetime. There is nothing artificial about this alternate lifetime. It is real and ready for you to access.

To begin, please take the C5 bus from your nearest bus stop on Tyler Street on Monday, 15 August at 8.00 a.m. Sign this letter below and bring it with you.

You can only make one visit, followed by an insight day at a later date where you will take part in discussions with fellow participants.

There is a war of ideas happening in Britain right now. Join our line of defence by taking part in this groundbreaking research.

Yours sincerely,
Olga Barker
UNCLASSIFIED

I stay up, reading the letter over and over again. This must be some kind of prank from someone who has way too much time on their hands, I think. I consider taking a picture of the letter and sending it to a friend, but I can't seem to shake the part of me that wants to believe it is sincere. Maybe there is *kheyr* in this, too.

A thin streak of light spears the window. Daybreak creeps into the apartment and my brother, Ahmed, along with it.

'Surprise, surprise,' I mutter at his hunched shadow. He's startled to find me in the dark living room, lying on the sofa in a daze. 'Is this how it's gonna be now? You just come and go like a ghost, without saying a word?' I fold the letter into the smallest square and tuck it behind my bra strap.

'Relax,' he says. 'It's Friday.' He drags himself to his room.

I catch my reflection in the darkened glass of the TV. My jaw-length, curly hair sticks up at angles. Bloated from the late-night eating, my stomach slightly protrudes through my clothes. An image of Winnie the Pooh pops up in my head, and I laugh at myself. I'm surprised Ahmed didn't take the opportunity to tease me about this.

I think about the letter. I wonder if it's one of his pranks. Whoever it is, they had me at *special journey*. I get up and open the window. The room becomes filled with sweet, cold morning air. Special sounds nice. Special is what I have been praying for.

*

On the Tube the following evening, I sit thigh by thigh with my old friend Rosie. We recently got back in touch and I agreed to meet her for dinner to see what has changed – and, more interestingly, what has stayed the same. On the way back from dinner, I have come to the sad realization that our friendship is disintegrating before my very eyes. I think we are both aware of how much we have outgrown each other. It feels like she is speaking in a new dialect that I can't seem to understand. After a while, she does most of the talking while I listen.

Opposite us sits a woman bouncing a baby on her knee: a sweet, drooling ball of fat. Rosie says that she feels like I've been avoiding her recently and, in my head, I agree; she can be insufferable at times.

'And oh! I forgot to tell you! I'm going to Rwanda next month to work for a nature conservation organization,' she says, smiling. 'The organization wants to preserve Africa's natural beauty. I'm going with a team of other expats from London.' She searches my face for a reaction.

I choose my words. 'Like one of those gap year things, except you're a grown woman?' I stare at the now sleepy baby across from us before turning back to Rosie. I think about telling her about the letter, but instead I make a face and say, 'Rosie, what do you know about Africa's natural beauty?'

'Well, I want to experience it. I want to immerse myself in another culture. Don't you think it would be good for me? I think maybe I could really figure myself out if I left for a while.' She puts her hands together and smiles.

I can feel my nostrils flaring. I think of Rosie 'immersing' herself in the whole of Africa like it's some kind of swimming pool. I wonder if she could have been behind the letter, too – but, frankly, she isn't bright enough to think of something like that.

'Oh please,' I say, trying to push down the envy that rises in my gut like acid reflux. Does she really think that Rwanda is eagerly anticipating her arrival? I stare at my feet. I suppose there are many things that people think a new place and a fresh start can offer them, but this conversation is planting something troubling in my mind. Something like resentment towards my own situation. I want to say something supportive, to congratulate Rosie in some way on the opportunity, but all I can think about is the fact that I will never truly know my own homeland in this cute, whimsical way. History will never allow it.

I take a deep breath and surrender myself to the thought that perhaps deep down, at my core, I'm suffering from the same ailments inflicted by city life as Rosie. The only difference between us is that she has the courage to at least attempt to seek some kind of cure.

I have to shout my words over the loud screeching of the Tube against the tracks. 'I'm glad you're doing this for yourself, Rosie. You deserve it.' I mean what I say, but it doesn't cool the raging envy.

In Rwanda, Rosie will get to be an expat. Here, after almost twenty years, no one sees me as anything but an immigrant. When I first heard the word *immigrant* used by Hooyo, I hated it. *Immigrant* – some kind of virus, some foreign body wishing to usurp its host. The whole country is talking about Brexit. The word *immigrant* features in almost every discussion.

I don't admit to Rosie that I hardly remember Somalia or much of my life there. I certainly don't lament out loud that soon Africa will belong more to her than it does to me.

'The next stop is North Greenwich . . .'

Together we weave through the tight patchwork of bodies to get closer to the Tube doors. As we stand tightly pressed together, surrounded by other people, I can't feel where my limbs end and where Rosie's begin. Each inhalation is a concoction of someone's cigarettes, body odour and perfume. The train stops and we all collapse harshly into each other.

Exiting the station, we hug each other and promise to text each other more. Rosie waits at the bus stop, but I don't want to hang around; I want to walk along the river and be alone. It's a quiet night, the air is warm and I need some time to gather my thoughts.

Even the silver outlines of boats bobbing on the river don't help to get Rosie's words out of my head. Where would I be if I had gone to university like her? If I hadn't told myself that I wasn't clever enough? Maybe I could have done pretty well for myself too. I never got along with the teachers, and looking back, I can't help but cringe at how I let their perception of me decide who I could become. I was the quiet, shy girl at the back of the class who often pronounced things incorrectly because that's how I had heard relatives say them. I was the girl who wasn't allowed to go on school trips if they required us to stay the night. I was difficult to engage, struggling to integrate, and eventually not worth trying to understand.

Music from the Greenwich Yacht Club slowly sinks into the water, along with the laughter of men and women. As I walk on, I start to calm down. Gazing at the glittery peaks on the surface of the river's tide is the closest I have been to starry nights. But so what? I have learned to love this place and its ugliness; the way that nobody really knows what brought them there and why they can't leave.

I start to think that maybe it would have been better not to have reconnected with Rosie after all these years. Boredom wasn't a good enough reason to call her. By now I should be able to sit alone in a restaurant, or read in the park by myself, while being wholly comfortable with everything that I am and all that life asks of me. When I met Rosie, we were twelve and both wore braces in bright, garish colours. She took me to her house in Blackheath, right at the top of Maze Hill, where we watched the sun set. She showed me her collection of *Girl Talk* magazines straight after the first day of school and we did the questionnaires, like *What does your hairstyle say about you? Which 90210 cast member are you?* In the middle of her large, messy bedroom, Rosie announced that I would be her best friend. I felt an enormous sense of relief that I'd managed to get the best friend thing out of the way much more quickly than I thought.

As time went on, we stopped reading *Girl Talk* and moved on to *Cosmopolitan* and *Glamour*. I read them until I stumbled upon the idea that 'dark skin' meant olive skin, 'sun-kissed', a 'healthy' brown. Girls like me existed at school and in the supplementary Sunday science and maths classes, but it seemed we never grew up to become the accomplished, beautiful women that featured in those magazines. We were born into society carrying all of our hopes and dreams, and then we dissipated into the air like mist.

Around the bend in the road, all of the residential buildings on the horizon slowly disappear from view, replaced with the portacabins on Salutation Road. I walk past the gate with the NO ENTRY sign and instead opt to cut through the trees, wading through the thick undergrowth and ducking under the branches until I disentangle myself at the other side.

An empty block of flats looms overhead, not a single window lit. Children's clothes still hang, stiff and bleached by the sun, on the washing line that criss-crosses above the concrete. A weather-beaten Spice Girls billboard from the late nineties is propped up at the side of the road, the wind rattling it to a steady staccato beat. Right underneath it is a Royal Mail van that hasn't been moved for as long as I can remember.

Objects are scattered around the area as though abandoned during some exodus. Furniture is grouped randomly in different corners of the car park. I love the bookcases and the little glass figurines, often broken, but still so full of charm. I walk over with a childlike sensibility, almost skipping, as if I am eight years old again. A Furby toy with a missing eye stares up at me from a plastic box.

It isn't long before the sickening feeling that I am not alone begins to set in. I turn to go back the way I came, quickening my pace. Something is watching me. Something or someone knows exactly who I am and why I came here.

As I run home, I can't feel my feet. I only hear them slapping the ground, hard. Past the roundabout I run, past the old clinic with its lavender bushes, past the car wash and the nauseating smell of industrial detergent that refuses to leave the place, long after it has closed down.

Eventually I'm locked inside the bathroom at home, shaken and knock-kneed. Yanking the tap open, I splash cold water on my face repeatedly until my eyes sting. Ahmed taps on the bathroom door and complains that I am taking too long. When I eventually come out he looks at my dripping face, his expression changing.

Going straight to my room, I turn off the light and draw my curtains together until they overlap. Under the covers I close my eyes, hearing only the thumping of my blood in my ears.

After some time, I get up, open the curtains and look down at the car park. I can see a group of hooded Somali boys on bikes, the tips of their noses lit by their phone screens. Their loud, uninhibited laughter and the sound of my mother tongue reassures me that nothing can harm me. This is my home and these are my people. In the distance, two police sirens harmonize, then split apart. The boys on the bikes stay there talking for most of the night. When they eventually cycle away, the silence that follows fills me with an inconceivable loneliness.

Chapter Two

*'Oh hyena, you cannot drag away hides
without making a sound.'*

Monday comes silently. The letter sits snugly in my pocket, but I'm on my way to work.

It turns out that the London Underground workers are on strike, so the rest of the city is having to rely on rail replacement buses. My bus is going straight to Stratford. I have never been on a rail replacement bus before, so the prospect of a new route to work helps to lift my mood.

As I'm boarding, the light on the travel card reader flashes red. 'You've got no money on it!' barks the bus driver. He settles his glasses on the groove of his bulbous nose.

'One second, that was the old one.' I rake my hand through the loose items in my bag: forgotten lip gloss tubes, crumpled receipts, a diary I've given up on, a half-finished packet of mints. The people behind me sigh and tut, causing my hands to become hot and sweaty. The line of people stretches as far as two sets of traffic lights.

I pull out my diary, shaking it by the cover to let the pages fan out. Someone's breath is on my hot cheek. Eventually I pull my card out from a forgotten compartment in my bag, and the driver waves me on.

Sitting at the front of the bus is a group of women wearing saris in complementary shades of green. A girl with long, glittery red nails taps away on her phone. Boys in school uniform hold a passionate conversation in the back. One boy, sitting slightly apart from the group but wearing the same puffy black jacket and green school tie as the rest, has his eyes closed under his hood. He nods his head from side to side to a phantom tune.

More people board the bus, but most of the passengers waiting at the bus stop don't get on. I find a space at the back, by a window. Relief spreads through my aching legs as I stretch them out before me, grateful to have a seat. A woman with vast hips eases herself into the seat in front of me and pulls out a thick, leather-bound book from her bag.

Outside, commuters watch the bus apprehensively. One last passenger hurries down the road and onto the bus just before the doors close. She's wearing a geometric patterned headwrap with thick gold hooped earrings, very similar to a pair I used to own before I lost them at a cousin's wedding last year.

The monotonous drone of the driver crackles over the speakers. 'The first stop is Mogadishu.'

No one reacts to this odd announcement, making me think I misheard the driver completely. There's no way he actually said Mogadishu. If he really did say it, it must be some kind of joke. I stifle a laugh. The girl in the headwrap keeps her eyes cast down and doesn't react. The women in the saris don't crack a smile either but begin to confer with each other, their expressions grave. The girl with the long red nails puts her phone down and stares pensively out of the window.

As much as I tried to forget all about the letter over the weekend, I couldn't. I try to put it out of my mind and focus on the day ahead, but the bus has barely moved in all of ten minutes. I realize that I'm going to be late again.

'Hi,' says the girl with the hoops, leaning over slightly with a soft laugh.

'Hi,' I answer, nervously. I wonder if I know her from somewhere.

'So, what do you think so far?'

'Well, I'm a bit pissed off actually. I'm going to be late.'

She raises a pointed eyebrow and laughs again. 'Hey, there's no such thing as being late to destiny.'

'Destiny? I suppose everything has something to do with destiny, right?' I begin to laugh as well, mostly at the randomness of the conversation. Her laugh is infectious. 'I mean, I get it. I support strikes, but . . . just not right now.'

She raises her eyebrow again as though not quite understanding what I'm on about. Then she unzips her backpack and pulls out a small photograph. 'This is my grandma.' She traces a finger across the surface. 'Wherever I'm going, I hope she's there waiting for me.'

I gather she means heaven. 'I'm sure she's waiting patiently for you.' I smile at her.

'I hope that's the case. What do you hope to find when you get there?'

I immediately want to say riches. 'Eternal peace, I guess?' I feel myself scrunching up my face in reaction to the conversation. It's completely bizarre, but the girl speaks as though it's the most typical exchange to have with a stranger.

She nods knowingly and puts on her headphones, turning back to face the front.

I cross one leg over the other, feeling unsettled by her directness. She caught me off guard. The bus picks up speed as the road clears ahead. We stop at a pair of traffic lights by

Salutation Road. To the right, a heavy sea of traffic approaches the Blackwall Tunnel. The girl with the hooped earrings is staring absent-mindedly at the patterned upholstery of the bus seats. In fact, she looks as though she can't take her eyes off it, and I let my gaze settle on it too. The red and yellow lines seem to merge into one moving entity of print, criss-crossing a stretch of blue like boats moving over an ocean. Sometimes they look like lines that could never meet. I blink slowly and look at them again. In some areas, the lines and circles seem to reconcile and I can make out shapes: the London Eye and Big Ben. When my eyes lose focus, the pattern is lost once again.

The bus careers down the slip road and begins to pick up momentum. The engine warms my seat and I begin to relax, feeling a little more comfortable now that nobody is talking to me. We plunge into the Blackwall Tunnel. The white lights overhead skitter off our faces and bounce around in the vehicle, lighting up parts of us at random. A sudden sleepiness overcomes me and I let it take over. Soon I will be at work, making myself a cup of coffee in the dirty office kitchen and typing numbers into spreadsheets.

When I wake up, I look through the grimy window smeared with fingerprints and dried raindrops. It seems much sunnier than before we entered the tunnel. Light pours through the windows, so bright that it's hard to see where we are.

I must have fallen asleep for a lot longer than I intended, because I can no longer recognize where the bus is taking me. My jaw drops open. White stone buildings with flat roofs blend into a pale oblivion. Brown cows and camels loiter by the roadside, as though waiting for someone to come and collect them. Everything within view looks like a photo being adjusted under a projector, lurching from left to right before finally settling still. I roll my eyes around under my eyelids, thinking that I must be in one of those sweaty anxiety dreams, but when I open them again nothing has changed.

A boy hurries along the street with a wheelbarrow full of large bottles of water. A frail white cat roots through an empty box of Pampers discarded on the pavement. A group of men sit at a patio under a tree, talking and laughing; one of them standing theatrically to address the group, prompting them all to erupt into more laughter. As the bus slowly passes, they look up, watching us cautiously through the window.

I examine our surroundings with fresh horror. Beyond the new-looking white buildings, separated from them by palm trees, I can see older, tomb-like structures. I have a feeling we're not going where we're supposed to be going. This is not any part of East London I recognize.

Checking my phone, I see that it's 10:45. I've been on the bus for roughly an hour. Somehow, while I've been asleep, something has radically changed. I consider the possibility that the driver has changed destinations and taken us to some underdeveloped suburb on the margins of the city. But the camels! Who can explain that?

'Is this bus going to Stratford?' I ask the girl with the red nails. She looks at me and shrugs, then returns to staring at the seats. I stand up and wobble up the aisle to the driver's seat, my legs shaking with every step. To my amazement, I find that he is now wearing a bulletproof vest over his uniform and a pair of black sunglasses.

'Stratford . . . not going to Stratford?' I can barely even form full sentences.

He doesn't look at me. Two beads of sweat slowly roll down his temple as he drives. 'Get back to your seat until we stop. I don't want to endanger my passengers!'

'But where are we?'

'Mogadishu . . . Wasn't I clear?' He looks me up and down with a glare. 'Do you have your signed letter?'

'Oh! Crap!' I dig my nails into my palms. The realization of what's happening is intoxicating; I'm still reeling from it as the bus comes to a sharp halt, jolting me out of my daze, almost knocking me over. I quickly wrap my sweaty hands tight around a handrail and steady myself as I pull the crumpled letter from my pocket. *A journey to somewhere both familiar and completely new . . . an alternate lifetime . . .* Everything that was both terrifying and exciting about the letter is now within my reach.

As I wait for the driver's guidance, the other passengers turn to each other in a frenzy of gossip. Except for the girl in the headwrap. She moves over to sit by the window, clutching her bag to her chest.

I notice I'm the only one standing, and people start to look up at me expectantly. A small girl in an emerald sari gives me a nervous smile, putting her hands together as if to say, *I'll pray for you.*

The crackling sound through the speakers returns. 'We have arrived in Mogadishu. *Ehmmm* . . . Sirad Ali, I believe this is your stop.'

The doors fling open, letting in intense heat and bright sunlight.

A great number of people – men, women and children – stand outside in long, orderly queues. Everyone is silent. The only voices are those of children. There seems to be a uniform look of anticipation on their faces. A woman raises her hand to shade her eyes and gives me a long, hard stare before whispering something to a man next to her.

'I don't know where to go from here,' I say, turning back to the driver.

'Keep them back!' shouts the driver. I follow his gaze and

see that he's addressing a group of soldiers. One soldier rests his finger on the trigger of an AK-47 that hangs casually off his shoulder. My excitement dissolves almost instantly. The soldier motions at me to step off the bus. Another soldier is collecting tickets from the people waiting, raising them to the sunlight, then ripping them in half. I look over at the girl in the head-wrap, hoping that she will say something.

'Off! How many times do you need to be told?' shouts the driver.

'Can you at least tell me where I'm supposed to go?' My tongue is so dry it feels like a rough blade in my mouth.

'Listen, love –' his voice softens – 'I haven't got the foggiest idea. I'm just a driver.'

I step off the bus. Things in my line of vision begin to shake again. I half expect a film crew to appear over the horizon. Maybe the person who wrote the letter is going to meet me at this bus stop and walk me through the next steps.

The guards let people move forward, one by one. There is a mixture of joy and tearful goodbyes. A woman in a black veil comes running across the street. In her slim hands she clutches a small, tattered notebook. She runs past the armed men and up to the bus doors as they close, gathering her many-layered hems up with one hand. Almost pleading, she knocks on the glass, but the driver simply shakes his head. 'Please!' she cries. She moves to stand in front of the windscreen and slaps her hands against the glass. Two armed men rush up to her in an attempt to coax her away. They grab her by the wrists and pull her away from the front of the bus. All of these people must have been hoping to get on the bus – the soldiers have clearly been sent to threaten them into staying exactly where they are.

An armed soldier walks over with a clipboard in his hand.

'Sirad Ali?'

I nod.

'OK. Stay here,' he says, in English. He walks off towards the other men. I watch him take orders from another soldier. He's quite young, probably no older than twenty years old. I brace myself as a wave of nausea spreads through my stomach.

'Your aunt is coming,' he says when he returns.

'My aunt?' I croak.

'Yes. Your aunt,' he reiterates bluntly.

Over by the bus, people are still clamouring at the closed door. The destination panel on the front still says STRATFORD.

'Could I have some water?' I ask the soldier hesitantly. 'My throat is so dry, I can barely breathe.' I can feel myself beginning to hyperventilate. I dig my nails into my palms and try to fight back tears.

He looks down at me with a sigh before turning away, crossing the road and heading into a small shop with pale pink walls and a bright green door – Noor Supermarket. A Lycamobile logo is stuck to the shop window and there are plastic-covered boxes of Tide washing powder piled up by the entrance. He comes out with a bottle of water and watches me drink until it's almost empty.

'Is that her?' he asks. A woman walks slowly and reluctantly towards us, dressed in a long orange and white garbasar and carrying a small leather bag.

'I don't know her,' I say.

The woman speaks to the soldier first. 'How long has she been here?'

'A few minutes.'

'Did you tell her anything?'

'It's not up to us.' He looks down at his gun, adjusting the strap across his shoulder.

I stand up and the woman steps back a little, looking at me, before slowly reaching for my hand. She forces a restrained smile and pretends to kiss the back of my hand, and I do the same out of respect. I desperately try to recall her face and fail. She is as good as a stranger.

She watches me intently, her face switching from mildly annoyed to a maternal concern.

'Let's go,' she says, already starting down the road. I hurry along after her.

'Where are we going?' I ask, stopping for a moment.

'To your parents' home. Where else?'

'Parents? The both of them?'

My so-called aunt cackles. 'They said you were British, not *dumb*. I'm taking you to the home where your parents live.'

The famous Liido stretches out before us. Inky dark bodies are swimming in a mellow azure. The sound of the call to prayer comes from a minaret across the street, soft and reassuring.

This is Mogadishu, Xamar, the place of my birth, the place I left at five years old before I could even understand why. Being here, despite its odd beauty, feels like visiting a terminally ill relative in hospital. I don't have much to say, but I look on with a sense of brokenness and feigned hope.

My aunt brings us to a narrow maze of off-white, crumbling homes. Women in colourful scarves sit outside talking. Their children chase a litter of ginger kittens. In the distance, the sea laps against the shore.

'Is it . . . *her?*' one of the women calls to my aunt. She is wearing large black sunglasses and has let a few strands of hair out from under her scarf. She flares her nostrils in subtle disapproval at the sight of me. They begin to talk about me, as if I can't hear and understand exactly what they are saying.

'Yes,' my aunt tells her. 'But don't say *a word.*'

'Oh, you have absolutely no idea what you have got yourselves into,' whispers one of the women.

'Does she even know Somali?' another says. They giggle among themselves and look back at me.

I stand there on the pavement, holding my work bag close to my chest, knowing that anything I could say about the situation would only further amuse them. Before I can think of a retort, I feel my stomach turn. Whatever I ate for breakfast is beginning to slosh around my insides. I press my fingers against a cracked wall for support. A woman in an indigo-blue baati steps out of the group, coming quickly to my side.

'Come on, dear. This is no time to be sick. Be strong.'

I cover my mouth, embarrassed, as my aunt begins reluctantly fussing over me in front of the others. She pulls out a phone and starts to yell at the person on the other end of the line.

The pretty lady in blue holds me steady as I struggle to keep my composure. Next to her, I realize she's hardly a grown woman at all – I doubt she is any older than me. I can feel myself weakening, on the verge of fainting, but her voice in my ear is clear: 'Please help us. Only you can help us.'

Chapter Three

'Let what is on this side of the bank be washed out by the flood, and what is on that side of the bank be carried away by the wind.'

As I fade back into consciousness, the first thing I become aware of is not the presence of someone sitting next to me or the feeling of the soft surface that I am lying on, but the smell of frankincense. I try to hold my nose and stop myself from letting it in, but it's too late. I completely unravel. I often don't realize the power that frankincense holds over me until I am forced to confront it again after such a long time. Until it makes me remember the things I desperately want to forget.

It was the Christmas holidays of 2005 when my dad gave up on life in England to go back to Somalia. The smell of frankincense burning that morning and his obscured figure in the smoky living room are etched on my memory. Some people find the scent soothing, but for me, ever since then, it has always been associated with powerlessness. This is something a dark part of my brain has decided for itself. It reminds me of the day my smiling childhood was snatched from me.

After that, whenever the semi-translucent crystals were

sprinkled over the hot coals on Sunday mornings, it would sting my eyes and make my nose run. The fragrance would smuggle its way into every room and demand acknowledgement. And it would cling to the walls for days.

I open my eyes to the unfamiliar face of an old man kneeling beside me. He rotates a set of prayer beads between his fingers while reciting verses from the Quran over my weakened body. As soon as he sees that I have opened my eyes, he retreats backwards on his arms in fright, like a struck animal.

'What are you?' he asks. His ancient eyes are filled with fear. 'If you're not Ubah . . . and she doesn't have a sister, then explain what you are. Are you human?'

'I'm just . . . Sirad,' I muster. 'I was brought here on a bus from . . . a different . . .' My voice trails off.

'I refuse to listen to this nonsense again!' He shakes his head, his body squat in a strange animal-like posture. 'You're a jinn. A filthy, imposterous jinn! That is the only truth.' It takes the effort of his entire body to shout at me. Sunlight filters through the wiry strands of his red beard.

He resumes reciting the verses, looking convinced that he can extinguish me, becoming progressively louder and more enunciated. Then he stops abruptly, wiping the sweat off his brow.

'Tell the truth, or I'll have to take further measures.'

'I'm not a jinn,' I croak. I pull myself to sit upright. 'This is my childhood home. Who are you?'

He closes his eyes and chuckles to himself. 'Your home? And how did you get here exactly?'

'I don't know the full story. Only that someone sent me a letter, and I somehow found myself here after catching a bus in London. I was . . . taken.'

The large living room has an arched window on the far wall.

There is a soap opera playing on a small, old-fashioned television in blurry, saturated colours over to my left. I recognize it as *Murder, She Wrote*, the detective drama that helped Hooyo learn English. There are low shelves filled with copies of the Quran and vases of various bright flowers dispersed throughout the room. The old man has stopped reciting and instead is staring at me – considering. He turns away and steps out of the room into a corridor. I try to call after him, but I struggle to form any words.

Gradually, now that I am alone, I begin to gain some control over my faculties. On the far wall is a cluster of family photos, arranged in a diamond. One of them features a woman with a ghostly powdered face and glossy red lips standing next to a man. It's me.

I gasp. I'm staring at a slightly younger version of myself. She isn't smiling. Her hair is brushed into a shiny, curly up-do, her chest adorned with yellow gold. By the style of her dress, it's clear this was taken at her wedding.

In the other room, I hear the auntie from earlier. 'Assalamu aleykum, uncle.'

'Wa aleykum salaam,' responds the old man. 'Where have you been? You left me trapped with her!'

'Don't worry,' she laughs. 'It's OK. She's not a jinn. Leave her alone. Let's just let her rest until her mother gets here.'

'She is not Bushra's daughter. Bushra only has one daughter, and her name is Ubah.'

'No, but you know what I mean.' He follows her as she steps into the room where I am.

Looking over at me, the old man says gruffly, 'If you're going to be here, just do one thing. Keep your mouth shut. Don't communicate with anyone outside.'

I nod. 'I'm sorry to intrude. I swear I didn't intend to.'

The woman brings me a bottle of water and a bowl of cut-up mangoes and papayas.

'Please eat something. And listen to Awoowe. He means well, he's just a bit –' She motions at her head with her finger. 'You know.' She gives me a big smile.

I let out a nervous laugh. The sliced fruit is cool and sweet. 'Shukran, habo.'

Without waiting for a response, she darts out of the room in a smudge of orange fabric. The old man continues to stare at me with a hard, serious expression.

'Look, I swear I didn't ask to be brought here! And I'm not a jinn. My name is Sirad Ali. I don't know what you're even talking about!'

I sit there eating my bowl of fruit, trying my best to tune out the old man's nagging voice, until a woman who looks exactly like Hooyo enters the room in a panic. At the sight of each other, our hands fly to our mouths in unison and we let out the same high-pitched squeal, freezing in shock for a moment.

The woman recovers first, turning to the old man. 'I told you! I told you so! I knew it was real!' She lets out a loud, triumphant laugh. It bothers the old man, who mumbles angrily under his breath.

'Hooyo?' I rush up to her.

'Not exactly. Just call me Mama. Welcome.' She draws me into a long hug and kisses me on the forehead. 'I've been thinking about you. I *knew* you would eventually come. I *knew* there was a reason.' She places her hands on either side of my face and levels her eyes with mine.

I have only ever called my own mother Hooyo. The word *mama* is vacant and easy to use.

She isn't exactly a copy of my mother, but something

uncannily close. The thick brows of the mum I know are two thin lines on her; the ring-shaped scar that my mum has on her temple is totally absent on this woman. The mole that my mother had surgically removed a few years ago is prominent on this woman's chin. I shrink from her touch, but she holds on tighter.

'Let me get you something to change into.' She takes long strides out of the room and brings back a baati for me: one of those traditional hid iyo dhaqan prints in red, yellow and gold. I throw it on over my white T-shirt and jeans.

Two young boys race into the room. They rush up to me, both amused and perplexed, as if they have just found a sea monster washed up on the beach.

'Wooo!' The younger of the two begins to jump up and down. 'Ubah is back!'

'Sweetheart . . .' Mama puts her hand on the back of the little one's neck. 'This isn't Ubah. This is Sirad.'

'Nice to meet you,' I say awkwardly, taking his little hand. 'And you are?'

The younger boy stifles a laugh and looks up at the older boy, hoping to find him laughing too. When the older boy doesn't so much as crack a smile, the younger one's face turns serious.

He completely ignores my question and looks over at my bag. 'Do you have games on your phone?' I shake my head. He rolls his eyes and pulls back his hand. 'Ubah always has games on her phone.'

Mama sits by my side on the sofa, and I start rambling an explanation. 'All I remember is being on a bus going to East London, where I work. In the same time it takes to make that bus journey, I ended up here! I don't know how that works.

It's crazy. But the letter says I'm only allowed to be here for a day.'

'London. Of course, it's London where you live . . .' Mama says, wistfully.

'What if I can't go back? What if I've done something wrong? Hooyo doesn't know where I am.'

'Don't be afraid,' she says, rubbing my hand. 'Without a doubt there is *kheyr* in this. Thank God for your safe arrival. Please don't worry about Hooyo, either. You'll be back with her by the end of the night.' Her voice softens with emotion, and she looks at the two boys. 'Take your brother upstairs,' she says to the older one. 'And you'd both better finish your homework, or you'll see what happens.' The older boy touches the shoulder of the younger one and they saunter out of the room.

Mama continues speaking as she stands up, her stately shadow rising up towards the ceiling.

'I know your life is very different over there, and I know you didn't plan to be here. I sympathize with you. This must be so confusing.'

I nod with a smile. 'Thank you. For making this easier.'

'It's not supposed to be easy, but we can try our best to make the most of the time we have together.'

'I hope I'm not being rude when I ask this . . .' I search for the most appropriate words, struggling with my limited Somali. 'Are you like my mother? Or similar? Or someone completely different?'

'Sweetheart, I can't say for sure. I think I am your mother — or at least, I'm your mother here, for today, and for as long as you want me to be.'

'What happens at the end of the night?' I ask. 'Will you just disappear? Will I go home and have my memory of the day wiped clean?'

Mama doesn't seem to mind my incessant questioning. She just lets me be. Whenever she doesn't have an answer, she scrunches up her nose and speaks with her right hand.

We sit there together, talking and laughing at the ridiculousness of the situation. She urges me to finish my fruit and water. For the most part, it's like having a conversation with my own mother. She talks about the weather, the herbs she has planted in the garden and what she wants to cook for lunch. Yet the difference between this version of reality and the one I just left is palpable. In slow motion, I become a part of a completely different timeline – one that has never existed.

'Let me finish preparing lunch – your father will be here soon. I can't wait for you to meet him. He is incredible.'

I hesitate. 'Does he know I'm here?'

'No. But just like me, he has been expecting you. Won't it be a pleasant surprise? Later, if you want, I can take you to meet Ubah.'

After Mama leaves the room, I'm so jittery I can barely sit still. To distract myself, I watch TV as the smell of her cooking fills the air.

The old man continues with his prayers. As I flick between a rerun of *Murder, She Wrote* and Spacetoon cartoons in Arabic, I can feel his eyes burning into my side.

During an ad break, I begin to panic about work. I think about getting up and leaving without Mama knowing. Then I remember the soldiers and their guns. It would break Mama's heart. I stay seated and watch this strange household go on around me. Wherever I am, I feel, deep in the pit of my stomach, that I have to stay.

When my father arrives, I am stunned into silence. He bears a great resemblance to my actual father, even more so than Mama to Hooyo. The first thing I notice are his heavy, slow footsteps. His head is entirely grey, and for the first time it occurs to me that my actual father is an old man too, not the thirty-something ghost of my memories. He doesn't look like the villain I have imagined, either; his limp gives him an air of vulnerability.

He greets the room without properly looking as he bends down to take off his shoes. I hold my breath. I don't want this moment to be prolonged, but it is unbearably slow. He unties the laces of his black shoes with difficulty, using one hand and then switching to two as his thick fingers struggle with the knot. His feet have callused heels, covered in millions of tiny cracks like shards of glass. There's something intrusive about staring at someone's scars, but I can't bring myself to look away. I want to know every mark.

Mama tiptoes from the kitchen and stands behind him. She has pulled up the long hem of her baati and tied it around her waist, exposing her slim shins. She stands on tiptoe and places her hands on his shoulders, smiling.

'Look,' she whispers, putting a finger under his chin and turning his head.

'No! No! It is not. It can't be!' he cries, staggering closer.

Mama nods vigorously. 'Yes! It is. It's *her*.'

My father rushes to my side on the sofa and examines my face with his hands, contemplating me as if I might disappear between his fingers. Then he reaches over and holds me in a tight embrace. I awkwardly place my hand on his back, startled by the sudden movement. I close my eyes for a moment and stand suspended in the bizarre feeling of being both right there with him and far away at the same time. All sorts of emotions overwhelm me at once – relief, embarrassment, anger. It hits me that whoever wrote that letter and called me here did so to mock me. I open my eyes before we pull away. I can still see the smoky living room of my father's last day in London and the back of his head fading away.

'Can I call you Aabo?' I blurt out. I am not sure where the question has come from.

He smiles. 'Of course you can. You can call me Aabo.'

Once, when I was younger and my father's presence was inconsistent, I repeated the word *aabo* over and over to myself, afraid that if I stopped using it, my father would disappear completely. There came a time when the word sounded like a word from an entirely different language. I couldn't mark exactly when, but it was a stinging realization. It stings now even more to say this to a man who isn't the father I was given. But perhaps he is the only one I will be left with.

A fat tear rolls down my cheek, catching me off guard. I scramble to hide it.

'Why are you crying?' he asks softly. 'Aren't you happy to be here? Because I'm certainly happy to see you.' He holds my hands in his rough palms.

'I *am* happy. It's not that,' I say, sniffling. More tears pour down my face. 'It's just that I haven't seen my father since I was twelve. And I haven't been back to Somalia since I left in 1998.'

He holds me as I finish crying. I don't know whether my tears are about the past or what I am being forced to feel right now, but I can't make them stop.

A green plastic rug is spread over the carpet and we all sit down around its perimeters, except the old man. He stays on the sofa, rolling the prayer beads between his fingers. Mama goes back and forth between the living room and the kitchen. I get up to help her, but Aabo stops me. He brings the rest of the food to the carpet and we sit together in a triangle around the food. I am a guest in their home, but it doesn't feel like a fitting position. I want to know what it would have been like to grow up this way, to be one of them.

Halfway through our main dish of rice and lamb shanks, Mama is the first one to talk. 'Things aren't always as simple in reality as they seem,' she says. It is as if she has read my mind. 'As blessed as we may feel, the truth is, our day-to-day life here is difficult. We often can't afford to eat more than one meal a day. If one of us, may God protect us, gets sick, we can't afford to seek treatment. But we trust God for our provision, night and day. And we love each other. That's more valuable than anything. Do you ever wonder what your life would have been like if you hadn't left Somalia as a little girl?'

'All the time,' I admit.

We eat in silence while I think about all the things that would never have happened if we hadn't moved. After a long time, I finish what I meant to say. 'But it's difficult to come to terms with the existence of a place where things turned out completely differently.'

'Of course! No one gets this kind of perspective. You can be forgiven for believing whatever you want. We are only given one life to live on earth, and even at the end of the night when you go home, you will still have only one life to live. But maybe you'll live it differently now.' I pour some bisbaas over my portion of rice. 'That's true. How did you know I was coming?'

'They sent us a letter. They told us about the university study and the opportunity they wanted to give you. We said yes right away. How could we refuse a chance to meet you?'

'Don't you think it's insane, though?' I ask, suddenly thinking of Hooyo, my real mum, at home eating dried fruit in front of the TV alone. 'I felt uneasy about it when I got my letter. Thought it was some kind of joke.'

'Me too,' says Aabo. 'I don't completely trust their motivations.'

He tosses half a lime onto my plate and watches as grains of rice fall from my hands and onto the carpet, not quite making it to my mouth.

'Would you like a spoon?' he asks, amused.

'No, no.' I hastily begin to tidy the mess I've just made. 'I'm a bit rusty. But I'll get the hang of it.' He refills my cup and continues to put chunks of tender lamb onto my plate. 'Come on, now. Eat well for me. You have a long night ahead.'

Mama leads me to her room to freshen up after the meal. She hands me a long scarf to wear outside, one that almost reaches my feet. I sit at her dressing table and begin to look through her collection of perfumes and creams, uncapping every bottle to smell them, searching more deeply into who she is. There is one bottle with just a few drops of perfume left: a woody, oudy scent that reminds me of Eid mornings. I dab a little onto the inside of my wrist.

In the top drawer I find several little glass jars of cream that each promise brightness, radiance or youthful skin. They have pictures of young, fair-skinned women on the front. There is an endless variety of them, each more fragrant than the next. Feeling guilty for snooping around, I quickly put everything back.

As I turn to face the mirror, I notice a photograph slotted into the edges of its wooden frame. It is a photo of Mama and Aabo. Mama is wearing a white cotton guntiino that clings to her slim frame. Aabo is holding flowers out in front of her. She is laughing at the camera, but his eyes are glued to her. Her smile floods my heart with a powerful burst of love, but also pain at how much it resembles my own mother's, only softer and brighter. I barely recognize the expression she is making, but somewhere deep inside me I know that my mother once wore it, tenderly and honestly, long ago. It was hers too.

Mama and Aabo encourage me to take a nap before we go out for the evening. Mama throws herself into cleaning while listening to an online conversation between two women that I don't quite understand. I don't want to waste even a second of my time here, so I decided instead to stay up, to help Mama clean and to people-watch through their window.

Eventually, I notice it's late afternoon. The sun perches on the old lighthouse by the shore. Mama joins me back in the living room and sits on the sofa. I want to fill the silence and say something about sunsets, but I change my mind and drink in the view. The water is getting darker and seemingly closer as the evening call to prayer is made. People bustle in the same direction towards the minarets, their figures replaced by slender seagulls as though they never existed at all. I watch as a little girl calls out to her brother. Before my eyes have a chance to adjust, two seagulls are skipping along in their place.

After we finish praying, the three of us go out together. We walk past a hotel overlooking the shore, where a wedding is taking place. Loud music and ululating women draped in glittering fabrics pour in and out of the front doors.

Taking a table in a quaint cafe, we drink tea from glass cups with peeling gold leaves. Aabo mumbles something about choosing this place for its view. The sharp taste of ginger slips through between the cinnamon and cardamom every so often. As it is poured from a teapot, I think about all the parts of me now healing. I surrender to the charm of the city. Mogadishu holds its place somewhere in the middle of tangible terror and extraordinary allure.

I have to keep reminding myself that this is not a dream. In dreams there are minor inaccuracies – sounds are never the right pitch, things are the wrong colours, objects don't have any texture when you touch them. In this world I've been thrust into, I'm experiencing the opposite effect. Everything is *more* real. I almost believe it more than the life I have already lived.

I watch in fascination as a man with a white beard drinks his tea alone at a table in the corner and scrolls through his phone. Everyone else has been coming in and out of the tea shop in groups.

'In peaceful times, things were so different here. It breaks my heart that you will never experience what that used to be like,' says Mama. 'There was a cinema across the road from here. There were theatres, art houses, beautiful places. The Cinema Equatore is where your father saw me and fell in love.' She smiles into her glass.

'We did not meet there,' says Aabo, glowing and stifling a smile. 'We met at her uncle's house, where the marriage details were finalized.'

'It was the first time I acknowledged him, so in my mind, that's where we met,' says Mama, looking down coyly.

'And then, just two years later . . .'

'Just two years married.'

'Everything changed in the city. Everything we had built and dreamed of was destroyed.'

They both hint at an intimate mutual understanding, their hand gestures mirroring each other. They speak of their memories in half sentences, in a way that makes sense to them the most. They are talking about the war, but in every way, they are talking about love too.

Mama changes the topic. 'There are different stories out

there about this bus service, you know. I heard the government accepted millions of dollars to be a part of the whole thing. They don't realize how dangerous it could be.'

'Is it a secret?' I ask.

'Yes . . . and no. Yes, in the sense that everyone is gossiping about it. No, in the sense that no one's allowed to report on it and there are still so many questions. The whole thing is a big mystery.'

'Anyway, let's take you back so you can meet Ubah,' says Aabo. 'Let's hope her husband isn't home yet.'

'Husband?' I murmur, remembering the wedding picture in the living room. It's so strange to imagine a version of myself already married.

'Do you remember that night in '98 when we almost left, but someone had stolen our car?' asks Mama as we finally untangle ourselves from a crowd of people leaving the mosque.

'How could I forget?' says Aabo. 'Everything was set for us to leave. And then, on the night we were supposed to go, we looked outside and our car was nowhere to be found. We were devastated because we had already planned so much. Your mother couldn't stop crying. I suggested that we go by boat – there was one setting sail the very next morning. But your mother didn't like that idea.'

'I was afraid of leaving by boat, so I convinced Aabo to let us stay and wait. The very next day, it was all over the news that the boat we planned to leave on had sunk in the Gulf of Aden that night, killing hundreds of people. Including babies. Including people that we knew!'

'I know it is difficult for you to understand our reality, Sirad,' says Aabo, noticing my shocked expression. 'And likewise, it might be difficult for us to understand yours. But I think we can learn from each other. Maybe if we had left Somalia a little sooner, or travelled despite the warnings, we could also be living a little better. But that's not how fate works. We had very little choice in the matter. In your version of time, you went with your parents as a five-year-old girl and left this place for good. In our version, we stayed.'

I wring my hands.

'You just have to accept that where you are is where you are meant to be,' adds Mama. 'But of course, not everyone finds that easy to do. Take, for example, our daughter Ubah. We love her very much and we've done nothing but care for her. She has been educated with all that we could afford. She has her family here, and her husband, who promised her a new life with better opportunities than she could ever have imagined. And he's trying – yet it's never been enough for her. She is deeply unsatisfied.'

'We've tried many times to stop her from doing something drastic,' says Aabo. 'I have caught her trying to sneak out in the middle of the night, too. Who knows what kind of trouble she would have got into if I hadn't talked her out of it?'

'Is she OK now?' I notice my heart begin to race at the mention of Ubah.

'Well . . . at least she's still here. But I don't know what it will take to keep her anchored for good.'

I know all too well that responsibilities don't always make people stay. I want to say to Aabo the things I've always wished I could say, as if he were my own father sitting in front of me – things I have rehearsed in my head many times before in our imaginary confrontations. But this man in front of me is not the man who packed his bags and left London all those years ago. He is not the one who called us from Somalia, every week at first; then on special occasions; then never again. That was someone else completely.

I don't know what to do with the anger in me.

'Come. Let me take you to Ubah's house,' says Mama.

*

Ubah lives in a modest home in another part of the city. We arrive in a three-wheeled bajaj and wait while a soldier asks the driver some questions before he proceeds on down the bumpy road. As we climb out of the vehicle, the street lights go out. By now the sun has completely set. Mama squeezes my arm. 'Don't worry, it's just a random power cut. They always seem to happen when you need light the most!'

'Don't worry,' Aabo echoes. 'Ubah is a nice girl. She's a bit sensitive these days, but she has a good heart.'

'Can you come with me?' I ask.

Mama's face turns sad. 'We are not on speaking terms right now. We love her, of course. But she doesn't want to talk to us.'

'What if I'm late? Do you know when the bus will be here to pick me up?'

Mama looks at Aabo, who answers, 'Midnight. We will come back for you when it's time to go.'

'OK. Thank you.'

Mama and Aabo walk me to the entrance of Ubah's home. Then they leave me there, alone.

Beyond the gate, the sky delicately shimmers with stars. Hanging on Ubah's pale blue front door is a plastic wreath of roses. As if on cue, the street lights flicker back to life.

I notice that the door is slightly ajar, but I make three firm knocks and step back. My mind begins to race. I want to be armed with the knowledge of what will happen after I meet her. Knowledge of how our lives will change.

Ubah, meaning flower. Maybe she lives up to her name in a way that I can't. Maybe she is waiting for me too.

I knock again.

'Ubaaaaah!' A woman's voice calls her name from inside the house.

I prepare a smile, not realizing that I am backing away until I feel a tree behind me. As I wait patiently for a sign that someone is going to answer the door, I try to accept that everything will change after this moment.

Chapter Four

'A sinking person grabs a straw.'

The housemaid makes me wait in the sitting room as Ubah finishes having her shower. Ubah takes her time with her shower, perhaps unaware that I'm on a time crunch. The housemaid doesn't say a word to me as she tidies the house, keeping her back to me for the most part. I perch on the edge of the sofa with my knees tightly pressed together and my sweaty hands placed on top of one another.

'I don't know if you know . . .' I start.

She startles, accidentally dropping a bag of charcoal all over the carpet, and stares at me. 'I'm her sister,' I say confidently. 'She's expecting me. Don't worry,' I lie.

The woman gives me a tight smile before rushing out of the room. She returns shortly afterwards with a tray of tea in a glass mug and some coconut biscuits.

'Thank you,' I say. 'But I've already had so much tea.' She shrugs and returns the tray to the kitchen. Her forehead has a dark spot, something that is supposed to symbolize a life of fervent worship. She looks deeply disturbed by me, but I am impressed by her composure.

She throws a long scarf over her clothes and races around

grabbing her things. 'I've got to go,' she shouts from down the hallway. Before I can respond, she has already left.

Ubah's living room is smaller than her parents'. There are no windows apart from a narrow, caged rectangle at the back of the room that reveals a small patch of night sky. There is a battered brown sofa for two, a carpet with a faded green pattern and a little herd of wooden camels on a low coffee table, arranged so that the baby camel seems to straggle behind. On the door hangs a worn, ornate display of Quranic calligraphy in greens and blues. The verse is *Ayat al-Kursi*, the Verse of the Throne.

The air inside the villa is balmy and heavy, like a tomb that hasn't been opened in centuries. There are no flowers or pictures of Ubah's wedding day like the ones displayed in Mama and Aabo's home, no shoes by the door or clothes lying around. No signs of a life being lived.

After a few moments I realize that I have been rocking back and forth, gripping my elbows tightly. I'm annoyed at how long Ubah is taking, but also a little grateful that I have some time to prepare myself. Her footsteps are heavy as she leaves the bathroom. I can feel my heart thudding in my stomach. The footsteps get louder, as though she is walking in my direction, then peter out as she enters a different room. I can't bear the anticipation. I gather the courage to walk up to what I presume is her bedroom and knock on the door.

'Come in,' she calls, in a smooth, low voice. I feel my shoulders begin to tense.

She sits by the window with her back to me. Her wet hair is dripping down her floaty white baati. I lean against the wall and look down at my feet.

'What do you want?' is the first thing she says, turning to look me in the eye.

Her eyes are dark and sunken, as if she hasn't slept in days, but she doesn't seem hostile. There is a disarming softness about her.

'Hi,' I respond. 'I'm sorry, I don't mean to just show up . . .' I catch my breath. 'It wasn't actually my idea to come here.'

'So why did you?'

'I thought I should come and meet you.'

'Well then, why are you apologizing?' She twirls a piece of her hair in her hands. 'You should only apologize if you meant to offend.' She covers her feet with the hem of her baati. 'I will spare you. You probably don't realize what you're being used for.'

'No,' I reply. 'Am I being used? By who?'

'The people who asked you to do this. They don't care about you or me. They only want to hurt us.'

'I can't speak for anyone else,' I say, defensive. 'I just came to greet you.'

'Under what circumstances?'

'I – I don't know.'

'Exactly. That's exactly the problem.' Ubah lets out a sigh. 'Welcome to Mogadishu. I hope you find what you are looking for.'

It is strange to watch her. It sends chills through my body.

'Listen, if you want me to leave, I can. I don't have a lot of time left anyway. The bus arrives to pick me up at midnight.'

She relaxes her expression and seems to smile through me. 'Calm down, Cinderella.' She pats the empty space next to her. I join her, sitting gingerly on the end of the bed. Somehow this makes me feel a little more at ease.

'This is the most bizarre thing I've ever experienced,' I say. 'But you – you're beautiful.'

'Don't make this weirder,' she retorts, throwing a pillow at me.

'This doesn't feel like a real place. I don't know how to describe it.'

'It's horrifyingly real. I guess from anyone's perspective, only the life they live feels real and complete.'

'But tell me,' I push. 'Why do you say I'm being used?'

'I've done a lot of research. It seems like, eventually, someone will get hurt.'

Ubah starts applying a qasil face mask from a small glass cup. She moves quickly and carefully, encircling her mouth and adding a generous layer to her delicate nose. 'If this was really a fair experience, wouldn't I be given the same opportunity? Shouldn't I be able to get on the bus too and see what my life would have been like in London?'

I think about her question for a moment. 'I guess you're right. It isn't completely fair. Maybe they're working on that side of things . . .'

Ubah laughs out loud. 'I'm amused by your innocence. If you stay here any longer, you will start to lose it.'

'I'm sorry,' I say sheepishly. 'I wish I had any say in the matter. I just wanted to go to work and have a normal day. I didn't choose this.'

'Do you even remember life in Mogadishu?' she asks. '1998 is a long time ago, right?'

She says something else too, but it's difficult to listen. Memories start to take shape, flooding my mind.

It was 1998, and I was just five years old. Even at that tender age, I had a strong awareness of the fact that we were living through times of immense difficulty. I was with my father in his restaurant as he served me a breakfast of canjero and kidneys sautéed in onions. I was just becoming aware of our sudden poverty and understood how hard my father had to work to feed us. I knew that my father was a kind man. I always saw him extend a plate to the hungry children that came into our cafe, and to surviving soldiers who were often missing a limb or two. In my eyes, he was the kindest and most generous person in the world. He loved our country unconditionally and his pride was intimately entwined with its beauty, with everything it had potential to become. Every other month, a family member would announce their departure to some faraway land, taking their children with them. Through it all, my father's love for our crumbling city remained constant.

But on that morning, something had changed. I noticed my father disconnect himself from life in Somalia all at once, visibly and painfully, as if turning his back on it. People came in and out of the restaurant all day long, and I remember feeling very small in the presence of so many loud, arguing men. A fight broke out. Someone had been pushed to the floor. Someone else had laid their hands on my father, grabbing him by his shirt. When the fight stopped and my father reassured me that it had just been a minor scuffle, I struggled to finish my food. I squeezed a piece of bread in the palm of my hand until it seemed to revert back into a warm ball of dough.

My childhood memories of Somalia mostly consist of pieces like that: fragments of near-death experiences and tense conversations happening around me. Second-hand moods and feelings; nothing I remember experiencing first hand. Sometimes, later, I would forget that I was even born there. Perhaps there was so much that I had suppressed, or perhaps I wasn't being entirely honest with myself about who I was and the reality of my beginnings.

I answer Ubah's question. 'When I remember Somalia, I remember my father. He was a huge part of our life here. He made it fun, even though everything was changing about the city. We eventually had nothing.'

'Where is your father now?'

'He left London in 2005, when I was twelve, and went right back to our childhood neighbourhood, got married, then eventually lost all contact with us.'

'Did you ever visit?'

'No. It was never an option.'

Ubah twirls the corner of her bedsheet between her fingers. 'Be glad, after all that has happened, that you got away from it all. You're quite lucky in that sense.'

'Well, not all of it. You can never really get away from things like that.'

At the foot of the bed I spot a plastic bag of clothes. I'm drawn to it because inside is a red puffer jacket with its sleeve hanging out. I wonder why someone living in Mogadishu would own a winter jacket.

'I saw the wedding photo in Mama's house. When did you get married?' I ask.

'Last year.'

'How is married life?'

'It's not what I thought it would be. But he's good to me. Sometimes I wish he wasn't. It would make it easier to leave.'

'And where is he now?' I ask.

'Working out of town.' She smiles at me as if remembering something. 'He's all right. He comes and he goes. When he's gone, I miss him bitterly and I just wait for him. When he's here, I am determined to run away. Isn't that strange? Come, let me get you something to eat.' She jumps up and adjusts her baati.

I keep repeating that I'm not hungry, but I seem to be following her into the kitchen. There is a pot of lentils on the stove. It's a small kitchen with a black-and-white chequered floor and a single wooden cupboard. Above the stove hangs a pink woven sign covered in soot: 'Home Sweet Home'.

She produces a chipped blue bowl from a cupboard above the oven where I can see a pile of other cooking utensils.

'I'm sorry I don't have anything else for us to eat today. My husband hasn't received his salary for five months. I apologize.'

'Please don't worry about it,' I say.

She produces a bag of bread from the cupboard and realizes there is only one piece left. 'OK. Let's go to the shop and get some more.'

'It's OK, Ubah. I'm not hungry. I already ate a lot with Mama and Aabo. You can eat that piece.'

'Oh, come on. The shop is just across the road!'

'But it's fine,' I insist. 'I don't want you to go out of your way for me.'

Her eyes widen when she looks at me. 'I'm not! I just need to get some bread. I've needed some for days now anyway. That's all that's missing and the dish will be complete. Don't make it a big deal.'

'All right, but can you at least let me pay? Maybe we can pass by an exchange shop?'

'Enough!' she hisses. I can't quite work out what has switched in her.

She goes to her room and comes out with all but her eyes covered. Her lithe, slender body disappears under the drapes of fabric. Her shoulders tremble as she ties the frayed laces of her shoes, and I realize that she is crying. Her quiet sobs are suppressed beneath her veil. She finishes tying the laces but remains kneeling on the floor for a little longer, completely exhausted. I reach out and put a hand on her shoulder.

'What's wrong?' I ask. 'Why are you crying?'

She drops onto her backside and puts her head in her hands. 'I can't do it any more. Please do me a favour and end it for me. Strangle me. It would be the easiest thing to get away with. You could leave me here dead and just go back to your life. No one would be able to hold it against you.'

'Ubah – I . . . I'd rather be kind to you instead.'

'You don't understand. That would be the kindest thing you could do for me.'

*

Stepping outside for a second time, it's harder to ignore the parts of the city that are determined to endure. There are scattered signs of a history that has outlived me and a future that I may never come to know. Now at night, the city of Mogadishu is defiant with youthful energy; the streets are crammed with cars and teetering new building developments that make a promise of peace over the mingling people. There are lambs and donkeys and people talking loudly to each other. There is hand-holding, shirt-grabbing, and armed soldiers lining the main road.

Ubah walks fast, dipping and weaving among the market shoppers. I trot along to keep up, my flat doll shoes failing to protect my feet from the sand. For a moment we are separated by three-wheeled minibuses crammed full of people heading towards the ocean. Out come a group of young boys in matching blue football kits, playfully pushing and shoving each other.

A young girl sits by a table piled with shoes for sale. A teenage boy walks around with phone cases and keychains displayed on a board that hangs off his body: the Empire State Building, the Sydney Opera House, the Eiffel Tower. Two women stand behind a table of jewellery; above them on the roadside is a sign saying 'Bishaaro Gold – Dollars Only'. Hawkers walk about, shouting their wares.

Ubah brings us back into conversation. 'I had a friend that made it all the way to America on her own with a fake passport. She met a guy with a lot of money and got married. She received her body weight in gold. She doesn't need to work; she doesn't have to do anything! It amazes me how easy some people have it because of their fate.'

For a long time, it was rumoured that my neighbour was a benefit thief. I've heard my mum and her friends talking about it before. Some of my mum's friends pitied her and some of them spoke about the story with rage in their voices. My mum always said that the food a thief buys with stolen money will never make them full; instead it'll make them hungrier and hungrier, body and soul. In those days, I thought it was always wrong to lie, but then I grew up and learned that a lie can sometimes be the only thing between life and death.

We arrive at the grocery store. Ubah puts a small loaf of bread wrapped in paper on the counter, along with the money. The shopkeeper bows his head disappointedly. 'You know, you still owe me from last time. And the time before that. And ah yes, the time before that too.'

Ubah, embarrassed, speaks in a low voice and leans in. 'Please, just this last time. I have a guest.'

The shopkeeper scrunches up his face. 'OK. But make sure you send me the rest before you set foot in here again.'

Ubah sighs with relief and grabs the bread. 'Thank you.'

As we leave, her eyes playfully dart over to me. 'Let's get some gelato.'

Her arm slips into the crook of my elbow. She leads me across the street to a small ice-cream parlour owned by the same family as the grocer's. She orders a Neapolitan ice cream;

I choose a vanilla and almond cone. We walk along the seafront, still arm in arm, right under the moonlight, until we have finished our ice cream.

'Is it midnight yet?'

'No. It's probably ten p.m. or something. Why?'

'Good. I don't want to leave yet.'

*

We return to the house. Instead of changing back into the white baati, my double wears a pair of light blue jeans and a slim-fitting tank top that shows off her tiny waistline.

I'm relieved to find she has forgotten about the dinner situation. She leaves the living room and heads to the bathroom, shutting the door with a bang. I can hear the sound of her vomiting, then a long trickle of water.

'Let's go to my room. I need the window.'

She hoists herself onto the window frame in her bedroom, half in and half out, lighting a cigarette. I try not to stare and instead pretend to occupy myself with re-tying my hair in the mirror.

'I'm sorry,' she says. 'I hate the smell too.'

'No! I can barely smell it. Do whatever you're comfortable with.'

She smokes it down to a stump. On her last exhale, she bares a gold tooth in a self-satisfied smile. Her face flushes red. She tiptoes towards me and lets herself fall onto the bed like a flaccid balloon. Both of us lie there, our heads touching.

'Sweet food makes me nauseous,' she says, groaning and rubbing her stomach. She wipes away the sheen of sweat above her lip with the back of her hand. 'I don't like feeling so heavy.'

'Is it always so lonely here?' I ask. 'What do you do about that?'

'I don't let it get to me. I try to keep myself busy.'
'Do you spend much time over at your parents' house?'
'Not these days. They're pushing me to start a family.'
'And you don't want that?'
'Not right now. I'm trying to escape that. There are places I want to go where I can't bring a family with me.'
'What do you mean?' I ask, rolling over onto my front to relieve the soreness in my hip from the springs in her mattress.
'I'm planning on running away soon and leaving the country.'
'But why? You have your own peaceful little place, and a good husband, and parents who are still blissfully in love.'
'Do you hear yourself, Sirad? Why can't I want more? Why should this be it?'
'No, I understand. But the journey – people often end up in worse situations.'
'It didn't stop your parents, did it?'
'No, but it could have ended badly for us too.'
'What's different about it? They wanted to change their situation, and so do I.'
'But where will you go?'
'I don't know . . . Italy, Sweden, maybe even London? I've always heard that Norway is beautiful, and I have an uncle who lives there who might be able to find me a place to stay. If I can get on this bus ride and get to London, then it doesn't have to be much of a journey.'
'Will you go with your husband?'
'God forbid, no!' She laughs out loud. 'And don't you *ever* tell anyone about this conversation – definitely not my parents.' She turns over onto her stomach too. We are eye to eye.
'Listen,' I say, grabbing her wrists. I am struck with deep empathy for her. 'You can't make the journey. You can't.'

'I'm not you, Sirad. We may look the same and all of that, but I am not you.'

'I just care about you.'

'Well, for your own sake, don't. We share nothing but a reflection in the mirror.'

I'm stunned for a moment.

'But we're here now, sharing the details of our lives with each other. That must count for something?'

She shrugs. 'I really do admire your determination to understand me. If there's anything I have learned about you today, it's that you care so much, but it's hard to pinpoint exactly why. You can soon go home and wash your hands of what happened today. You can forget my story.' She turns to lie on her side with her arm propped under her head. 'Were you told that old bedtime tale about the half-bodied woman?'

'I don't think so. What's it about?'

'It's about a woman who has half a body and wanders the city at night. People are afraid of her because she's only half a woman, but so powerful. She's a villain in the story. And because people are afraid of her already, she uses that power to keep herself safe from other dangers. She makes people give her their money and she eats them afterwards.' Ubah squeals with laughter.

'You were told stories like this as a child?' I ask, thinking of my battered copies of *Biff and Chip*, bought at the school book fair.

'It's my favourite story. It is the most honest thing anyone has said about our people in centuries. It is more truthful than history.'

*

Outside Mama and Aabo's house, we huddle together to say goodbye as the soldiers wait by the gate. It is a bittersweet end to a long and extremely surreal day. I start crying. I cling to these alternate parents as we embrace and I weep shamelessly in front of them. Each time a tear slides down my cheek, a new one follows in its path.

'Go and make something of yourself. Don't worry about us. We'll always think of you,' says Mama, with that same motherly concern. I bury my tearful face into her neck as we hug each other.

'Think of us often, as we will think of you.' Aabo's voice follows closely behind.

'Will I be able to come back again?' I ask him. 'I *have* to come back. They can't just bring me here and take me away!'

He places his hand on my head. 'Why would you want to come back, dear? You had today. Keep the memory of us close. You still have your family on your side of things. Take care of them. Make peace with where you have been.'

'Things won't be the same. How can I go back there and expect things to stay the same?' My voice is shrill. I notice that I am grabbing onto Mama's arm with both hands. I am fighting a force bigger than them – I want to fight the air. Anything to vent my frustration.

'Your life was never meant to stay the same, Sirad,' says Aabo. 'It just has to be righteous and honest.'

Ubah stands awkwardly to one side, watching me. I let go of her parents and move towards her. She holds me tightly.

'You have no choice but to be strong for yourself. I'm coming. One day I'll show up in your city and maybe we'll find each other.'

'Am I able to call you, or reach you in any way in the meantime?'

'It won't work.'

'Well, if you get to London – *when* you get there – come and find me.'

'Hurry up!' call the soldiers, waving at me impatiently.

'Here.' Ubah passes me her phone and prompts me to save my number. 'Now go look after your mother and that brother of yours.'

We hug one final time before I follow the soldiers to the bus.

The driver rests his head against the steering wheel as I search for my travel card. In the split second I place my card on the reader and watch it turn from red to green, something inside me comes undone. I watch the driver search for my name on his clipboard register and mark a tick against my name.

Some of those on the bus are the same passengers I saw earlier. The women in their green saris have since changed into various shades of pink and gold. The boy in the hooded jacket sits up in an unnaturally upright posture. Each person's face tells a separate story, stories that could probably fit together seamlessly, end to beginning, like one long, continuous fable. Now we are homebound. Everyone on the bus is silent, deeply aware of what this journey has unleashed within us.

I take in the scent of Mama's baati before taking it off, searching for the faintest scent of frankincense, hoping that now it can take on a new meaning. But I can't smell anything. It's almost as though the memory of the day is slowly beginning to distance itself from me.

Ubah is right, I think, as I make myself comfortable in my seat. This whole operation is unfair. If I am allowed to walk into her world for a moment and witness her pain and sadness, only to leave without being able to change anything – then I become an active participant in it.

I accept the fact that this visit has not been about finding something but about taking it forcefully, as though it has always been mine. Mama, Aabo and Ubah never belonged to me. I wish I could say that visiting them will be my only crime. I know from the moment I take my seat that it won't be.

Chapter Five

'When a man sleeps, he is the same person when he wakes up.'

The bus stops on Salutation Road at almost 1 a.m. I feel my stomach drop as the driver announces the end of the journey. Some of the passengers who rode the bus with me are getting picked up by relatives. I decide to walk home, picking up the pace as fast as I can, struggling to ignore the ever-present feeling that I am being watched. When I get to the end of the road and see the residential homes come back into view, some of them with their lights on, I relax a little bit. A sour smell of rain and dirt hangs in the air, but it is a relief to know that I'm not far from home; and that, on this side of things, my brother exists, and I still have somebody to call Hooyo.

As I push forward, a cool, strong breeze picks up behind me, rustling newly dried leaves as though propelling me further along my journey, urging me towards an inevitable confrontation.

Still reeling from the shock of the experience, I don't have the energy to face anyone just yet. Evidence of where I have been clings to me as I make my way towards our building; I can still feel Mogadishu's sand in between my toes. I'm carrying Mama's baati in my bag. Even the moon in the sky that lights my path home is the same wafer-thin crescent I saw in Mogadishu earlier tonight.

Pushing the warm, stagnant air with my arms, I walk briskly down the street, confirming with relief that everything is exactly the same as I left it. Every so often a car zooms past me with its speakers blaring loud music, then the bleak stillness returns. I'm still wearing a pair of black flip-flops I took from Mama's house. I decide to stop by a 24-hour McDonald's to change in their toilets.

I consider whether my every step is being recorded. It isn't too far-fetched, perhaps, considering everything that has happened today. My reflection in the toilet mirror catches me off guard. I trace big dark rings around my eyes with my index finger and notice that I'm bleeding from a crack in my bottom lip. I take off my scarf and retie my hair before pulling on my cardigan. Seeing myself in the mirror after spending a day with Ubah feels like she is staring back at me; I half expect my reflection to talk to me.

Leaving the restaurant, I see two men in fluorescent jackets tearing hungrily into burgers. They look up at me as I pass them. Picking up my pace, I continue down the street, intending to go home until I pass Emre's coffee shop. It's one of the few coffee places close by that I know stays open until the early hours of the morning. It is safe and familiar, and those are two feelings I desperately need.

In the daytime, Emre's operates as a standard cafe, serving the usual hot drinks and Turkish pastries. In the evening, it transforms into a shisha lounge where university students often gather. Despite the loud students, the place usually has good energy. They run a weekly soup kitchen and food bank for the homeless and struggling families. The owners don't seem to mind if you spend hours in one place with a cup of tea and a book.

The neon lights of the sign flicker in the darkness. There aren't many students inside as it's nearly closing time. Duman, the cafe's ginger cat, stretches out on the counter and rolls into the shape of a croissant, his fur blending in with the terracotta walls. I reach over to stroke him between his ears and he responds with a loud purr.

'Are you OK, darling?' says the barista. 'It's a bit late, isn't it?'

'I know,' I reply, 'but you're not closing now, are you?' I try to disguise the desperation in my voice.

'No, no, of course not!'

I order two potato boreks and a glass of pomegranate tea.

'Take away, or . . . ?'

'No, I'll just stay here for a bit, if that's OK.'

'Sure! Of course!'

I pull out my phone as it buzzes with delayed messages. Two messages from Rosie, two missed calls from my boss and three missed calls from Hooyo. I send Hooyo a message, worrying she will start calling everyone I know, if she hasn't already. *I'm OK, Hooyo. I'm coming soon.*

Duman follows me to my seat, perching on the ground beside me in the hope of some scraps of food. The snack pacifies my anxiety and helps to alleviate the taste of metal on my tongue.

The laughter of a few students in the back trails through the cafe. I can hear a few words of Somali here and there. I wonder if they know about the bus. Maybe they do. Maybe by the morning it will be national news.

I begin a hopeless investigation online into the bus and the letter. Someone, somewhere, must have answers. I check the Transport for London website and sift through countless updates on the Tube strike to look for anything even remotely connected, but there is nothing. I apply every keyword I can think of to a new Google search – *Stratford rail replacement Mogadishu* – and look through several pages of results.

My tea is now cold, but I finish it anyway and sit there perusing the drinks menu and fiddling around with the salt and pepper shakers. I look up and out of the high windows at a tiny triangle of sky left between the new building cranes. The barista begins to spray and wipe down the front counter. I catch her stealing a few glances at me. Could she know something? I wonder. Each time she looks over, her gaze hovers for a bit longer. I scoff the rest of my food down and gather my things.

*

On my way back, I pass the town hall where we were given our British citizenship one sweltering summer's day. It still has its lights on. *Naturalized.* I love that word. It sounds so crisp and clean. I am a citizen of this city and it feels natural. Mogadishu is the past, and I won't get it back. Ubah is a figment of something I can't yet figure out. But *this* is home.

I can recall that day clearly. They gave us tea and small slices of Victoria sponge in the foyer. There were lollipops for the children. Hooyo twirled around on the sunny street with a girlish joy. She felt as if she had graduated from university, her course a long emotional battle with paperwork and arbitrary questions.

My dad was annoyed by her apparent glee. I could see that he was putting a damper on her mood. I flounced around in the ugly pink tulle dress she had made me wear. I'll twirl too, I thought, just to make her feel better.

I remember the days we lived in our uncle's house, the first place we lived when we arrived in London after months in a cramped Dover detention centre. We slept in the living room, which had a fireplace and a bookshelf filled with my uncle's university books. His wife didn't like us being all up in her space or me playing with her children's toys. She tried her best not to let it show, but I sensed it anyway.

Some nights, I lay dreaming about all the possibilities of life after our arrival. Usually these were good dreams. I had heard about Hamley's and I dreamed about buying toys and teddies three times bigger than my body. Often, I dreamed of walking with Hooyo for hours on end along a motorway and then arriving at a house filled with sweets.

One night I suddenly woke to find my entire body drenched in a cold sweat, reliving the scenes of a recurring dream. It would always start with a knock on the door. Even at a young age, I was afraid of people coming to raid our room in the middle of the night and take us away. I had heard the adults talking about them. I began to think that maybe we had overstayed our welcome, that maybe our papers would one day mean nothing. After all, it was just paper to me. You can rewrite anything that is written on paper.

*

At the end of the long road, I eventually arrive at our estate. In the centre of the car park, where the concrete cracks and dips into the ground, is a wide and deep puddle of rainwater. Our tower block trembles in the reflection like a teetering stack of Jenga.

I run up the stairwell inside. From another home, the sound of the television erupts out into the hallway with laughter, applause and whistles. I felt like I'm on a game show myself, being heckled and jeered at by a crowd. Just before I reach our floor I rest a short while, gripping the metal banisters. A current of panic passes through my chest as I try to think of some kind of explanation for where I have been.

My mum is sitting cross-legged on her bedroom floor with the safe open and her gold jewellery on the carpet.

'Sirad, where have you been? What time do you call this?' She lifts her chin pointedly at the clock above her door. I rush to embrace her, hugging her so tightly that I can barely hear what she's saying.

'I – I had dinner with some friends after work. Sorry.' I'm smiling at her like a maniac. I kiss her on the forehead and squeeze her arm, making sure she's definitely my mother and not some strange copy of her.

'Friends? At this time? Sirad, what has gotten into you?'

'Sorry, I forgot to call.'

'How irresponsible! I was getting worried! You never disappear like that. What makes you think it's OK to do that now?'

My palms begin to sweat, making the keys in my hand slippery.

'You should be careful about where you walk when you're alone,' she continues. 'You don't own these streets. They're dangerous.'

'OK, Hooyo.'

My mum returns the gold to the briefcase. She produces a calculator from her lap and narrows her eyes in focus as she taps in the numbers, glancing from the calculator to the gold and then back again. She rubs an open palm over her face with a yawn. I can't help but compare her to Mama. Despite her troubles, Mama looked radiant. She was hopeful, with a serene spirit. Hooyo, sitting on the floor in her tiny room, is like a dolphin that has been taken out of the ocean to swim in a cramped glass tank. Noticing the difference between the two makes a tear swell in my eye. I want so badly to sob into my mother's lap like I am a child again and tell her everything that has happened.

'Sirad, dear, I haven't got any energy left. Will you heat yourself up something to eat? There's some chicken in the oven.'

'OK.' I hold onto the door frame, leaning on it with all my weight.

'I was on the phone to the council for over an hour today and couldn't get through to anyone about the boiler. Did Ahmed tell you about the books he needs for his psychology revision? He has a whole list of things he needs. Can you help him out with some money?'

'Of course.'

'You know he has nobody but you and me.' She stretches her legs and gets up off the carpet. On goes the dressing gown again, wrapping itself around her, tranquillizing her. In a sleepy voice, she asks me to turn out the lights.

Clothes are strewn around my room. I throw myself onto the bed and read the unread text message from Rosie: *Hey! Up for meeting up this week?* I delete the message and grab my towel to go and take a shower.

Under the falling water, I sit on the floor with my knees up to my chin, letting the hot water soothe my aching body. A new feeling of sadness spreads through me as I remember my evening with Ubah. I let the hot water hit the top of my head until I can barely feel it any more.

*

In the morning, my alarm rings in my ears on the highest volume. I can't bring myself to eat breakfast, so I pick at a bowl of trail mix that has been sitting on my bedside table and occupy myself with further bus journey research until it is time to get ready.

Attempting to go back to life as normal, working in a dingy

office selling magazine advertising space and living as I have always done seems ludicrous now, but I know I have to approach my life with a new sense of responsibility. After yesterday, I am craving some normalcy.

*

I arrive at work fifteen minutes early. The man who sits next to me, whom I refer to in my head as 'lipsmacker' because he chews loudly when he eats, tips his head towards me and smiles mischievously. 'Well, well. Where have *you* been? Miss I-Never-Take-a-Day-Off.'

'I'm not in the mood this morning, Kevin,' I snap, just to get him off my back. He raises his eyebrows and opens up a packet of prawn cocktail crisps.

My manager hovers around my desk. I didn't even notice her walk up to me. Earlier this morning I sent her an email about my absence the previous day, and I took it that she accepted my excuse: something about a family emergency that I didn't go into. As she rifles through some papers on my desk, I silently pray she won't ask to speak to me in her office about reducing my shifts. She jokes with the others and shows them her new necklace that her boyfriend bought her. There are murmurs about a leaving do last night that left some of the executive team in a sorry state.

I get up to make a cup of coffee and help myself to a slice of cake that somebody has brought in. Listening to the kettle boil, I wonder anxiously if I should actually go over to my manager and explain myself in person. Eventually I decide against it and return to my seat.

The day drags by. I work through all four hundred of my unread emails and a never-ending stream of telephone numbers on a spreadsheet. The executive team pretend not to watch, but they are always watching. One of them has sent me a message asking if I have booked in my shifts for the week. I'm deeply exhausted and can no longer manage to fight to stay awake. I only notice that I have fallen asleep when I feel the drool on the back of my hand. Once again, there is the heavy presence of my manager standing behind me like some kind of shape-shifting ghoul. My colleagues and I secretly call her Mad Mandy when she does things like this. Aside from that, she is quite nice and mellow. She gently puts her hand on my shoulder and crouches down next to me.

'You dozed off. Is everything OK, Sirad?'

I sit upright and wipe my mouth. 'I did?' Blood is thudding through my ears. 'Sorry. I didn't get much sleep last night.'

'Really?' She purses her lips and places some loose papers for filing on my desk. When she walks away, I load up a new tab and continue my fruitless research into UNCLASSIFIED.

*

Throughout September and October, the world holds its breath, eagerly awaiting the outcome of the US presidential election in November. This is bigger and darker than Brexit, I think. Something is changing globally, or perhaps I'm just more attuned to it. One morning I sit in the kitchen while Hooyo makes malowax with Nutella. Each time she finishes one, she slides it onto my plate straight from the pan and I smother it in brown sugar or chocolate spread. Ahmed pops up out of nowhere to steal a piece from my plate until I slap his hand away. Hooyo shows me a picture on her phone of an empty piece of grassland surrounded by a wire fence.

'What am I looking at?' I ask.

'I'm going to purchase this land one day and build a house.

That's where we're going when they eventually kick us out of here.'

I want to laugh, but she's serious. It doesn't seem like a bad idea. She scrolls through her phone for pictures to show me the kind of farm she envisions. The more I see of it, the more I buy into the idea. If that's what will make her happy, then she deserves it. And I want to be the one to give it to her.

*

November eventually arrives like a burst of cold water from a faucet. The short afternoons and the impenetrable grey fog on the way to work each morning only intensify my melancholy and my desperate longing for answers about the bus journey. Who is Olga Barker? Why hasn't she written to me since August? And what was the point of the bus journey if they weren't going to get back in touch?

I can't bear the anticipation. I can't stop thinking about Ubah, Mama and Aabo. I ache to know if they're OK and if Ubah has succeeded in making her journey.

In the evenings we huddle together in our small living room under electric blankets. My mother watches the Somali news channel, her icy toes tucked under my thighs on the sofa. For the first time in my life, I take a genuine interest in what I am watching. Unsurprisingly, they're talking about the US election results. In between the election updates are reports of bomb explosions in Mogadishu. They seem less important somehow. There are no mentions of the names of the deceased or anything about who they were. I'm angered by this; it's the first time I've reacted so strongly to this kind of news. If I had been a girl in Mogadishu, this could easily have been my fate.

In the corner, at the dining table, my brother tussles with his new revision books for his mock exams. 'Ahh, this is so stupid!'

I'm relieved to see him trying, at the very least. 'What's the matter?' I ask, from the other side of the room.

'I don't get it. Why do we need to memorize all of this? When are these things going to matter in the real world?' He slaps his hand against the table.

'Hey, lower your voice!' warns our mother from the sofa. She's still watching the news, her eyes scarily wide. She doesn't take her eyes off the screen. 'Don't break my furniture. And don't lose focus.'

I go over to him. 'Look, just memorize the most important ones first,' I say. 'Learn those properly and once you've done that, you can move on to the others.'

'I want to give up. There's no point. I've still got biology and physics to do and I haven't looked at that work since May.' He puts his face in his hands.

'Don't be silly, Ahmed!' our mother shouts from the sofa. 'You're my last hope. Sirad already ruined her chances. Don't mess this up.'

I brush off her comment. Since coming back from Mogadishu, I've had a new appreciation for my little brother. I sit next to him at the dining table to arrange his flashcards. I begin to write equations down for him.

'What are you doing?' he asks.

'Helping you,' I reply. 'Hooyo's right. You're our last hope. She wants to start a farm and I want to live in a cottage somewhere by the sea. You better buckle down.'

This makes Ahmed smile, but he pretends to turn up his nose in disgust. 'A cottage? What are you, eighty?' He takes the flashcards out of my hands and starts to fill them out himself.

My mum switches back and forth between the Somali and English news channels. One channel shows the aftermath of an air strike in Syria and another shows a raging fire in a mosque in India. 'How wretched is this world,' she mutters, without taking her eyes off the screen.

I take the remote from her hands. 'Hooyo, you can't watch this all day. It's not good for you. Why don't you show me those farm pictures again?'

'How can I ignore this, Sirad? Look at these innocent people. It could be any one of us. That's what I can't ignore.'

'Look, I'll put on the nature channel. Let's watch the one about the lions.' I switch over to the Discovery Channel. A pride of lions laze about on golden plains. The mother stays close to the cubs as the father sleeps nearby.

'Sirad, you're getting on my nerves. Change it back.'

'I'm actually trying to concentrate,' hisses Ahmed. 'I can't get anything done in this house.'

I hand the remote back to my mum. Ahmed puts his books to one side, stands up, and puts on his jacket.

'Where are you going?' I ask.

'Out. I have to take a walk. I can't think in here.' He pulls his hood over his head and makes for the door.

I follow him into the hallway as he puts on his trainers.

'Ahmed, wait.'

He pauses. I think about telling him everything, about the bus. He would believe me. He would understand. But somehow, I just can't bring myself to do it.

'Hey, be careful out there, yeah? Take your walk, but come straight back. Don't talk to people you don't know and don't go anywhere near Salutation Road.'

'Don't tell me what to do,' he retorts. 'Anyway, why the hell would I go to Salutation Road? There's nothing to do there.'

'Good,' I say, relieved.

Ahmed closes the door behind him.

Chapter Six

'To be without a friend is to be poor indeed.'

Many early winter mornings find me alone on the balcony with my duvet wrapped around my shoulders and a cold cup of shaah held between my knees. I am cold, bleary-eyed and yawning. My sleeping pattern is next to non-existent after late nights and early mornings at work or looking up the UNCLASSIFIED project, hopelessly wondering if some truth will find me. But there are only incongruous rumours that crop up here and there. I hear them via my mum as she retells them to her sister on the phone. They say that a large number of undocumented Somali migrants are popping up all over the city, particularly in our area. When asked where they have come from, they refuse to answer and give nothing away about who they are. Of course, my mum knows very little more than hearsay. Illegal immigration isn't unusual, so it doesn't attract unique attention. When things fail to progress beyond these snippets of information, I take a break from research. Financial burden is powerful enough to squeeze the joy out of even the most eventful situations. I succeed in catching up with some of the household bills, but we are still behind on rent by about four months. The succession of more bills makes it impossible to even make a dent in the debt, and it doesn't help that my manager hasn't yet approved my requests for shifts in the coming week.

I don't care about the specifics of the UNCLASSIFIED project or whatever the university wanted to get out of it; I'm more concerned about Ubah. I want to know where she is, or ended up, and if she's OK. I want to know how Mama and Aabo are doing and how they are filling their days, but I feel I have somehow abandoned them, even in my thoughts. In truth, the more time that passes without any contact from Olga or her team, the less I think about them. I attempt to coax a new Sirad back into being, slowly but surely. On the weekends I rise early, leave home around 9 a.m. with my books, and sit in the community cafe while it's still quiet, drinking their pink Himalayan chai, reading and circling things with a pencil. I exist in my own bubble, impermeable to anyone or anything around me.

At the start of the winter season I signed up to volunteer at Emre's community kitchen. On weekends I harvest the frost-hardy vegetables for soup. Plunging my hands into the cool dark earth feels like a kind of returning to something, like I am digging for things the past has robbed me of. I am filled with gratitude on these mornings, albeit temporarily, but it seizes with a newness each time. Sometimes, when I want to kill some extra time, I help in the canteen and dish out the food. I like sitting with the elderly and listening to them natter in surprising amounts of detail about the most random memories.

Sometimes, when they're really comfortable, they tell me their secrets. I tell them my secret too, loudly and animatedly, over plates of Sunday roast. And they drink it all in with delight. 'So what does she want, Ubah? What will she do?' They speak about Ubah like she is a character in a story

I'm writing. I look at their earnest expressions and half-open mouths.

'I don't know. To live fully, maybe? To feel at home. Isn't that what we all want?'

'I suppose so. But the question is, how is someone not at home in the only place they've ever known?'

I'm stunned by this question. It comes from Bertie, a seventy-eight-year-old retired crochet artist. I'm so inspired by it that I write it down in my phone. There is enough food left for seconds. What I notice is that no matter who I speak to, they all wish for it to be spring again soon. They just ask me to tell them about Ubah each time, over and over again.

The year is finally coming to an end. We are restless, keen to get it over and done with and ready to begin the new one. Most days, our apartment is packed with relatives and their noisy children, and I let myself be consumed by the hubbub of it all. It can be helpful in that it quiets my thoughts – until I feel the inevitable effects of cabin fever.

Family life is mostly a performance, I realize. It can be tiring, like the performance we have to put on to be respected at work. I watch relatives display overwhelming ranges of emotions only to abruptly cut them off with remarkable stoicism. They talk about Somalia every day, sometimes all day. There is a desperation in their voices when they speak about going back and being a part of the rebuild for a better future. They find great pleasure in embellishing these plans with minute detail and then tearing them all up at the end with hopeless talk of systemic corruption that will never let the people thrive. Maybe this is it, we all wonder. This small, cold island.

'Bring your aunt some salad, Sirad,' whispers Hooyo, trying to be discreet.

My mum has invited her half sister Najma over with her

two little girls. All morning I have been helping to make them lunch and preparing my bed for the girls, who will most likely end up sleeping over. We eat lasagne for dinner while watching *The Prince of Egypt*.

Aunt Najma and I have a difficult relationship. She approaches me with love and wryness in equal measure. She makes jokes about how I have to put some weight on and stop starving myself into thinness. When she embraces me, her bony fingers dig into my sides as though she's measuring the fat on my ribs. If it's not the lack of fat on my bones that concerns her, it's apparently my dull skin. She is especially unrelenting when it comes to the topic of marriage. Everything I do in her presence is somehow linked back to marriageability. Every time she sees me, she tips her head up at an angle, squints, then goes into a long spiel about the possibility that she knows someone who knows someone who could introduce me to a suitable young man. 'Walahi, he's got a lot of money! Walahi, bilahi, talahi, you would love him!' Her gold earrings jingle with every word. She can't believe that I'm not interested, but I know better than to take suggestions from someone whose marriage I wouldn't want mine to resemble.

It isn't long before my mum gets tired of Aunt Najma's constant comparisons and unsolicited advice, but I can tell she needs her company. She is comforted by those who can understand her experience, so she draws them close, even if they sometimes sting her. I think she would have loved to meet Mama. I imagine them both sitting by the sea with cups of tea, engrossed in endless conversation.

This time, something is different. I watch my mother begin to withdraw and tire of the meaningless chatter and bottomless cups of shaah. Aunt Najma pulls out her phone to show us some pictures she took at a wedding the previous night.

She looks at my mum, back at her phone, and then back to my mum, each time expecting an enthusiastic response but getting nothing. Eventually she diverts her attention to me.

'You look exhausted, my dear. But what does a young woman like you have to be tired about? You're not married and you don't have kids yet. You're supposed to be lively and energetic.'

I say nothing, hoping she will get the hint and stop.

'Still, I don't think you're tired enough. Your family is your first priority. You're all they have. Your mother . . . I'm worried that maybe you haven't been there enough.'

'Sorry?' She is talking as if my mother isn't in the room with us. As if she's dead.

'I mean, she's lost her job and she's not –' My aunt pauses. 'She's not feeling very well. So now things have fallen on your shoulders. Learn to cook a few things, help her tidy up around the house. Look after your brother and make sure he isn't up to no good. I say this to be nice. I'm your aunt, aren't I? I'm her sister.'

We both look over at my mum, who has moved to sit closer to the TV. Last night, I helped her wash her hair and scrubbed the dry skin from the soles of her feet with a pumice stone. Now she sits inert on the sofa like a china doll, with her kohl-lined eyes smudged.

'I do everything for my mother, actually. I'm here for her, and my brother.'

'You may well be doing all of that and more! It's just a harmless reminder. I don't mean to scold you, if you think I am.' Aunt Najma looks around the room sheepishly. 'I know your mother is very proud of you. She's always saying that you're her pride and joy.'

'I know.' I harden my voice.

'Good. And you know what else? When you get older and raise a family of your own, you'll know exactly what to do when times get hard because you've been trained, sweetheart, *trained!* – through experience. You're not like the other girls who have been raised here. You know how you're going to raise a family one day. Have you thought about that yet, Sirad? Have you thought about starting a family of your own one day?'

'I'm only twenty-three. So no, I haven't thought about it.'

'Twenty-three? I was a mother of four by your age!'

I want to say something slick, but I spare her the anger that has been mounting within me. God, give me strength, I think as I leave the room to make some more tea. Aunt Najma calls after me, 'Make it black. Add some honey if you have some. My throat is starting to get a little sore.' She hands me the glass tea cup she had been drinking out of and stretches herself out on the sofa. Her daughter Hanna crawls onto her lap and curls up against her chest. 'Darling, bring some milky tea for this little one too. I'll ask God to make all your prayers come true.' She laughs into her daughter's hair.

The kitchen floor is covered in onion skins from the lasagne and cake crumbs from where the girls have helped themselves to some chocolate brownies. I clean up the mess as I wait for the tea to brew. From the kitchen I can hear my aunt singing along to a Somali song on TV, encouraging her daughters to join in.

I carry the tea out on a tray.

My mother has resumed talking to Aunt Najma. The conversation seems tense now, spoken in low, hushed tones under the music. I think I hear the Somali word for money, but I'm not sure. They sit close to each other. Aunt Najma places her hand on my mum's wrist and watches her with wide, pleading eyes.

'But you seem so lonely and distant these days.'

'I have my children.'

'I know, I know, but . . .'

My mum shakes Aunt Najma's hand off her and sits straight up as I walk into the room. 'Oh look, your tea. Be careful when you're passing it to the girls, Sirad. Don't stand over them like that.'

I put the tray down and remember what I wanted to ask Aunt Najma. I'm looking for answers to the rumours.

'Aunty, I don't know if you've heard the talk about all the new Somalis in the area who claim to have come here from Somalia just recently. What's that all about?'

She perks up in her seat. 'Sirad, please be careful. I've heard some scary things. These poor people have probably been victims of human trafficking, and here they are destitute and terrified. God knows how they got here. Someone said they came over from Somalia on a bus!'

I do my best to sound shocked. 'A bus?'

'They expect me to believe that. I tell you, social media is destroying our people's common sense. Oh, there have been all sorts of theories. But the thing is, nobody knows for sure. They don't speak.'

'What do you think they want?'

'I don't know. But they're everywhere on the west side of Greenwich.'

I am jittery as she talks more about it, but I don't want to ask too many questions in case she grows suspicious.

Hanna tugs on my arm. 'Sisi, do you have a charger for this? I couldn't finish my game.' She holds up her iPad, now drained of its battery. There are bits of food stuck to her Hello Kitty T-shirt.

'No, honey.' I prise the iPad out of her hands. 'Why don't you sit properly so you can drink?'

When my mother has re-engaged with the conversation, she

changes the topic. The two of them are becoming engrossed in another discussion, so I put on my coat and scarf, deciding to take a walk.

*

I savour every step towards the riverbank. On the way, I buy myself a mocha from a small Colombian cafe where the barista speaks passionately into her phone as she makes my drink. I thank her and she flashes me a beautiful, bright smile. She wipes her wet hands on her apron and resumes her conversation.

After a while of just being outside, away from my aunt's ceaseless lectures, the fog in my head begins to lift. I enjoy the cool, brilliant air. I walk up to a charity shop that I often frequent and stop to root through the box of free books by the door. Most of them are yellowed and slightly bloated, but I never pass this box without giving it a thorough search. Crouching by the pavement, I look at each book, one by one, before settling on a bilingual collection of poems in Arabic and English. The book is in decent condition, save for a few marks along the spine and a slightly bent cover. I look for somewhere to sit and read.

I find an awkwardly placed bench by the entrance of the empty Greenwich Market and sit with my poems and my mocha, immersed in the beauty of the words on the pages.

I have almost reached the end of the poetry collection when I look back up at the street again. A middle-aged Somali woman walks hurriedly towards me. Nothing about her seems particularly out of place. She wears a long, puffy black coat and brown boots. I stand up and greet her.

'Assalamu aleykum.'

She returns the greeting but walks straight past me, towards the post office.

I sit back down, embarrassed. I don't know what I expected. That was just a random Somali lady going about her day. She didn't even ask for my help.

Yet I continue to sit there expectantly, waiting for some sign of people who have arrived on the bus. In the hour that I sit there, a young German couple ask me for directions, three homeless men ask me for change and a teenage boy on a bike mutters something inaudible at me.

Give it a rest, I think to myself, over and over. Just focus on yourself.

*

The next day is Sunday, so I decide to try again. I wake up on the living room sofa and leave the house before Aunt Najma and her kids are up. I walk briskly towards the river and get there in about ten minutes. Something tells me that this is where I should wait. I find a wooden bench and watch the slow *slosh, slosh* of the river against the rocks. Along its bank come an elderly couple, walking briskly at a steady pace. Two Somali girls pass by but, judging from their fashion and make-up, they're from this side of time.

Around 10 a.m., the riverbank begins to liven up with people. It is Sunday, after all, which means the international food market is open and thriving. People holding paper bags of delicious food walk towards Greenwich Park. A man stands nearby making bubbles with a large rope tied between two sticks, undaunted by the bitterly cold wind. By his feet is a paddling pool full of soapy water. That's someone's father, I think. He has a fatherly look about him. Maybe it's his style, a beaten brown jacket paired with straight-leg blue jeans. He submerges the rope in the water to make the bubbles. Nobody but me stops to watch how he makes them travel with the wind.

I sit on my bench, facing the water, watching the man loop and unloop the rope through the paddling pool. Each time, the bubbles are smaller than the last ones and skitter over the water with the wind, away from the passing children. He curses frustratedly under his breath. He slowly lowers the rope into the water and lifts it over his head, his energy waning rapidly.

'Assalamu aleykum,' comes the voice of a woman next to me. It's a Somali woman. She is holding a large plastic bag over her shoulder. She looks like she is in distress.

'Wa aleykum salaam.'

She smiles warmly, showing white teeth and dark gums. 'Abaayo, I'm looking for a hostel. I'm told there is a hostel somewhere near here . . . for work.'

'A hostel? What is it called?'

'It's called Sayn . . . Sayn-something? Uhh, sorry darling. I don't know how to say it.'

'Sayn?' I try to sound it out. 'I can't make out what you're saying.'

'Here, look.' She pulls out a business card from her pocket and hands it to me: Saint's Inn. It's a hostel about a minute's walk south of the high road.

'Saint's Inn. Ahh!' I enunciate each letter. We giggle at her previous pronunciation. 'That's very close by, actually,' I say. 'Come. Let me show you.'

'Would you? That's so kind of you.' She laughs in relief and lifts her bag back up. I walk her up the road, adjusting myself to her incredibly slow pace.

'What's your name, abaayo?' she asks when we eventually arrive at the hostel. It's a small building that looks like a Victorian dollhouse, tucked away on the corner of the street.

'My name is Sirad.'

'That's a beautiful name. Thank you for helping me, Sirad. You have no idea how difficult it has been to find this place. May God always keep you safe.' At points she seems to lean her weight on her left leg.

'Thank you,' I reply, unsure what else to say. I wait until she gets inside the building before I walk away.

Maybe I am just tired, but the bizarreness of the situation doesn't hit me until the next day, when I am doing the washing-up after breakfast. *'Of course!'* I hiss at myself. *'Of course, of course, of course!'* I don't think any further, but put my shoes on and practically run all the way back to the hostel.

I am panting like a stray dog by the time I reach the entrance. People glance at me cautiously as they pass through the entrance – women – Somali women in all shapes and hues and heights. It isn't just their clothes or their lack of proper winter jackets for the most part; they have a certain energy about them that is unmistakably out of place. I see one woman who looks barely older than eighteen, wearing a threadbare orange cardigan and a black hijab. Something doesn't seem right about the hostel, so I summon the courage to walk up to her. She glances at me apprehensively, keeping her eyes downcast.

'Assalamu aleykum. Can I ask what is going on in this hostel? Are you all staying here?'

The woman studies my face. 'Yes, we are.' She's short with me and turns away untrustingly.

I think about going in but I am afraid of potentially putting the women, or myself, in a compromising situation. I can see through the glass that the reception area is poorly lit.

I sit on the low brick wall outside, watching people go in – again, mostly women. There is the occasional man, mostly in uniform. The women look weary, as if they have been through unspeakable struggles to get here.

Eventually, after some time, I back away and walk back home.

The next day, I stay in my room. I don't leave except to eat. My manager still hasn't responded to me about my shifts, and the office will be closed for a few days for Christmas and the New Year. Around noon, my phone starts ringing with a number that isn't saved. I let it ring until it stops, but then they call again.

'Hey!'

I recognize her voice immediately, my heart leaping with joy.

'I've arrived! I'm finally here!'

'Really? What?' I'm practically screaming down the phone. *Oh my God,* when?'

'The bus! I got here last week, but I only just got settled and managed to buy myself a cheap phone.'

'You've been here a *week?*' I am breathless. 'Tell me exactly what happened!'

'I have to keep my voice down, Sirad. I can't talk about these things where I'm working right now. All I can say is that I'm relieved to be alive.'

'I'll come and get you tonight, when you finish. Let's have dinner. Where are you staying?'

'At a hostel. Where I also work.'

'Saint's Inn?'

'Yes, I think that's the one.'

'No way! I live near there! In fact, I was there yesterday. What's going on inside there?'

'I wish I could stay to talk about it, but I have to go to work now. Let's meet tomorrow. I'll meet you here at ten in the morning.'

'I just can't believe you came. I can't believe you actually did it.'

She's laughing quietly. 'I'm glad I finally found you, Sirad. You can't imagine how hard the past week has been for me.'

After we hang up, I lie in bed for a few moments in complete disbelief. The rest of the day passes by in a blur.

That night I find myself in the middle of a dream that seems to bring together so many of my main anxieties in one short vision. I am in a garden enclosed by rosebushes in red, yellow and blush pink. The sun shines down on me and warms my face as I lie on my front in the tall grass. Every detail feels real, like the sensation of my eyelashes brushing against my hand. I roll onto my back as large shadows overhead block the path of the sun and intermittently leave me cold. Strange half-woman, half-bird creatures are flying in the sky above me. Their voices form a song. I touch my arms and can't feel the wings the other women have, just the goose bumps on my skin. I wave my arms, finding them short and bony. I scream. I lie there for what feels like hours, wildly hoping that my feathers will materialize before me. The bird-women sweep off towards the horizon, and I remain alone on the grass.

Chapter Seven

'Either be a mountain or lean on one.'

The waitress goes back and forth, to and from our table, bringing tiny jars of Bonne Maman jam. Ubah finds the little jars extremely cute. She sits across from me and spreads butter carefully on thick hunks of bread before layering a fried egg on top and drizzling it with sriracha. She tucks her red puffer jacket under the seat next to us, the same jacket I saw folded away in her bedroom in Mogadishu. Her hair is wrapped in a stylish blue satin scarf and she's wearing a knitted turtleneck jumper with a long black skirt.

She is supposed to be at work this morning, but has decided to come and spend the day with me instead. My workplace is closed until the New Year. Neither of us slept properly the night before. I called her in the early hours and she cried to me on the phone when I asked about her parents. She didn't get the chance to say goodbye to them. She didn't know how to.

Now she's laughing freely. I notice that her pink lipstick leaves stains on her teeth. Somewhat embarrassed when I point it out, she wipes them away with her thumb.

The early afternoon sun, unaccompanied by a single cloud, shines through the restaurant window, right across us. We shield our eyes with a copy of the *Metro* that we picked up on the bus ride here. Somehow, Ubah appears to have aged backwards since I last saw her. I think it's partly to do with her cute, childlike mannerisms that come out now that she is more relaxed. She sits on her hands and taps her feet against the floor. As we eat, we people-watch through the window. She comments on everything and asks a lot of questions. We gossip freely in Somali. Sometimes it seems as though people around us understand what we are saying. They swivel their heads around to look at us while we suppress laughter until it feels like we could burst.

So this is how it feels to have a sister, I think. I feel an inexplicable sense of satisfaction as I notice how much she is enjoying her breakfast. We are sitting in a new cafe on Greenwich High Road where they have been playing Sade's greatest hits all morning. Ubah clears her plate well before me, so I offer her my Portobello mushrooms, which she accepts shyly with the end of her fork. We warm our hands on the bone china teapot and play Never Have I Ever. The small, unbalanced table we sit at is our own tiny island of joy.

Ubah excuses herself to go to the toilet. People roll lazily into the cafe like marbles, savouring the public holiday. Being there with Ubah feels like we are sharing a private joke. It's exhilarating. There is a whole reality that others around us would never believe. It feels as though we have found a cheat sheet to time.

And yet, I'm consciously trying not to focus on the looming elephant in the room as it gets harder to ignore.

'Do you think your parents will ever forgive you?' I ask, when she returns to her seat.

'I know they will. If I wasn't sure of that, I might have never left.'

'What about your husband?'

'He will never forgive me. And likewise, if I wasn't sure of that too, I might have never left.' She hides her hands in the sleeves of her jumper.

'What are you going to do now that you're here?'

'What everybody else does, I guess. Work, eat, sleep. Study? I have to make something of my life now that I'm here. I've got nothing to show for twenty-three years of existence.'

'How do you think you'll do that if you're undocumented?' I lean in. 'You can't even buy a lighter in this country without showing ID.'

She swallows a great big gulp of orange juice and scoffs. 'There are people that can help with that. Fake ID, passport, even a driver's licence. There are people who put themselves at risk every day to make all the right kinds of papers. That's all I need.'

'So you're going to create a fake identity?'

'Oh Sirad, you make me laugh. *Everything* is fake now in this world we're living in, no matter which side of time you're on. It's all the same. What's a passport other than bits of paper and plastic that somebody glued together? That's all you need for people to take you seriously and decide whether you're worthy of a proper existence.'

She's right. The gap between the world of illegitimacy and legitimacy is just an office somewhere filled with important papers.

'These people in charge want to play and control by bending time, but it doesn't belong to them. Just like their man-made borders that don't belong to them either. I realized on my way here that I was one of the luckier few because I managed to find the money. I watched a little boy being dragged out from under the bus where he had clung to the axle overnight in the hopes of sneaking on. He was shivering. A child! They took him away. They tortured him. I know they did . . .' Her voice trails off. She squeezes her eyes shut for a second. 'We're both here – we got here in different ways, but we're here. What makes your journey better than mine? If I wanted to, I could have taken the route through Libya like others have. But to what end? Death? Slavery? It would be one or the other. I got on the bus because I wanted freedom to live more than one kind of life.'

When we finish talking and digesting our food, I take Ubah through a shortcut to Greenwich Park, avoiding the main road in case anyone from the hostel sees her. We race each other up the hill to the Royal Observatory and collapse on the grass, gasping. She is silent for a while as she takes in the skyline and the insect-like cars zipping up and down the road below. I fall silent too. Even though I have lived here almost all my life, the view always seems to take my breath away. It is a mixture of awe and *what the hell am I doing here?*

Rosie and I used to roll down the hill all the way to the bottom, aeons ago. I would come home with grass stains on my long-sleeved school uniform shirt and hide the evidence at the bottom of the laundry basket. Once, on the heaviest day of snow we had ever witnessed, we used recycling bin lids as toboggans and hurled ourselves over the hill into a white panorama.

'This line, the Greenwich Meridian, runs right through the whole world; it's supposed to separate the East and the West,' I say, pointing to the Royal Observatory, where tourists form a long queue for admission. 'So right now, we're right in the middle of the world.'

'I feel invincible right now,' whispers Ubah. 'Nobody will find me here.'

'Me too. It's my favourite place. Ironically, it's the only place where time seems to wait and just let me breathe.'

'One day I'll learn English properly, so I'll be able to describe exactly how I'm feeling to you. But I heard an expression once in a movie that's close to what I'm feeling, I think – I'm the cat in the cream.' She says the last part in English.

'You mean the cat who got the cream?' I laugh, splaying out my arms and legs in the grass, snow-angel style.

'That's what I mean.'

'*Cat in the cream* sounds better. The cat got so much cream, he had enough to bathe in.'

'I like these little proverbs,' says Ubah. 'I didn't know the English could be so poetic.'

The first place Ubah asks me to take her is Woolwich. It takes me by surprise. I expect her to say Mayfair or Notting Hill, somewhere more polished and a lot closer to whatever ideals someone might have of what London is like. She says she wants to see the closest area that is densely populated with Somalis; that she is just curious about how we are getting on here, curious about what almost two decades here looks like. I think the truth is much simpler – Ubah misses home. Technically, she can never go back. That's something that would be difficult for anyone to come to terms with.

Woolwich was my city centre for a long time – not Carnaby Street or Oxford Street, but the shabby markets and the halal meat butchers, the mosque, the money transfer shops where we'd find ourselves each month while our mother pacified us with Starburst sweets. Sometimes we'd even be allowed to get the ferry boats to the East End, which always made me feel like I was in some kind of war movie, leaving behind a loved one. This is where we used to hang out after school until sunset, where girls would meet their crushes in groups just to walk past each other without a word, where the big screen displayed the World Cup as people napped in the grass.

Ubah stares hawkishly at the mums walking their children through the centre of Woolwich. A look of pain flashes across her eyes for a few seconds before they return to her vacant default. She observes everything intently as we walk along the high street. I catch her staring at a homeless man fast asleep on a street corner in a pile of boxes.

'I never imagined that London could look like this. It's a bit ugly.' She is taken aback. This stings a little. I internalize it as though I am part of the ugliness.

At the market, the stall sellers shout the same things they've shouted for years – a kilo of oranges for a pound, a kilo of apples for two. Hearing them shout the same thing over and over feels like I'm in some kind of simulation. Their words no longer sound like the names of real fruit. They sound like desperate cries for help.

We eventually arrive at the African hair shop. The Indian shopkeeper stands behind the till as she has done for years, ever since I can remember. She never smiles, but she has a kind presence. Her assistant busies himself by restacking the shelves, but I notice he has his eyes on us.

I explain to Ubah that I can find the best hair oil here, the stuff that is designed for our kind of hair. The shop's owner watches us closely too. All the years of spending my lunch money here and she still has to make sure that I'm not stealing. It fills me with a quiet rage. I used to come in alone after school for a tub of gel and some conditioner. She hovers in the background of my memories of a time when I was just discovering eyelash curlers and how to wing my eyeliner.

I buy Ubah the same carrot oil conditioner that I used growing up. I open the lid just to smell it again. There seem to be hair products here from every stage of my life, all arranged on the shelf in exactly the same way as they have always been. Each one is a kind of artefact along a timeline, from when I was fifteen and obsessed with taming my hair straight, to when I cut off all the dead parts at twenty to embrace my curls and start over again.

The Indian shop owner bags up our purchases and furrows her brows, her eyes flicking between us.

'Is this your twin?' she asks, pointing her chin at Ubah. 'I didn't know you had a sister.'

'Yes. We've been coming here for years . . . haven't you noticed?'

Ubah starts to giggle. She can tell what is going on. We leave the shop in a hurry.

It's not too different in the Somali clothes shop where I take Ubah to buy some new baatis. The owner here is normally very talkative, but the shop is busy. She eventually helps us work our way through her stock for sets of baatis with matching garbasars. I can tell by her expression that she wants to ask who Ubah is, but before she can say anything, a customer asks for her help finding a pink silk garbasar.

Ubah seems embarrassed to let me buy her some clothes to wear. It's the least I can do to help her settle in, I keep repeating to her. But she struggles to accept it. During the walk to the clothes shops, she pleads with me to stop, suggesting she can wear the clothes she brought until she gets paid.

'Absolutely not.' I fight hard against her excuses. 'You'll freeze to death if you don't have enough layers on and a new, *proper coat.*'

'Let's just go back,' she insists. 'I don't want to make you feel like I've just dropped into your life for you to take care of me. Remember, I chose to come here on my own.'

I pull on her arm and get her to walk with me through the

double doors and into Primark. The security guard watches us squabble at the entrance.

'Just choose a few jumpers and something to sleep in for now, then. It's so cold and you don't have clothes! Stop feeling bad about my help.'

Eventually she stops digging her heels in and follows me around the shop. We have to guess her bra size. I find her some socks, leggings and a few pairs of tights. I put them all in the basket for her and guide her by the elbow to the flannel pyjamas.

'I've never worn a set of real pyjamas,' she says, feeling the material between her fingers. She chooses a pair embroidered with cat faces.

'Try them on if you want to,' I say encouragingly. 'And don't forget to get yourself some warm socks too. You can try some dresses on as well, just so you know what to get next time.'

She begins to relax a bit. I think she might even be enjoying herself a little. Each time she passes a floor-length mirror, she stops to check her reflection. She holds an array of dresses and jackets up to her body and tries on a pair of black suede thigh-high boots.

The shop assistant wearily shows her to her changing room. I wait outside and look through the discounted clothes racks. Maybe these short bursts of meaning will be enough, I think. Things will get clearer. I'm certain of that. I will look after Ubah and help her settle in. That could be my purpose.

I return to the entrance of the changing rooms and wait for Ubah for a good half an hour. She has still not come out. I think she must be trying on the rest of her clothes so I wait some more, flicking through the jackets and coats. Twenty more minutes pass. As soon as the shop assistant moves from the changing-room doors, I walk straight through to find Ubah's cubicle. The curtains are drawn, but I can see her red jacket in a tiny crack between the curtain and the wall. I call her name and wait while the worst thoughts swim around in my mind.

'Ubah?' I put my ear close to the curtain. 'What's taking you so long?' She doesn't answer. 'Ubah? Let me in.' I can hear her shuffling around. She eventually pulls the curtain back.

She is sitting on the floor in a bra and jeans. Her face is buried in her hands and she is sobbing.

'What happened?' I crouch down to sit beside her on the floor. She pulls her face from her hands; a thick vein stands up on her temple.

'I was putting these clothes on when it hit me. It's exactly a month since it happened. I was crying so much that I could barely stand.'

'What happened? What happened to you a month ago?'

'I lost her.' She points to her abdomen. 'I lost my baby.'

'Ubah!' I throw my arms around her. 'I am so sorry – I had no idea.'

She pushes me away. 'Don't be. This is unlike me. Don't mistake these tears for regret. I never regret anything.'

'But it's OK to grieve,' I reason. 'That was your baby.'

'I'll finish getting dressed. Just wait outside. I'll be OK.'

I wait for her to finish up. I pay for the clothes, and we leave Primark with our arms linked.

On the bus back to Greenwich, Ubah suddenly bursts into random chatter, speaking quickly and jumping from topic to topic. She remarks on the traffic, the Christmas decorations on people's front lawns, and her memories of New Years in Mogadishu. As she speaks, I watch her carefully; her little hands, the dark puffy rings around her eyes. She is so delicate and so vulnerable. I feel like I'm staring at the saddest version of myself.

'You're going to make it out of this, Ubah. I just know it.' I try to speak some life into her. 'Both of us are. One day you'll be exactly who you want to be and you'll have a nice career, and fall in love, and you'll have a beautiful family of your own.'

She smiles sadly and looks down at her hands in her lap. The truth is, I can't even begin to imagine how she will get there. With her status, or lack thereof, she can't even visit a doctor if she needs to. What kind of life is that for a young woman? But I can tell that she's feeling defeated, and so I have no choice but to feign some hope for her.

I see her off at the entrance of the hostel.

'Be careful. Don't trust anyone you meet here,' I warn her, just before she goes inside. 'I don't like the way that security guard is looking at us.'

It's one of the men in uniform I noticed the other day. He hasn't broken his gaze from the moment he noticed us walking up to the entrance.

She laughs. 'I'll be fine. Now go away before he gets annoyed! I'll call you tomorrow.'

We meet again the next day and take the Tube to Oxford Street. We try on countless dresses and pairs of shoes that we have no intention of buying in fancy shops that neither of us can afford.

'I made a friend at the hostel.' Ubah is proud of this piece of news. 'He's a photographer from Bulgaria. Or is it Belarus? It's one of those.' She smiles dolefully as she tries on a pair of black patent heels. 'We got talking and he said that he is pretty sure I could be a model. Runway, he thinks. I have the legs for it. Editorial is possible too, he said. I just need to experiment a bit. He has a studio in West London. He wants to meet me tomorrow after work to take a few photos.'

I can't believe what she's saying. 'What did I tell you yesterday? Didn't I tell you not to make friends with strangers? And you've gone and done exactly as I told you not to.'

Ubah makes a face. 'He's a professional. He wasn't being disrespectful.'

'I don't care!' I blurt out. I don't intend to sound so blunt. 'The point is, he might really be a photographer, but we just can't trust anyone here. The risk is too big.'

'Look, he knows my situation. He's in a similar boat. He's not going to hurt me. What would he get out of that? I'm going to a legitimate shoot which I will pay for with my own money.'

'Who do you think you are?' I scoff at her, incredulously. 'Iman? This isn't a Hollywood movie. This is London. At best, no one cares about your dreams. At worst, they want you dead! Do you understand?'

Ubah stares at me, obviously confused as to where I've found this new tone. 'Just stop it! Stop worrying so much about me! I'm not your little sister! I'm not your daughter! Remember who you're talking to! I've survived all this time without you. I've been through my own challenges and learned my own lessons. I'm barely even your friend! I'm not you, Sirad. I'M NOT YOU!'

She tells me she wants to go back to the hostel. She says she's tired and doesn't want to eat. She tells me not to go all the way to the entrance of the hostel with her. That the security guard is on duty and would recognize me. We stop short of the building, around the corner, and Ubah turns to face me.

'Sirad, I don't mean to sound ungrateful. The past couple of days have been wonderful, and you have been so kind and generous to me. I'm so glad I found you again.'

'It's OK. You were right. I overstepped a line.'

She smiles in response, and the tension fizzles out. 'Next

time we see each other, I want to see Buckingham Palace! I want to feel like a princess for a day.'

'Your wish is my command,' I say. She curtsies playfully, giving me one last hug, and skips off towards the hostel.

I am exhausted by the time I start my walk home. I remember something Ubah said to me earlier: 'I wish I was as light as smoke. Or fumes. Dark and formidable, rising and rising, snuffing out people that hurt me.'

The sky is bruised black and blue. Thick droplets of rain begin to fall, so I quicken my pace towards home. People scurry past me and disappear into cracks in the concrete. I won't be able to make it home without getting soaked, so I run for cover at the DLR station.

There is a Somali woman standing there having a cigarette. I know immediately that she's one of those who has travelled over on the bus. She pulls her hand down away from her face, awkwardly trying to hide the cigarette. I avert my gaze.

I stand there under the roof of the station, my shoes in sticky, blackened water on the floor, listening to the *ssshhhhh* of the rain.

The lady with the cigarette begins to sing quietly to herself, but I can just about hear it. I recognize the song but don't remember the name. Overwhelmed with emotion, I remember Mama and Aabo, and wonder what they're doing right now. I wish that I could say sorry to them on Ubah's behalf. They don't deserve to lose their daughter.

Chapter Eight

'One cannot obscure the sun with a mere finger.'

It never gets easier; waking up and having to remember that things *aren't* OK. As a child, I could spend the whole day skating outside or eating my body weight in sweets while dangling my legs from a tree – pretending the world was perfect. Now sadness seems to co-exist with every other emotion until it finds itself reigning supreme.

Everyone has their own quicksand, but sometimes we're able to find a rope, something with which to drag ourselves out from the pit. For some, that rope might be the arms of another person, or money, or drugs. For me it's as simple as closing my eyes and letting myself dream. Sometimes the dreams are about things that have already happened and sometimes they are images of things I feel are yet to come. My dreams now are more confusing than ever – I get lost in the chasm between who I think I am in my waking reality and who I really am as a result of my experiences, fears and desires. And now there is this added layer of who I was when I journeyed to Mogadishu that manifests in my dreams too. It leaves me with endless questions: has seeing what I've seen and choosing not to share it with my mother made me a bad daughter? Am I withholding something from her that could potentially make her happy? Am I selfish for doing that? The more I try to ignore these questions, the more they haunt me.

One morning, while I'm having breakfast with Ahmed and my mother, I zone out of the conversation to think of Ubah. I haven't seen her for a few days because we have both been working some long shifts, but I can't wait to see her again. I'm so engrossed in my thoughts that I miss the heated conversation starting between my mother and brother.

My mother is pacing about the apartment, following Ahmed and yelling hysterically. It turns out he has planned a trip to Scotland without asking her. 'With who?' she demands.

'With my friends!'

'And you didn't think to get my permission?'

'I'm sixteen! None of my other friends live under this much control! I can't stand it!'

'Ahmed. I'm only going to say this once. You're not going.'

It turns out that Ahmed already has an overnight bag packed. There is a long, tense moment of silence. Ahmed looks down at his overstuffed Nike gym bag and then sprays some cologne on his neck in front of the hallway mirror. He leaves with confidence, shutting the door behind him with a bang.

I stay sitting in front of my cold fried eggs, saying nothing. I can hear the stove's incessant ticking noise coming from the kitchen.

'What does he get out of torturing me like this?' asks my mother, joining me at the table with a packet of custard creams.

'He's going to take photos. It's his hobby.'

'He's out of control. Who does he think he is?' Tick, tick, tick.

'You know you can stop that ticking noise by flicking off the switch on the wall,' I say, irritated.

'Oh. I barely noticed it.' She glances back towards the kitchen. 'There will be more visitors today.' She says this like it is bad news. 'So I need to do more cooking. Go on, get dressed. I need you to go to the shop for two boxes of eggs, plain flour, cinnamon sticks, olive oil, fresh coriander leaves and aluminium foil.'

'Hooyo, you need a break.'

'From what?'

'From this!' I say, motioning my hand towards the kitchen. My mother just shakes her head.

We work all morning to prepare lunch and deep clean the apartment. I do the shopping and the cleaning as my mother continues to cook and listen to the Somali radio. For the millionth time in my life, she gets me to watch her as she hovers over the stove, concocting familiar meals.

'Learn with your eyes and measure with your heart,' is what she always says. 'Learn from your mother. That's what I'm here for.'

*

With Ahmed gone this weekend and Ubah still busy, I feel lonelier than I have in a long time. I decide to visit our local library in an attempt to fill the void. At least then I can see Maxine, I think, pleased with my new plan. Maxine has been a librarian at my local since I was still in primary school, and we have shared a special friendship ever since. I used to love the way she would tilt her head to one side and say, 'I've got time for you, star. I've always got time for you.'

The East Greenwich Library is a low, red-brick Victorian building with a door that is always wide open, showing a glimpse of the bookshelves inside. Footsteps are muted by the thick forest-green carpet, making it easy for a painfully shy child like I used to be to move from shelf to shelf without attracting attention. A few people sit around on big beanbags, deeply engrossed in their books. There is always music playing in the library, coming from Maxine's computer or the radio. Today it's Anita Baker. Whenever I can't see Maxine at her desk, I look around for the red mug I gifted her when I got my first ever job, or her gold-rimmed glasses perched across the pages of an open book.

The shelves are still decorated with tinsel and fairy lights, despite the fact that Christmas is over. Just as I expected, Maxine's chair is empty, but her red mug sits on the desk, half filled with black coffee. It isn't long before she pops her head around the office door and makes a soft squealing sound. She seems pleased to see me. Her enthusiasm and warmth are as consistent as a prayer.

'I'll be out in a minute, star. I'm just on the phone.'

Maxine is sort of like a village elder. She has always been right there at the centre of things. She runs a breakfast club for local kids and after-school homework clubs three nights a week for the children whose parents can't help them with their homework. She writes poetry and social commentary blogs. She leads a small group of local Black activists and deeply cares about things that the average person doesn't have the emotional capacity to care about. She's always there – so much so that for years I was convinced that the library was where she actually lived. If I came and didn't find her, I would immediately want to go home. She was the first person I would seek out if I felt down or was in trouble. I would sit by her desk and listen to sixties Motown, hanging on to lyrics and second-hand feelings I didn't understand.

Growing up, the books in that library were my only way of learning to understand people that I would never meet, and I hoped, in some strange magnetic way, that they would understand me too. I became fascinated by the lives of strangers. I piled together dusty memoirs and took them home, their worlds coming along with me. My mother couldn't understand what was in those books for a young Somali girl like me. She was worried, like a lot of Somali parents who were new to the culture and were apprehensive about the ways their children could be influenced. The more obscure the writers and stories, the better, as far as I was concerned. I loved the memoirs of unknown local writers. I cared about the mundane details of their lives and the self-grandeur that led them to write about themselves. That kind of courage wasn't lost on me.

Maxine finally finishes her phone call and comes back to her desk. She has a way of walking that looks like she is dancing.

'Star, where've ya been?' she asks me. I often feel as if she's addressing me with some kind of intimate, indoor voice, a voice reserved for family members.

'Maxine! It's been too long. I'm so sorry.'

'What you sorry for, love? Life happens to us all. And that's OK.'

I've established a sort of pattern over the years. For a while I will come in at least weekly, sometimes two or three times a week; but then, after a few months of that, I will disappear for a while. Maxine and I seem to understand each other despite our thirty-five-year age difference. She is the daughter of a Jamaican miner who came to England on the *Windrush*. My father was a sailor too, back in Somalia.

When we came to London, Maxine was one of the first people my mother became friends with who wasn't a relative. We went to the library one day when I was five years old, and I climbed onto Maxine's desk and refused to get off. Maxine greeted me as I sat there with my legs swinging. I said nothing back. I was mute then. It must have been the ordeal of this strange new land, or the trauma of the war, that rendered me mute for an entire year. I didn't say a word; I couldn't make anything make sense. Two very different worlds were coming together in my head: the life we had hastily abandoned in Mogadishu, and this new one in cold, rainy England. There was a painful eclipse of languages and truths.

'Fee-fi-fo-fum,' I said to Maxine one day, echoing her as she read aloud from *Jack and the Beanstalk*. Maxine read to me some afternoons even though I'm sure it wasn't even in her job description. She did it in the hope that it would inspire me to say something eventually. I knew I was being treated differently from the other children. I sat close to her on the carpet, almost on her lap.

'Fee-fi-fo-fum,' I repeated. It was the first thing I had said in a year, and the look on Maxine's face was pure euphoria. I remember how her dark brown skin suddenly gained this rosy quality. 'What's that?' I asked.

She clutched the book hard and leaned in to whisper, as if telling me a secret. 'It's a nonsense rhyme. You can make it mean whatever you want it to.'

That afternoon she stood up and did a dramatic reading of 'The Jabberwocky' along with interpretive movements that left me in hysterics. I laughed so hard that I cried, and after a while I didn't know if I was crying from despair or from a deep-seated longing that I couldn't articulate.

Those nonsense rhymes eloquently revealed the truth about life in those early days. Things here in England would not always make sense, but there would always be the library and Maxine with her sixties music reverberating through the room.

After that, I would race to my mum's bedroom on Saturday

mornings, begging her to take me there until I was old enough to walk there by myself. Each time I came through the doors, I cast off the world along with my coat. To me, reality didn't matter unless it existed in a book. On summer holidays I was often the only child in the library, and in these periods, even the best book failed to steal me away from my thoughts. I would walk around the shelves like I was a small silver ball caught in a maze. Maxine would call me to her desk. Without words, she understood what I was going through. Without words, she told me that I didn't have to stay on the estate throughout the summer if I didn't want to. There were books. Books could take me wherever I wanted to go.

'What's with the face?' teases Maxine now, with an eyebrow raised. She is wearing a red turtleneck, quite a change from her usual black or white. 'Has it got anything to do with a *man*?'

I touch my face. I hadn't realized how harshly I was frowning. 'Hell no,' I reply. 'I know you wish it was, but it's not.' I sit down across from her at her desk.

She reaches into her desk drawer, pulling out a packet of sweets. 'So what on earth is stressing you like this?'

'Nothing. Maybe I'm just a bit tired. It's getting to that time of year. Exhausted is the word.'

Maxine laughs her deep, buttery laugh and takes off her glasses to rub her eyes. 'See now, you could probably get away with nonsense like that if I hadn't known you half your bleeding life! Hang on.' She jumps up from her seat. 'Wait there while I bring us some tea. And have a good proper think about what you just said.'

I groan and put my face in my hands. This time there is no way I am going to let Maxine in on what I've been going through. As much as I trust her, I'm not ready to share anything with anyone yet.

Maxine returns to her seat with two cups of peppermint tea. 'You stay away for months, come in screwing up your face, and now you want to convince me that everything's fine?'

Her voice is a little louder than I'm comfortable with, so I'm more determined to stay quiet about everything. A teenage girl holding a stack of books walks past the desk, clearly eavesdropping on our conversation. 'Tell me the truth, girl child.'

'OK, so here's the thing,' I reply. 'I'm not lying. But things are still a bit fresh, so . . . you know . . . when I make sense of it all, I will tell you exactly what is up.'

She nods her head and laughs again. 'Mm-hmm. Sure you will.'

'There's a lot going on. I'm stressed out. Mum has lost her job and she's spiralling. We've got all these bills, and I just hate my job. I hate the fact that I'm not managing well. I feel selfish because I'm still so wrapped up in my own world.'

'You poor baby. You're not selfish! You're doing all right. You've been holding it down for so long without any complaint. I don't know how you do it, honestly. You poor thing.'

'But I am selfish. This doesn't feel natural to me. To be needed so much all of a sudden. You know my mum. She was never like this.'

'She's just going through a rough patch, love. You get to that certain age when everything feels so overwhelming. She'll come out of it.' Maxine rubs my arm and slides me another sweet.

'It's not just a rough patch, Maxine. She's actually sick. Mentally. And it's breaking me.'

'And who said that can't just be a rough patch? There is healing. Hang in there. She'll be all right. You have to truly believe that things can change, for her and for you.'

'Why do bad things always happen all at once?'

'For the same reason good things happen all at once. Sometimes you have to properly feel all those difficult things to know what ease feels like when it comes. Your only job is to take care of yourself, be truthful to *yourself*, when you know you're not OK.'

'I know. I just don't want to disappoint her. That scares me more than anything.'

'She won't be disappointed in you. You know that. So, relax yourself for a bit. You'll be fine.'

A group of teenagers walks into the library, swinging their arms and chatting in raised voices. Maxine gestures at the quiet zone signage on the wall. They settle down on a sofa in the far corner, sniggering, and begin to activate the games console.

'Listen,' says Maxine. 'You are well overdue a break. When things get a little calmer with you, promise me that you'll take a moment for yourself.'

I've been pushing myself to the limit for months. The constant pressure of everyday life, compounded by the gut-wrenching memories of Mogadishu and my other parents, are beginning to take a toll on me. I sit in front of Maxine a mere shell of myself, with hollow dark shadows under my eyes that I have failed to cover even with the thickest concealer I could find. Maxine sees through my facade. She isn't fooled one bit. Her computer keeps pinging with emails. Other people need her, other causes, things that are more deserving.

'I'll consider it.'

Maxine raises her eyebrow. '*Consider* isn't good enough.'

'OK. I promise I'll do something fun when things get a bit better.'

Maxine closes her eyes and takes a satisfied sip of her tea.

The gold specks on her eyelids reflect the light. 'Better. You're far too young to be feeling like this. For once, I need you to act your age.' She stifles a smile and tries to look serious. 'You're going to better places. This library, and this crazy Jamaican lady, will be long gone.'

'Come on now. You're going nowhere. You'll be sitting here for a hundred years!'

Maxine walks with me to the door. 'Shush now, no more excuses. Get out there and enjoy your life before you end up wishing for the old days.'

I stand for a moment outside the library, taking a deep breath of fresh air. The sun is beginning to set, casting a warm glow on my body. Talking with Maxine has brought me a sense of peace I haven't felt for days. The weight that has been suffocating me seems to have lifted. I look forward to seeing Ubah soon and having more adventures together in the city.

*

In the evening, I listen to the sound of my mother shuffling around to settle down for her usual early night. I promptly leave the house and begin walking to the hostel.

'I'm here to see my sister,' I say, rather confidently, to the woman behind the hostel reception desk. Before I go in, I peer through the glass to make sure the security guard from the other day isn't on duty. 'Is she here?'

'I'm afraid I can't give you any information about our guests or staff. It's our policy.'

'I'm not asking for information. I already know she stays here. I'm just asking if I can see her.'

'Sorry, I can't help you with that. If she's bringing a guest, she knows that she has to notify us.'

'OK. I just want to check if she's safe. Can you at least confirm that for me?'

'I'm sure she's fine. I have no inclination to believe otherwise. I'm going to have to ask you to leave before we forcibly remove you.'

Chapter Nine

'Make your presence known, or be absent.'

In the last few months of 2005, my father moved out of our home bit by bit until all that was left of him were his old jackets in the hallway, hanging there like shed skin. First he took his clothes, then he took his letters, but throughout much of that period, his red Toyota Corolla remained parked in the estate car park.

 I was twelve then, chubby and angsty, with a penchant for journals that I discreetly wrapped up in old copies of the *Greenwich Times*. Every day, as soon as I woke up, I would climb onto the windowsill and look down at the car park to check if the car was still there. Then I would pull out my journal and write. One day I wrote that, if his car was gone, it would mean my father had truly left us for good – that was the final stage. And sure enough, I peeped through the curtains one foggy morning and the Corolla was nowhere to be found. I spent many mornings thereafter staring at the empty concrete space where it should have been.

 On New Year's Day 2006, he came back for just a few hours. It was a Sunday morning, and my mum was in a bad mood. As children we thought it was because we had woken up late, bickered at the breakfast table and watched cartoons instead of reading or drawing. She finished cleaning the kitchen and bathroom and put some coal on the gas cooker for the uunsi. When she wasn't looking, I would poke the whitened parts of the coal with a fork and watch the embers shoot out of it like molten birds. This was thrilling because it could get me a sharp clip around the ear. It became a little game; my mum would turn around, and I would make the sparks skitter through the air without her noticing.

Quran played on the radio. My mother recited along to the verses until her memory failed her, sometimes going on for as long as an hour. We had kept those cassettes since our days in Mogadishu, so the voice of the reciter had become intimate and familiar to us. He was like a family member, even though he was Egyptian and long dead.

'I don't want to stay here,' said my father. I remember not knowing what he meant by *here*, and to this day I'm still not sure. Did he mean *here* as in the home where my mum had started to burn the frankincense resin on the coal, so that it became difficult to breathe? Did he mean London – or England, the country itself, and what it stood for, and the fact that he never quite learned to be a part of it? Or did he mean here with us, as a family? Did he no longer want to be a part of our tragic situation?

I took note of the differences in their tone of voice – my mother's curt and sharp like a knife compared to his slow, soft voice. This time my parents did not close the door. We were free to witness all of it.

What I find strange is that I can't remember what my father said to me before he left, but I remember fragments of the conversations he had with my mum and brother. My mother bit her lower lip as she spoke calmly about the money that he owed her. She told him he needed to send the money first, and he promised that he would. There was some disagreement about how much it was and what it would be used for. She told him that everything was *khasaaro*, a waste, and he replied by saying that there was nothing wasteful about the family they had made together. Through their parting argument, I was learning the definitions of words I had never understood before. I learned that optimism can be violent.

Ahmed carried on watching cartoons, and I merely pretended to. The whole time, my parents sat close to each other in the living room. I don't think I had ever seen them sit that close together, except in faded pictures from a time when I was not yet a thought in my mother's mind. I think they sat that close in an effort to keep their voices low. Maybe they wanted to make it look like everything was OK, like Hooyo and Aabo were just talking, and not discussing the logistics of a man ripping himself away from a family and a country.

Ahmed, then six, asked us to watch him climb the door, jump, and spin a web like Spider-Man. My dad clapped his hands in a theatrical display of awe. Ahmed tried to ask him about superheroes and which one was his favourite, but all he could do was laugh and pat Ahmed on the head.

I sometimes wonder if he said anything to me at all. With my mum, he knew how to be serious when they discussed money and matters of the household, and with my brother he put on the silly, overly impressed act that grown-ups adopt to play along with small children. For me, he could never find that middle ground. I was old enough to be slowly becoming aware of the world they had constructed around me. I saw the holes and the seams in the structure that we called family life. I questioned things more, and most importantly, I knew which questions never to ask.

Once he left, we spent the rest of Sunday cleaning. It went on for hours, past the normal time that my mum would allocate for things such as hoovering our rooms and folding our school uniforms. I had never cleaned so much in my life, and even when I showed my mum that I had done enough, she would find something else for me to clean. I got on my hands and knees to wipe off the felt-tip pen Ahmed had scribbled onto the skirting boards in the kitchen. I tried all kinds of solutions – washing-up liquid, bathroom detergent, wood polish – but it wouldn't come off.

My father stayed in touch for a while after that. He would call us from Mogadishu every weekend, giving us updates on how the country had changed and the many ways it would change again when things got better. All of the neighbours we had known left the country in the nineties, around the same time we did. Some had gone to Denmark, Sweden, the Netherlands, the States. A new family had moved into our childhood home in Xamar Weyne. My father promised to send things over to us, but he never did. I didn't hold it against him, though. I decided that maybe we had everything we needed in England, and that things from Somalia would only remind us of the life we had left behind.

Very quickly, he got married again and had children. He told me the story over the phone as if he was telling me a bedtime story. The new woman was kind, beautiful and fair. Their home was by the sea. His daughter had fine, silky hair, more hair than he had ever seen on a newborn baby, and they called her Nour – light. Light of his life, perhaps.

I looped a lock of my hair around my finger and passed the phone back to my mum.

After that phone call, my mum told us that we didn't have to talk to our father every weekend if we didn't want to. He was busy with his new family and wouldn't have much time for us. I think she made excuses for why we couldn't come to the phone when he called. We were doing our homework, or we were playing outside. The phone calls began to dwindle down over the years until we only heard from him on Eid or on birthdays. And then the calls stopped completely.

'Is he even alive?' I asked my mum one day, when we hadn't heard from our father in over a year. There was a lump in my throat.

'Yes, he is, but he won't ask to see if *you're* alive. And he doesn't care, either.'

'Will you get married again?' I asked, cautiously, but with genuine curiosity.

'I don't know. Maybe I will, maybe I won't.'

'Why did you get married to Aabo, if he's so bad?' I asked her another time. I believed she had a role in why he was the way he was. Could she have not been wiser in her decision to love him in the first place? Why did she do whatever she did that led to their union? There would be no pain if she had thought twice. No quiet suffering, no children, no me. I was sitting on the floor between her legs as she rubbed almond oil into my scalp.

'For love,' she said, and I was shocked. I hadn't expected her to say that. I was fifteen at the time and to me, love was a Jennifer Lopez movie at best. Love, as I understood it in terms of flowers and dates and romantic walks, only existed in Hollywood or Paris. I couldn't imagine my parents participating in love.

'And where did you meet him?'

'I met him through my brother, Aadan. They worked together on a ship.'

'When did you realize you loved him?'

'When he asked me to marry him,' she said. I didn't know what to ask after that. I was waiting for her to describe their long telephone calls, the gifts that he would buy her, and the way he would say her name, but all she said was 'Turn your head.' She grabbed a strip of my hair between her fingers. The formation of a new braid was always tight and painful.

When I was seventeen, my mum was engaged to be married again. She announced it to my brother and me, along with some of our aunts, on a July afternoon when the sun was at its highest point in the sky. We were sitting in a relative's garden, eating watermelon on the grass. The women made high-pitched ululating sounds with their tongues against the roofs of their mouths, a sound I had heard at weddings. It was a celebratory sound. It was primal and passionate, nothing like the delicate, soundless tears that flowed at white people's weddings. We are loving people, I learned. I took in the sight of a house full of people gathered for love.

I know that she definitely loved this man because she would spend hours talking about him on the phone, and how he reminded her of Michael Jackson – in her words, when Michael Jackson was still Black and beautiful. She cooked for the extended family and filled many dishes with food and Somali sweets. The men came. And then the women. Negotiations happened behind closed doors.

Many years later, she told us why she broke their engagement. It was because he didn't believe that girls should become educated. My mother had dragged herself through nursing school and worked two jobs. She had a family to send money to back home, an example to set, a life to look forward to. She wasn't going to throw it all away. Not for this man. Not for anybody. She spent months in bed, when all was said and done. I couldn't understand why her choice had filled her with so much sadness and fatigue. I couldn't understand a lot of things back then.

I think of that July still, years later, when it rolls around and the sun is bright and unrelenting. And when I think of December, the month my father left us, I remember the emptiness of the car park space where his Toyota belonged. I catch glimpses of his non-farewell in the speech of other people. I pay attention to how people say goodbye now, even if they aren't loved ones, even if they are simply colleagues I am fond of moving on to new jobs, or old classmates I have never connected with in any special kind of way. I ache after parting from near-strangers because of what they force me to remember.

*

When I leave the hostel without seeing Ubah, the cars and buildings are bathed in a purple light like the one from that evening at the junkyard: soft Ribena purple.

In the days that follow, I keep calling her, but she never calls back. Then, one afternoon, I get a text: *Sirad, I hope you receive my message with an open heart. Lately I haven't felt very safe. I encountered many close calls with some serious danger. I am writing this because I care about your safety. I can't let myself put you in danger because of my own choices. Because of this, I have gone into hiding. This is my way of protecting myself and protecting you. By the time you receive this message, you won't be able to respond, as I will have changed my number. Take care of yourself.*

I read it over and over again. I remember the photographer she gushed about. Surely she couldn't be so naive? Maybe she trusted him with her secrets. Maybe he hurt her. I am powerless in this moment, knowing that I can't even file a police report if something has happened to her, because she is technically not supposed to exist. She is as good as a figment of my imagination.

I ask the Somali migrants about her, without tiring, for days. In local newsagents, stations, coffee shops and back at the entrance to the hostel. None of them will even commit to a full conversation with me. One of the ladies says that Ubah distanced herself from everyone else from the moment she first arrived, and they never got to know her. She worked, ate, and slept as far away from the group as possible and was uncomfortable talking about herself. She trusted no one. Of course, I know that I was the exception – until she decided to distance herself from me too.

'What about the bus?' I ask one of them, the youngest of them all. Her name is Hajer. She is about nineteen years old, with a warm smile. We are sitting in a restaurant; I have offered to buy her dinner in the hope that she will tell me as much as she knows. She speaks highly of my double. It is clear that they at least got along during the short time that they spent in each other's company.

'Do you know anything about the buses and the system that brings people to and from Mogadishu and here?' I press.

She pushes fried aubergines around on her plate. 'Everybody wants to get on the bus. I was told that it was all part of this technology that somehow tracks who would be best suited to making these journeys. I don't know how they get that information, if that's what you're interested in. At first, the buses only went one way, taking people from London to Mogadishu and not back. It was intended to be this short-term project by some university academics to connect people with their roots for a day and see if they felt grateful for being here.' She scoffs.

'But then it backfired on them. It was only a matter of time before word spread about the bus route. An underground company was set up to smuggle people over here and put them to work as cheap labour in certain places.'

'But what is the point of it all?' I ask. 'What are we supposed to realize at the end of this?'

'I have no idea. But what is it to us? Why should we be burdened by trying to discover that? All I know is, so many people want to be in my position. I won't waste it. You and others are tragically wasting your lives asking too many questions.'

I am offended, but she is right. Some things just don't need my interrogation.

'In every situation, we should always put our own best interests first.'

'Did you come here alone?' I ask.

'I was with other people, but I was the only one from my family. I left in the middle of the night and slept beside the station until morning.'

'And did you ever see Ubah with anyone else? Maybe she disappeared with a man, or was taken somewhere in a car?'

The girl stops chewing and stares at me, wide-eyed. 'I can't say any more. I am so sorry. Thank you for the food. It was very kind of you, but I have to go now.' She stands up and stuffs a bread roll into her jacket pocket.

'Wait!' I plead. 'I promise I won't say anything to anyone. You can trust me.'

'It's not that. I can't. I feel uncomfortable involving myself in other people's affairs. Please forgive me for talking about her in the first place. I can only worry about myself. Thank you and goodbye.'

Smoothing down her skirt, she leaves the restaurant. I

watch her walk up the high road until I can only see glimpses of her head bobbing through the crowd. Very quickly, she is enveloped by swathes of people.

Chapter Ten

'A word is yours when it's still in your stomach.'

I offer to take Rosie to the airport on the day she leaves for Rwanda. I feel guilty about deleting her message after we last met, and about generally ignoring her earnest efforts to stay connected. I feel even worse about this when I think of how much I had hoped to develop a normal friendship with Ubah, only for her to distance herself. No matter how much has changed, Rosie is one of the only people who knows me for me.

At Green Park station, we board a busy Piccadilly line train to Heathrow. In our carriage are a group of loud Italian children wearing bright orange jackets and carrying luggage bigger than their bodies. I nibble lazily on a croissant as I listen to Rosie making conversation with a couple of Americans. Unsurprisingly, she is talking about her internship. They listen intently, all wide-eyed and impressed. Rosie has a remarkable way of striking up a natural conversation with almost anyone, even this early in the morning.

'Are you excited?' asks the woman, leaning over her husband's lap to smile at me.

'Actually,' I respond, with croissant crumbs falling over my jacket, 'I'm not going. But I'm excited for her.'

'Yeah, it's just me,' Rosie chimes in. 'She's a great friend for seeing me off at the airport, though.'

'So what will you be up to, then?' asks the man in a friendly tone. 'What's your name?'

'Sirad.'

'Lovely name. Are you also into saving natural habitats?'

They both seem very sweet. I can tell from their faces that they expect me to say something exciting too. 'Actually, I'm involved in a university research project on time travel.'

'Oh, wow!' they both say, at the exact same time.

Rosie's jaw drops open. 'What? Sirad! You never told me!'

'It's just started,' I reply, with as much smugness as I can manage to help disguise my trembling voice. 'Actually, I wanted to tell you all about it today.'

The Americans exchange awkward glances. 'Sounds like you're both going on to great things,' says the woman. The train pulls into Hammersmith station, where they alight with enthusiastic goodbyes.

'A research project about time travel, huh?' Rosie prods. Her face gives away her disbelief. 'What's that all about?'

'I'm not really allowed to say a whole lot. But it's about finding out whether there are alternate dimensions.'

'Oh, there definitely are. Who's doing the research?'

'UCL,' I reply, without skipping a beat. The same university Rosie went to.

'Really? I'm surprised I haven't heard about this. Good on you!'

I cock my head to one side. I am having too much fun with this. 'Like I said, the research is in its early stages. We haven't put anything out yet.'

'So, what are you doing for it?' Rosie takes a bite of her croissant and brushes flakes of pastry off her chin.

'Outreach, something along those lines.' I'm waffling, and she can tell.

'Good on you,' she says again. 'Let me know how it goes.'

Rosie eats the rest of her breakfast in silence. I begin to reflect on what I have learned over the years, throughout my friendship with Rosie. She is beautiful and kind, but deeply lonely. Even when surrounded by people, she is lonelier for it. They are never the right sort of people. They enjoy what she can offer them, but they don't seek to understand her. I realize as I'm sitting with her that I have perhaps behaved the same way towards her in the few months we've been back in touch. I picture her alone in her flat after one of her nights out, sitting in front of the television with her blanket around her shoulders.

'Thank you so much for coming with me, Sirad. I'm going to get you the loveliest gift from Rwanda.'

'You don't owe me anything. In fact, I want to apologize.'

'For what?'

The cuff of her jumper is wet and threadbare from her anxious habit of picking at loose ends with her teeth.

'For not making much time to hang out with you over the past few months. I have to admit, I was a bit jealous when you first told me about Rwanda. It's disgusting, and I'm ashamed. I think when you told me all this amazing news, when I was sort of going through it, I misdirected all of my resentment.'

'Wow,' whispers Rosie. 'Really? I had no idea you felt that way.'

'Yeah. I can't believe I'm saying this. But I hope you can forgive me.'

'Sirad, I'm literally heading for the airport, about to say goodbye to start a new life. Of course I forgive you!'

'You're not saying goodbye!' I laugh, but tears spring to my eyes. 'You're only going to be gone for a bit.'

'I'm being dramatic, aren't I?' Rosie gives my hand a squeeze.

'If you weren't dramatic, then you wouldn't be you,' I say, teasing her.

When she called me at 9 a.m. this morning, I hadn't slept for more than an hour – I was tossing and turning all night, thinking about Ubah and whether she was safe or not. Hearing Rosie's voice on the other end of the line just as I felt forgotten by the world was strangely comforting.

'You know,' she continues, 'sometimes I think I'm crazy for doing this. What if I go out there and realize I made a massive mistake? What if I end up feeling more lost and useless than I've ever felt before?'

'Lost?'

'The feeling comes and goes.'

'What about right now?'

'I don't know. Everywhere I've ever gone, there has always been someone I know, someone to make me feel at home. I went off to university with the school lot, you know, Benjamin and Grace. I always felt that without that familiarity, I wouldn't be able to make it anywhere.'

'Really?' I accidentally make brief eye contact with a man sitting across from us. He's wearing navy overalls splattered in paint and sits with his arms crossed and his head resting on his chin.

I have never imagined that Rosie could feel lost. Her life has always gone according to plan. It's as if everything she has ever done has been organized in some long, colour-coded to-do list.

'Yeah . . . I mean, I was constantly making sudden and dramatic life decisions. I once thought that I could do the whole vegan thing; then I tried to convert to Buddhism. Now I'm wondering if all of this will be a phase, too.'

'I don't think this is a phase. I think you're really passionate about this.'

'Remember that game M.A.S.H.?' she asks, looking blithely out of the train window.

'Of course I remember. You would always add my crush's name onto your list of future husbands.' We giggle without making much sound.

'It's quite sad if you think about it. We were only kids. Why was there so much pressure to think about the future? They never expected that from the boys. What were *they* doing while we were picking baby names?'

'Playing football and eating grass.'

'So, nothing much has changed then.' We laugh together and suddenly I notice a lightness.

'I wish I could get rid of those M.A.S.H. questions at the back of my mind. It's like all of that crap has somehow been chiselled into our heads. Even now, I'm on my way to start over in a new and exciting place, and I've got those stupid bits of paper folding and unfolding in my imagination. Which man? What kind of home? And will I have kids? I've got all these inane questions going round and round in my mind.'

M.A.S.H., like life, was a game of pure chance. Our futures revealed themselves under the folded bits of paper, in glitter gel pen: a big detached home for me, a shed for Rosie, a Lamborghini for Rosie, a smelly bus seat for me. We used to be in fits of giggles by the end of each round, especially about the boys we were 'destined' to marry, this part more fun than anything else. We didn't realize then that real life wouldn't be much different, except more tearful and riddled with even more irony.

'Why does it feel like I'm running out of time?' I wonder out loud.

'Hmm.' Rosie tugs on a loose thread from her jumper cuff until it comes off, limp in her palm. 'Same. I think that's probably something we're always going to feel, right?'

'Right. But I feel it now more strongly than ever. I just want to get out of this rut.'

An elderly woman boards the train and stands expectantly to one side.

'You will,' says Rosie. 'I have no doubt about it. You're amazing. You just need to give yourself some grace. See, for me, I've realized that my greatest responsibility is to make sure I'm happy. No one else is going to care more about that than me.'

Rosie appears to think deeply about what she has just said, as though second-guessing herself. It must be really nice to come to such a well-rounded realization, I think. It must be so freeing not to feel a crippling sense of responsibility towards anyone else. I am nowhere near understanding what it means to prioritize happiness. Small moments of enjoyment, sure. But not happiness. I haven't even begun to define that for myself yet. And here is Rosie doing it so boldly, all by herself.

Someone's playing music loudly out of their phone. We all look at the guilty offender with no intention of asking him to stop.

Rosie begins to go on about some feminist authors I have never heard of. She rolls up her jumper sleeves. Around her wrist is a tattooed chain of daisies, looping round the raised outer bone and joining the inner side along her green veins. She got the daisies done a few years after brandishing the initials of her ex in the same place. They disguise a past she hates talking about, but so often does. A C for Chris and an L for Linton can be made out beneath the petals. They dated when Rosie was eighteen and he was well into his twenties – twenty-six or twenty-seven, she was never firm on which one. He would go through her phone every night and often he deleted the numbers of friends and family, mine being one of them.

One aggressive push against the wall from him was all it took for her to change the course of her life, move to the other side of London and call off everything they had planned together. I get the impression that Rosie never dares to look back on the past.

When we eventually make it to the airport, things are unusually quiet. Inside, people yawn and hold each other tightly. We make a beeline for the first coffee shop we can find. In the queue, a man pulls a woman into his arms by the tips of her fingers and they stand like that for a long time, his body curving over hers, covering her face. It is obvious that she is leaving. It is also clear that she secretly wants to let him go and never come back.

'I'll send you pictures of the cute animals,' Rosie smiles, sipping on her coffee and leaving a smudge of lip gloss on the rim of the cup.

'Listen, Rosie. There's something that's on my mind. Something I've recently discovered.'

'What is it?' Rosie narrows her green eyes at me.

'I recently found out that I have a twin.'

'WHAT?' She slams her open palms on the table in shock, her jaw swinging open.

'Yeah . . . We were separated at birth. My grandma took her and raised her when she was born. We left her in Somalia.'

'When did you find out?'

I feel sick to my stomach for lying, but I go on. This is the only way I can even begin to talk about what happened. 'A few months ago. It completely turned my world upside down. But I've grown to really care about her.'

'Where is she now?'

'I don't know. We haven't spoken in a while. I guess because we spent so long apart, it's impossible to really share anything now.'

We chat over more hot drinks and pastries, keeping our promise of making the goodbye short and fuss-free. When she pulls away from our hug, I feel like she has taken a load off me that I have been dragging around for a long time. She takes with her a little portion of my childhood, effectively freeing me from it. *Goodbye*, she says with her walk – *we never have to be those little girls again. Let go*, she also says with the way she lightly swings her free arm – *you too could be weightless, if only you could be brave.*

Rosie never looks back the whole time she walks away. I slowly begin to realize how much her leaving has shown me about who I am and what I want.

I arrive home after the long Tube ride back to find that my uncle Farah has come to visit.

'I was messaging back and forth on WhatsApp with Halima this morning,' my uncle says. Halima is one of Hooyo's oldest friends in our local area.

'How is she? She never picks up my calls these days,' says my mum.

'Not great. I worry about her, you know. The things she goes on about . . . We called a sheikh to bring holy water and read the Quran over her a few times . . . to help her with her issues.'

'What are her issues?'

'She kept going on about the bus business. People appearing out of nowhere who had fled the city decades ago, dazed and confused, claiming to have caught a bus from London and then been dropped off in Xamar Weyne.'

'God,' says my mother. 'I heard about a similar thing from

someone else. I can only empathize with the poor woman and others like her.'

'I had to ask her if she was telling me a joke or not, but she was serious. She really believes it's true. Apparently, the people who arrive on these buses are not allowed to stay, so they get taken back to London the same mysterious way they came.' He shakes his head. 'Why would anyone be taken to Somalia just to be brought back? What's the point of it? Where is the logic?'

'Our community operates in incredible ways. I don't understand us any more,' says my mum.

'What a sad state of affairs,' says my uncle. 'The truth is so cheap, so easily traded in for entertainment and gossip.'

'It's not entirely unfathomable either. I tell you, nothing shocks me these days.'

'The people of Xamar are vulnerable and stressed. Conspiracy theories are the last thing they need right now. All these stories are taking advantage of their sense of what is real in the world.'

After we finish drinking tea, I go to bring my uncle some water for his blood pressure medicine. I come back to find him and my mother in fits of laughter. They are looking at something on a phone.

'What are you all laughing at?' I step over my uncle's outstretched legs.

'It's a video of a cat speaking Somali!' laughs my uncle, with his eyes scrunched shut. 'How strange are God's creatures?' He slaps his leg and erupts into a series of deep, scratchy laughs. Using a cigarette he has pulled out of his pocket, he points at the phone screen and lets out a bellowing cry. 'Look! The cat speaks Somali better than you!'

Chapter Eleven

'One refusing a sibling's advice breaks his arm.'

It's Maxine who finds me a new job. Every week she has been forwarding me a list of job advertisements that she thinks I should apply for. I think it is just her own special way of building up my morale. She can't possibly believe I have a flying chance at any of these jobs – Assistant Editor, Production Assistant, Features Editor. Good God, I think – I love Maxine. Everything from how she prefaces her little messages of encouragement with a heart, to how she will sometimes check on me a few days later to see if I have actually applied for anything. She never fails to show me that she is right behind me.

I am half forced into going for this job – *Executive Assistant wanted for a brand new women's magazine.* 'APPLY!' is all Maxine writes at the bottom of her email.

She calls me just as I open the message, and I laugh in disbelief. 'Maxine. Are you sure they'd want me? It's in the City, so I'm sure they're getting hundreds of applications. And – well, I'm barely the kind of candidate they want.'

'Don't be silly. The deadline is tomorrow. Do you want a job or not?'

'Of course I do! I'm just so done with putting my heart

and soul into an application, only to be rejected or completely ignored.'

'You're going to have to come up with a better excuse than that.'

I know she won't let me off easily. 'Fine. I'll apply.'

But I take too long procrastinating and doubting everything, and I end up missing the deadline. My laptop's charger stops working, and midway through a draft of my application it gives up on me. I half run to the shop first thing in the morning to buy a new one and finish the application by breakfast. I write the accompanying email and hit send, the whole time believing I have completely ruined my chances.

Two weeks later, I receive a call from a woman named Rita, who introduces herself as the CEO of the magazine. I sit up straight on the sofa and clear my throat.

'Are you able to come in for an interview tomorrow?' she asks. Everything else she has said is a blur; *tomorrow* is the word I fixate on.

I go to three interviews before I am given the job. The money isn't anything spectacular, but it's money. *Think of the prospects*, I repeat to myself as I sit in the office foyer each time they call me for the next stage of the process. I wear brand new blouses each time. I dry-clean my blazers.

I hand in my notice at my old job and let the team know. After a gruelling week of tying up loose ends, I am finally free.

'I got the job!' I scream as I run down the street and into the library. Maxine does an endearing happy dance. She compliments me on my shoes, a pair of shiny black brogues with a platform.

'Now go out there. Do big woman tings!'

For the first time in my life, I'm looking forward to work. I hope that long, busy days at my new job will help to take my mind off the bus and Ubah, and most importantly, that it makes me feel like an ordinary adult with ordinary responsibilities.

On the morning I start, as I get ready for my first day, I push all my worries to the back of my mind. I can barely afford the train journey there, but I make it on time and that's all that matters.

As I wait in the lobby for a lift to the third floor of the office building, a girl in a hijab walks past. We exchange quiet salaams and nervous laughter. A sense of calm has already begun to descend and envelop me.

Rita's office seems to magnify what little January morning sunlight there is. The light comes through the bare windows, bouncing off the shiny white surfaces, leaving shadowy patterns on the walls. She shows me where to hang my coat as if she is welcoming me into her home. And like an awkward guest, I sit on the very edge of the plush cream sofa as she briefs me on my responsibilities for the day.

Rita speaks in a loud, jokey voice. 'If you don't go running for the hills by lunchtime, it'll be a good sign.'

I laugh in response and let my shoulders relax. I like her already. Her kind, pixie-like face and messy hair are putting me at ease.

'I'm just kidding. You look like you're raring to go. I *love* that blouse.'

'Thank you.' I touch the buttons of my plain white blouse, the one I had almost wrestled out of the hands of an old woman at the charity hospice shop. 'It's vintage nineties.'

'Oh God! Are the nineties really vintage now?' She unscrews the cap of her metal flask. 'I want you to be as comfortable as possible here, so I'm going to take the time to really help you understand the set-up. Let me know if there's anything you're unsure about, and I'll go over it. Anything at all.'

She sips coffee from the flask and then laughs to herself. 'You know, I couldn't sleep last night. I read something awful online. Something *so* awful, I think it inspired a potential cover for next month.'

'What was it?'

'The sudden influx of refugees – lots of them, mainly women and young children – they're being smuggled here, apparently. They're completely voiceless and invisible to passers-by. And they're on the streets begging for work, a home, food. I can't get it out of my head.'

'I heard,' I reply, with my eyes downcast. My chest begins to ache. I think of my double and her wounds. I remember her helpless tears. 'I can't seem to forget it either.'

'In the blistering cold! Children! Oh, it's *dire*.'

Rita has a sparkling diamond ring on her finger. I can't help but gawk at how perfectly small and dainty it is and how it seems to bend the sunlight that touches it.

'I got engaged over the holidays.' She runs her finger over the diamond, noticing where my eyes have wandered. 'We were in a cabin in Finland, surrounded by snow. He left it in the fireplace because he knew I would get up early to go and light it. And when I saw it there . . . I just broke down.'

'It's such a beautiful ring.'

'Thank you. I'm still not sure what this marriage thing means in a world as crazy as this. But it feels so good.'

She glances over at the clock and jumps, startled by how much time has already passed before she has even said a word about my induction.

'Jesus Christ, I can talk! Ever so sorry, let's get back to work. Feel free to stop me if I ever go off on a tangent like that again.'

'No, I enjoyed that. But you're right. Let's get started.'

'Great.' Rita pulls out a thick pile of papers from one of her folders. 'This is your induction pack. Let's start on page three.'

Her notepad flings open. In thick black marker, she has written 'ISSUE THEME: SOCIETY'S INVISIBLE WOMEN'.

My heart sinks. All I can think of is Ubah and the women from the hostel. Who will ever see them? Who will ever answer their silent cries? Here they are, alone in a new world, a new city, trying to fulfil some sense of a tomorrow. They are nothing but a means of making money for someone higher up. They have no rights over here, and even fewer where they have come from.

At home that evening, I find my brother sitting at the dining table, resting his head against his forefinger and his thumb. His first mock exam is a matter of days away. This is the first time I've seen him with his books out for months. We see less and less of him these days. Hooyo and I are still not quite sure where he went with his camera that time, but it was clear that he was exhausted by life and needed an outlet, somewhere to go just to breathe.

I have a newfound appreciation for my brother since Mogadishu. I think it's the knowledge that there is a version of my life where he doesn't exist that suddenly makes me feel more protective of him than I ever have before.

'How much have you got left to learn?' I ask, pulling out a chair beside him.

He makes an exaggerated gesture of clearing his throat. 'Two hundred and seventy-two pages.'

'Ah. So you haven't put a dent in it, is what you're saying.'

'I'm not trying to.' He pushes the books away. I push them back towards him.

'Come on now. Just put in the time. These are your mock *exams!*'

'And what happens if I don't put in the time?'

'You'll fail!'

'And what happens after that?'

I pause, irritated by his smart retorts.

'And then you can't do the things you really want to do. People won't respect you when you're a failure. You'll be poor. You'll be . . . invisible.'

'Huh?'

'Look, just get on with it, will you? Exams now, picture-taking later.'

'It's film photography.'

'Yeah, whatever.'

I prepare a bowl of chopped fruit and bring it to the table to munch on absent-mindedly. Ahmed reaches into the bowl to share.

'I just feel dumb investing time in something that I don't care about at all. I feel like I'm constantly pretending.'

'Who are you pretending for?'

'I don't really know.'

'So why pretend?'

'Because I have to. Since Hooyo lost her job, I've felt so pressured to do well – for her. And the more I feel pressured, the harder it is to do anything at all. It's like life has become about passing or failing. But I don't want to buckle. I want to make it out of here – far, *far* from here.'

'Hooyo isn't well. She doesn't want to admit it or find a word to define her struggle right now, but you know she's not OK. She's got a lot on her plate. The only thing that you need to show her is that you're trying. How will you ever know if you're not meant for something if you don't try?'

'I have tried.'

'No you haven't. Open your book and stop moping.'

He opens his book at a random page and stares down at a picture of baby monkeys being fed from milk bottles hanging from a metal cage. Then he looks across the room at the TV. The sound was off, but the screen shows a busy Times Square from a bird's eye view.

'I forgot to tell you, this letter came for you.'

'What is it?'

'Haven't opened it. Read it for yourself.' He passes me a brown envelope, addressed to me in curly handwriting. There's no return address or any sign on the envelope of who it could be from. My pulse thuds in my ears. I rip open the envelope.

Dear Sirad Ali,

We hope this message finds you well.

As a valued participant in the UNCLASSIFIED project, we would like to invite you to join an upcoming focus group session at our offices. This session will bring together a small group of participants who, like you, have embarked upon unique journeys through our project. The purpose of this session is to gather insights and feedback on your experiences, which are invaluable to the continued development and success of the UNCLASSIFIED project.

Your voice is important to us, and we believe that your perspective would greatly enrich the discussion. The session will be an opportunity for you to share your thoughts, connect with others and help shape the future of our initiative.

The details of the focus group are as follows:

Date: 9 February

Time: 10am
Location: UNCLASSIFIED Project Headquarters, 10 Salutation Road, London, SE10 0AT
Duration: Approximately 2 hours

Over the next few days, I read the letter countless times. I wake up with it and go to bed with it under my pillow. As the days pass and I get closer to my meeting, 9 February becomes a slowly approaching dark figure from a sleep paralysis episode.

Hooyo receives an email from my brother's teacher requesting a meeting about his academic progress, or lack thereof. The meeting is arranged for the 8th and I take the day off work so we can go together, without Ahmed. My mum puts on a smart black coat, conceals under her eyes with light make-up and blots some lipstick across her lips. She even brings the old leather handbag she used to use for work. Her termination letter is still tucked into the inside pocket.

We sit at the back of the bus and are silent for the whole journey. Her whole body faces the dirty windows and she scrolls through text conversations on her phone. I sense her reluctance to talk to me about whatever is on her mind, and I am equally reticent.

As the bus crawls up the hill towards Ahmed's school and the gates of the entrance come into view, a childhood anxiety revisits me. This is the same place I attended between the ages of twelve and sixteen. I can still hear the old noises from the front playground, now empty. There's the roof where a boy from the year above threw himself to his death. A hedge of barbed wire now lines the edge. And there's the school coat of arms. I find myself standing in front of the building's entrance with a faint, inexplicable longing for those days.

The corridors are lined with examples of pupils' work: photography, paintings and poetry. We arrive at reception fifteen minutes early. From where we are sitting I can see a glimpse of the library where I used to spend many lunch hours wedged between bookshelves, sitting on my bookbag.

Mrs Singh summons us to her desk. She puts on her gold-rimmed glasses as we sit down and doesn't waste any time getting to the point.

'We're certainly very concerned at this stage. Ahmed hasn't been to a single science class for weeks, and the mock exams are fast approaching.'

'That can't be,' says my mum, shaking her head and closing her eyes. 'I send him to school every morning. He goes.'

Mrs Singh puts her elbow on the table and narrows her eyes. 'That's not what the register says. I mean, we've been sending you messages about it and you haven't responded. Is everything OK with him?'

My mum shakes her head in disbelief. 'I haven't seen your messages. You should have called me. I have been – so busy. Does he go to his other classes?'

'According to the register, he has been missing a few other lessons too.' The teacher rubs her eyes with her ring finger under her glasses. 'You see, these mock exams are very important because they give us an idea of how we can support each child. We can't stress that enough. You'll need to talk to him in any way you know how.'

'Is there still time to get him back on track? Can he get himself together in time for the real exam?' asks my mum.

Mrs Singh purses her lips. 'To be honest with you, I don't anticipate that Ahmed will achieve his predicted grades if he carries on like this. But look, miracles happen every day. If he fixes things now, he can turn everything around by the time exam season kicks in. Just let us know how we can support him. We have a team now in the library for the independent study sessions. I know it can be tricky sometimes to help with GCSE homework; I struggle with it too sometimes with my own son. And if there is anything else we can support him with holistically — breakfast club is free now for some students from lower—'

'He has breakfast at home. I take care of that, thank you.'

'I'm sure you do, Mrs Ali.'

'Mrs Hirsi.'

'I apologize, Mrs Hirsi. You can reach me via email if you need anything.'

'Have I failed?' my mother asks me, as we ride back on the bus. We are almost home. Her question is completely out of the blue and unexpected. We are the only ones on the bus. My mum looks like a lost little girl. Her eyes fill with tears that threaten to spill over.

'You haven't failed,' I offer. 'Ahmed is just growing up and finding some parts of that a bit difficult, that's all.'

'But everything started with me. There has to have been a root cause, and I think that root cause is me. Me, me, me. When I lost my job and gave up, I could have tried to be better, but it's so hard. It's just so, so hard.'

I feel my heart soften towards her; a flutter of heat in my chest and then a cooling sensation. 'It's not your fault,' I reassure her. 'You didn't bring it upon yourself. You can't make yourself responsible for the choices your children make.'

'I just want you both to remember that it wasn't always like this. Sometimes I get flashbacks to how life used to be when everything was all new and exciting here. We went on long walks together after dinner and to the museum. We were young, your father and I. We had dreams too. We wanted all the same things that every twenty-something in the world wants – a home, a family, some semblance of a future. It wasn't all just struggle, struggle, *struggle*. That is what people think it was all about back then, but that is not true, not every day at least. There was something very beautiful there in the beginning.'

'So do you regret it? Do you regret coming over here?'

'I regret how we went about it. Your father and I, we made it harder on ourselves.'

'How?'

'We turned on each other at every obstacle.'

'That's human, you know.'

'I know.'

We stop at the local Turkish butcher's for some chicken before we head home. My mother holds a five-pound note tightly in her hand. I don't have to ask to know that it's all she has left of what I gave her last week.

'How much money do you think it will take, Hooyo?' I ask, while we're standing in line.

'For what?'

'For us. For your everything. How much is enough for us to keep our heads above the water, at the very least?'

'Why stress yourself out about it, dear? Life is nothing but survival, and provisions come from God. We should be careful not to lose ourselves in constant questioning.'

By the time we leave the shop, it's dark outside. My mum searches for my hand as we wait by the traffic lights before crossing. I hold hers in mine, her fingers bonier and harder than I remember them. How long has it been since I was just a little girl?

I think carefully about the letter and what it might mean.

Both of us look left and right for oncoming traffic. We hurry along the street with the wind in our faces, no longer sure who is leading and who is being led.

Chapter Twelve

'You don't go searching for bones in a lion's den.'

I curl up in a ball in bed with my phone gripped tightly in my hands. I'm grateful that Rita didn't ask me to elaborate on what I meant by 'a family situation' – she just told me to take care and give her a call at the end of the day to confirm that I could come in for work the next day. It's 7 a.m. on 9 February. The fierce winds bring the pungent smell of cannabis into the living room. I gaze out of the window at the very road that I am going to walk along in search of UNCLASSIFIED's research offices. As I eat breakfast I rock back and forth, waiting for a sign to turn me away from my decision – a way out from something that could eventually be a violent and unforgivable act of betrayal.

When the time comes to leave the flat, I find myself uttering prayers of protection under my breath. I look behind me, over my shoulders, as I walk towards Salutation Road, even before I get down the stairs of the tower block. The sound of school-children laughing in the distance on their way to the bus stop helps to calm me down ever so slightly. I hope, almost foolishly, that Ubah will appear at this point to help me, guide me, or at least turn herself in.

I get closer to the Spice Girls billboard; I can read the words that are scrawled all over it in faded black marker. Tied to a lamp-post is a wreath of dead flowers. There is a poster for a missing child, then one for a dog, and then another. Most of the words have eroded away.

The place is drenched in silence. The junkyard furniture is all gone, except for a ripped armchair poking out of an almost-full skip of rubbish. I keep walking through the car park until I reach the exit at the back. I haven't gone further than this since I was a child.

Outside the UNCLASSIFIED offices are a fleet of buses. Interestingly, each of them has the same destination displayed on the front: Stratford. The building itself is extremely underwhelming – it's simply a large, unmarked porta-cabin of offices. I can see old phones and printers through the windows.

'You lost, darlin'?' calls a man from behind me. I walk briskly to the door and push the button before glancing back at him. He stands staring at me until I realize that the front door is unlocked and go inside. The man staggers away.

A young woman is sitting at a reception desk reading a book that has been covered in black tissue paper, obscuring the title. She tells me where to sign my name and shows me where to sit and wait, then goes straight back to her book. I sit on a hard chair in the foyer and wait with my legs tightly crossed, listening to the clock ticking above her desk.

After a while, a young woman enters through the front door. She is petite and Middle Eastern-looking, with long, curly black hair and an evil eye necklace.

I hold out my hand. 'Olga?' I enquire.

She shakes her head. 'I'm supposed to meet someone called Olga here, too. I've just used the toilets. They're filthy! What are you here for?' She takes a seat opposite me and fiddles with her loose plait.

'I'm not quite sure. I just received a letter a few days ago.'

'So did I.'

'You took that bus?'

'Yes! I think we were on the same journey? I remember you. You got off first in Somalia. I think I passed out for a while after that, just out of pure shock.'

'Oh God,' I whisper. 'Where did you get off?'

'In Baghdad.' She huffs and tugs on her plait. 'I have no flippin' clue what this is all about or what they want from us.'

She looks like she hasn't slept very well. She's extremely fidgety. She opens her mouth to speak again, but it's a while before any sound comes out. 'Ugh! Where is this damn woman?'

'I had to lie to my boss to take a day off from work.'

'Me too. A research project, you know! I swear this whole thing has ruined my life.'

'They've got a lot of explaining to do,' I say, awkwardly. The girl pulls thinner strands of her hair by her face. She taps her feet against the carpet.

At last Olga appears, and she looks almost exactly as I imagined her. She's on the younger side of middle-aged, with short, sleek brown hair that sways with every slight turn of her head and a squarish jaw. Her grey blazer and skirt set looks quite dated and uncomfortable, but she has an air of authority about her. She is shy as she approaches us and apologizes for keeping us waiting, ushering us into a stuffy room containing nothing but chairs and two large filing cabinets. Olga pulls some chairs out from a store cupboard and begins arranging them into a semi-circle.

'How many are we expecting?' I ask.

'Four or five others. If they're still coming, that is.'

The girl and I give Olga a hand arranging the chairs into a circle. Within the space of a few minutes, the rest have joined us. All of them complain about the difficulty of finding the place and the strange man outside. One woman has brought her dog with her, and Olga tells her she has to tie him up outside. She makes a big fuss about this before eventually giving in.

'Good morning, all. My name is Olga, and I'm head administrator of the UNCLASSIFIED project and your facilitator for the day. I know this may be very daunting for you all, but before we get into the nitty gritty of it, I'm going to go through some house rules with you. I need you all to pay attention to them, because they're very important.'

Sitting next to me is the girl I spoke to on the bus. She is wearing the same gold hoop earrings and geometric patterned headwrap. When she came in, we exchanged looks of relief and said hello. At least we recognize each other. At least we can testify for each other if we have to, for that small part of the journey we shared.

Olga goes on: 'To begin, there is some important housekeeping to go through. This environment is totally confidential. Anything that is said in this room must not be shared elsewhere. Anything that is said in the outside world about UNCLASSIFIED, you must ignore unless you hear it from us first. I have to make this bit very clear: we have some strict policies to ensure your safety and wellbeing. I'm going to pass around some pens in a moment. Please have a read through our privacy policy and sign the dotted line. Once you've all done so, we can begin.'

Olga swiftly pulls out some documents from a clipboard and begins passing them around the circle. Reluctantly, I skim-read the policy, finding nothing out of the ordinary in it. For the most part, it reads like something I would expect. They aren't liable for any loss or damages, and they reserve the right to use our stories to further their understanding of the parallel worlds.

I'm distracted by what's around me. From Olga's clothing to her clipboard to the filing cabinets, it all feels like we're in some kind of time capsule.

'I really have to emphasize the third paragraph of the policy. We strictly prohibit sharing or discussing anything about this project on social media.' She pulls her chair closer to us. 'Does anyone have any questions or concerns about what I've just said?'

'Nope. Just kind of want to get to the point, really,' says the girl with the long plait, drumming her fingers on the arm of her chair.

'Well, I was just about to do that.' Olga forces a smile. 'We were running our research project as part of the Centre of Migration Studies at the university, which I can't name. We've carried out decades of research into the significance of time and space in migration and worked with some incredible minds, all of whom will remain anonymous. It started off as a sort of fascination with migrant people's perceptions and beliefs about time and space, and how this adds to their experience of belonging, loss, grief, love and feelings about the future. Then we took our research to new heights and, long story short, we discovered a way to jump between timelines and gain some kind of control over this variable.'

Nobody says anything, but Olga takes a long, emphatic pause.

When nobody speaks, she continues. 'When this project began, it was the seventies. If you know about this bit of history, you'll know that things got very heated in London between minority communities and the far right. People were no longer sure whose country this was, and what it even means to own a country, if there is such a thing. Meanwhile, UNCLASSIFIED was only just beginning to define itself in light of these new parallel worlds that we gained access to.'

Just as Olga finishes her sentence, someone knocks on the door, and she jumps right up to answer it. She returns to her seat with bottles of water for us.

In between large gulps of water, Olga finishes her introduction. 'So, as you can see, our work felt incredibly pertinent at the time, but we were struggling to pinpoint how our theories could be made into praxis. We're humanitarians as much as we are academics. We wanted to provide some sort of relief, some sort of impact. We thought that perhaps we would see if a glimpse into this world could offer immigrant communities some sort of healing and understanding.

'Our original hypothesis was that, by providing a controlled experience to a parallel world, young people from migrant backgrounds would be able to gain a unique perspective on what it means to be who they are, allowing them to create a strong sense of identification with both here and elsewhere.'

'So, was your hypothesis correct?' asks the girl in the hoop earrings.

Olga smiles. 'That's a great question. What's your name, dear?'

'Ruth.' She looks around the circle. 'What is the purpose of UNCLASSIFIED if we never get the answers to all our questions? I got off in Lagos, whatever happened there *happened*, and now I'm here. There was no time to make sense of it all. No time to sit with my thoughts or change anything. What was the point of it?'

'Thank you for saying that, Ruth. You've made a very good point, and actually, it's one that we ask ourselves from time to time. That's why we find it so important to talk to you and get a sense of how we can improve this project.'

We all look at each other, hesitating. The tension is suffocating. I can tell everyone in this room has a lot to say, but doesn't know where to begin.

'Why don't we go around the circle? Please say your name and where you went before you chime in with your thoughts on the experience,' says Olga.

'Dimple.' The first girl to speak is one I also recognize from the bus journey. She's wearing a pair of light blue jeans and a white T-shirt. 'I went to Calcutta.'

'OK, Dimple,' says Olga. 'How do you feel now that you've had some time to think through the experience?'

Dimple seems to hold back a lot of her words. She speaks slowly and carefully. 'I just don't know how I'm ever supposed to be the same again. I'm sorry, that's the only thing that I can say right now. I'm struggling to find my words.'

'It's OK, Dimple. We can come back to you. Ruth?'

Ruth lets out a long, audible exhale. 'I went to Lagos. Yes, it was beautiful in some ways, but mostly frustrating. Like I said earlier, I don't know what could possibly be achieved in just one day.'

'Less than a day, even,' someone else chimes in.

We go on like that around the room, each person saying their name and where they went, and offering slim vestiges of their stories – but all too afraid to say anything substantial. I notice that everyone in the room is a woman.

'Where are the boys?' I wonder out loud.

'Aha. We did have a couple of young men in this cohort, but unfortunately they weren't able to make it. But that's OK. It's beautiful to be in a room of women from such diverse cultures. The research group is very passionate about getting women, in particular, to share their thoughts and feelings about the journey. It appears to be a little more difficult to engage men.'

'Good for them,' says Ruth. 'Because this has been a waste of time. I was perfectly content before I went on your project. Now I can't sleep at night because of all my worries.'

'Me neither,' says Dimple. 'I just got back from Calcutta with more questions and more confusion about whether I'm supposed to be— look, basically, I'm having an existential crisis.'

I am hesitant to comment. All I can think about is Ubah. It seems that Olga can sense this, because she ignores everyone else and picks on me. 'And you, dear? What's your name, and how was the journey for you? Did you find that you left with more questions?'

'My name is Sirad,' I reply. 'And no, not questions, but more responsibilities.'

Olga's interest is piqued by my answer. She tosses her hair back. 'Can you elaborate? I know you're in a slightly different situation to the rest – your double crossed over to this side, didn't she? Do you want to talk about that a bit?'

I shake my head. 'I don't want to, no. She has a lot to run away from. I don't want to get involved. I don't think it's appropriate.'

'And that's OK. In fact, you are entitled to your feelings. But remember, this is a confidential space. Everyone in this room can relate to your sense of unease.'

Yasmin, the girl I first spoke to in the reception area, begins to defend me. 'She doesn't have to share a thing. You can't force her! She's clearly struggling with what happened. We all are!'

Olga straightens up in her chair. 'Your honest thoughts

help us learn, to see what we can do to improve your overall experience.'

Yasmin shoots a glare at Olga. 'And what have you offered us since we came back? Nothing! No support. No check-ins. After we all go home today, what are you going to do to tidy up the mess you've caused in our lives? What have you got to stop us from going crazy?'

Olga takes a long pause. 'That is still being figured out.'

'But you had decades! Right?' Ruth lets out a laugh of disbelief. 'Are you just here to mine our feelings for your own curiosity? You've made a mockery of us.'

'Listen, I too went on a journey to my homeland when I was a young woman, around your age,' says Olga. 'Don't get me wrong – I was confused about it for a little while afterwards. I'm not saying that you're all supposed to get it right away. But I can say now, looking back, that it all made sense—'

'We don't want to hear it,' says Dimple, cutting her off. 'Save your sorry story for someone else.'

'This is just sickening,' mutters Ruth. She gets up from her chair and prepares to leave. 'At a time like this? I can't feed into this rubbish. I'm done.'

The rest of the girls follow suit. I hover above my seat, unsure of what to do. Then I see the blank expression on Olga's face, as if she's nothing more than some kind of automaton running out of power. Before I know it, I'm the last one left in the room with Olga.

'Sirad, do you have a moment? I want to talk to you privately.'

The loud conversation of the girls filters back to us as they leave the building, leaving an unsettling silence in the room. I stand up and nervously hold my bag up to my chest as though shielding myself from Olga, my heart still racing from the heated exchanges.

Olga looks weary and entirely harmless. Pieces of sweat-drenched hair stick to her forehead.

Before I can respond to her, Olga's voice cuts through the silence.

'We received some information about your double, Ubah. Our security team have asked you to comply with us in our search to bring her back.'

'I don't know where she is,' I respond.

'That's fine. But I take it you know something about where she was working? Hundreds of people have crossed over and have been working illegally in local establishments. This is human trafficking.' Her gaze is intense, as if she's searching for something beneath the surface of my eyes. 'Look, this can't be easy for you. I get it. And I understand that today's session didn't go as planned. It's not easy to be candid when emotions run high.' She pauses, letting the words hang in the air. 'But I'm asking you for a completely different kind of input here. I need you to tell the truth.'

I swallow hard, feeling a knot of anxiety tighten in my chest. 'I am telling the truth. I don't know where she is. I hung out with her for a bit, yes. But I haven't spoken to her in a long time.'

Olga stands and steps forward slightly. 'What would it take for you to work with us a bit more?'

I shift around on my feet uncomfortably. A feeling of disgust washes over me.

Olga's gaze sharpens. 'I can offer you twenty-five thousand pounds for pertinent information,' she says, her voice calm but with an undercurrent of pressure. 'All we need is a written statement. It doesn't have to be fancy. Just the name of the hostel, what she did there and what you saw in the area. We want to help Ubah return safely, and make sure no one is being taken advantage of.'

Afraid of the seriousness of her preposition, I walk towards the door, but the sum of money she has just mentioned seems to slow me down. I find myself holding onto the door handle and turning back to her.

'A statement? Is that all?'

'That's all.' Olga gives me a smile of relief. 'Come here tomorrow morning. Alone.'

'I have to get back to work. How much more of my time do I have to waste on this?'

'Then come by before work. Does seven a.m. work for you?'

Stunned at my decision, I nod back at Olga without saying a word. As I walk out of the building, I'm overcome with a heady mix of fear and shame.

Outside, a crow picks food out of a bin. I see the man who called out to me earlier loitering nearby. All I can think about is the sum of money Olga offered me, as though it's written into the clouds. Twenty-five thousand pounds would be a fresh start for us; we could pay off our debts and sleep properly. With the money, I could be the one to lift my mother up out of whatever she has sunk into.

As I exit Salutation Road, I fill my lungs with fresh air. I feel dirty, but something in me begins to settle. From where I'm standing, I can see our estate ahead of me, and my neighbourhood, beyond this no man's land. I have to keep up, I tell myself. There's no time to be sentimental and no room to worry about anyone else. Time itself has abandoned me. I am all alone in my wickedness and in my joy.

Chapter Thirteen

'An old wound will not go away.'

'**N**ow some half a million and more, as we know, are coming.' The BBC news report I'm watching on TV shows drone footage of shoes, clothes and life jackets abandoned on a shingle beach. The correspondent's voice is urgent. The cuffs of his khaki trousers are wet as he walks along the shore. A large crowd of people wait on land, cheering and clapping as the lifeboats get closer. One by one, the survivors wade onto land, some of them crying into the shoulders of their partners and clutching their children tightly. These people arriving on boats on TV are not too different to the ones crossing over on the buses; both groups are desperate to reach safety, to be seen as more than a piece of debris bobbing up and down in the sea.

Keeping my promise to Olga, I prepare to visit Salutation Road for what will hopefully be the last time. Aunt Najma and her daughters have stayed the night again. She is up early watching the news, rambling on as usual. I'm ironing my clothes and hanging onto every word from the TV.

'And where are you going so early this morning?' quizzes Aunt Najma. She watches me iron my clothes, piece by piece.

I've already prepared myself in case anyone asks this. 'I

have an early work meeting today,' I reply, making direct eye contact.

She narrows her kohl-lined eyes and tips her head to one side. My blood is pumping forcefully through my veins. I turn up the volume on the TV.

'I see.' She twirls a strand of her hair. 'You're quite important at your new job, then?'

I don't say anything to this. In my rush to get ready, I accidentally knock over a silver cup of water on the coffee table. Najma jumps up and makes a big fuss of wiping it up. I turn back to the TV.

'What would push them to do this? Why would they risk their lives?' the correspondent continues. Now that I have turned up the volume, his voice rings through the entire apartment. 'Anyone would be moved by the atmosphere behind me right now if they were here. Dehydrated, weak, even wounded – it doesn't stop them from keeping on. They know that many others aren't so lucky.'

The survivors are received with an incredible display of warmth and emotion. Ordinary members of the public offer their hands and shoulders to lean on as the survivors collapse with exhaustion and tears. I find it difficult to continue watching, but the strong force of guilt forces me to listen. Aunt Najma crunches loudly on pistachios. 'How beautiful humans can be when they actually care.'

'Where will they go now?' asks the correspondent. 'This is just the start of their journey through Europe. For many, this is no resting place.'

My mother comes in with a tray of tea and biscuits. I kiss her on the forehead as she sits down. Aunt Najma's girls trail after her with mini yoghurt pots in their little hands. My aunt and my mother launch straight into a conversation about one of their long-time friends, who has recently lost a sister.

As I finish getting ready, something the news correspondent says catches me off guard: *'Every day, at the moment, an average of six people die in the water.'*

I'm suddenly tearful at this. I think of how each of those people had a family who loved them, who awaited news of their safe arrival, and who are now perhaps deep in indescribable grief.

I refuse the tea. My stomach is beginning to cramp up. A young man with long mouse-brown hair forces his way through the crowd and begs to speak to the reporter. Excited by his enthusiasm, the reporter holds the mic up to his mouth.

'I just want to say, it's completely different when you're actually here and you can see what these people have gone through. When you can see someone suffering right in front of you, it's not so easy to pretend their life doesn't matter. You want to make sure they're safe and OK. This isn't about politics, for goodness' sake. It's about human lives!'

A girl comes up beside him and hugs him. She is wearing a large yellow REFUGEES WELCOME T-shirt over her jacket. *'We're Christians,'* she says. *'What kind of Christians would we be if we didn't show up to help in some kind of way?'*

'What's one thing you want these people to know?' asks the correspondent.

'That there are people like us who want them here,' says the man. *'It's as simple as that.'*

I find myself moved to tears at the sight of a woman in the background who is struggling to breathe. She is having a panic attack. She is holding her baby tightly in her arms as two women stand with her, trying to help. Their expressions are calming and reassuring, as if they know exactly what they are doing. I can't help but picture Ubah in the Primark changing room, crying with sadness and fear.

'To a new and better life, says almost everyone I have spoken to this morning. The destination is the same for everyone.'

The report changes location to a busy market in Goslar, Germany. A young couple walk hand in hand, smiling. The woman wears a white scarf and a black oversized NYC hoodie. The man carries a blue plastic bag filled with fruit.

'Here at this farmers' market in the medieval town of Goslar, Germany, Mahmoud and Leyla are far away from the olive groves of their home country, Syria. Together, they're planting the seeds of a new life. With their children, they are surviving, but beginning to thrive. For them, it has been important to find a place their three children can call home.' Inside their tiny kitchen, the couple prepare breakfast with the food they have bought from the market. Mahmoud boils water on the stove as his daughter eats toast at the table. The camera zooms in on her large blue eyes. She's watching a cartoon on a small TV as she eats.

'On this crisp winter morning, the children prepare for a school drama production. Their youngest, Jalila, is the leading lady, Mary. She's a bubbly and intelligent child, and just like any other five-year-old, she enjoys playing with her friends. At first glance, this could be the household of any German family – but most German families don't have a family therapist to help them cope with the effects of having survived a war.' Those last few words pierce through me. Nobody thinks about how difficult it is to realize you are a survivor of the very things that have killed others. Even as a child new to the country, I was aware that we had left so many loved ones behind. It never felt right.

The first time I took part in a school nativity, the year after we arrived in England, I too played Mary. I could barely string an English sentence together. My teacher gave me a sand-coloured shawl to drape around my head and placed a little white baby doll into my arms. I beamed with pride. I thought I was supposed to dress up as my mother, so I spoke like her and ignored the script, making everyone in my class laugh.

On the day of the performance, I opened the heavy red curtains by an inch to watch the hall fill up with parents, grandparents and squealing babies. Beside me on the stage was my acting partner as Joseph, a mixed-race boy with green eyes and curly hair.

He crossed his arms and said in a hostile voice, 'You look like you're from another country.' He was pointing at the scarf on my head. I had known all along that I was different from the other children in my class; even though they came in all shades, something made me stand out. Now it seemed clear that my cover was blown. No child at that age wants to be reminded that they're different.

The teacher appeared and got us to assume our positions and get into character. The curtains drew back, and the warm spotlight shone on my face. I had forgotten my lines.

On the news, little Jalila climbs onto a school bus. In a school hall, parents politely greet each other and make small talk over cups of coffee before the play starts. The Syrian couple sit together silently; language is a barrier, physically isolating them from everyone else. The camera implies that there are other unseen barriers. People walk around them to get to their seats without speaking to them or acknowledging them, as if they are a part of the furniture.

'The thing that worries Mahmoud and Leyla most is the future of their children. Here, at this local Catholic girls' school, they struggle to understand the system by not speaking the language or sharing the same religion as everyone else. Even so, it's

a place of solace. School means structure, hot meals and somewhere where their children can be safe as they figure out their next steps.'

There was an empty chair beside my mother when she came to watch me perform in the school play. Later, she made friends with other Somali and Asian mothers, but I still remember the look on her face in those early days. I would watch her from the classroom window, waiting in the playground to pick me up at three thirty in the afternoon. She looked like a lost child on their first day at school. She looked like she had been rushing to get to me, and she often was. My mum was always rushing. Rushing to catch the bus for work, rushing to get home before it got dark so she could pray on time; rushing, always, towards something better somewhere else.

*

When I arrive at the UNCLASSIFIED offices, I'm still thinking about the news report and Ubah. The receptionist gives me a big, fake smile and tilts her head towards the hallway. 'Come this way.' She leads me to the same room I was in the previous day.

'Do you need any support with your statement?' she asks.

'No, thank you. I don't have a lot of time.'

'Don't worry. It won't take more than a few minutes.'

There are two pieces of paper I need to fill out. One is filled with lots of tiny boxes I need to tick and a line for me to sign. The second gives me space to describe what happened during the time I spent with Ubah in London. It all seems so simple. I take a deep breath and sit down on a chair, using a clipboard the receptionist provides. After I've finished, I hand over the paperwork and leave the building. I promise myself it's the last time I will ever return to this place.

Any mention of refugees reminds me of Ubah. The topic is being discussed everywhere – I can't block it out. I feel like a fraud whenever I find myself in the midst of conversations about relatives or people in the community who are facing hardship after immigrating to somewhere or other in search of safety and freedom. I have cousins who have successfully crossed to Germany, Turkey and the US. I have neighbours who, just a few years ago, escaped the war in Syria and are struggling immensely.

Something is gnawing away at me, bit by bit. I can't place where my guilt lies. Part of it is due to the fact that I had to try to erase Ubah from my own memories in the same way that UNCLASSIFIED wants to erase her presence here. I can't think about her the same way while doing what I am doing. It's torture.

The money has already been deposited into my account by the time I arrive at work. I stuff the memories of Ubah, Mama and Aabo into a dark and quiet corner of my mind. It's the only way I can carry on.

*

It takes me some time to gather the energy to leave the house and force myself to meet a friend. I head to the library to see Maxine. At first, I can't imagine how I'm going to face her. Even if I choose to keep a secret, I can't hide my emotions from Maxine.

I sit behind the rows of people at the desks in the quiet area, reading. By 5 p.m., people are beginning to leave, one by one. Eventually it's just me, Maxine and the cleaner, who circles around us with her vacuum wires.

'Come on over here, star.' Maxine coaxes me away from the books I have been listlessly piling together.

I feel completely defeated. I am just moments away from telling Maxine everything. I just want to hear, in her words, that I am not evil – that I can somehow be good again.

'You know you can't sulk away by yourself for very long. It'll take up all your energy.'

I rush over to her.

Maxine lets me into the small office behind her desk area. I sit down on a velvet two-seater sofa. The room is colourful and vibrant. It doesn't look like it belongs in a community library. It's tastefully kept and smells faintly of oud. A single candle burns on the radiator.

'So, star, what's the matter?' Maxine says it as if she already knows. She pours peppermint tea from a silver flask and hands it to me in a small mug. 'How's the job? Please don't tell me someone's being horrible to you.'

I take a long sip of tea, and she waits for me to speak.

'You know, I think I'm the problem. I'm the one that's hurt somebody. I'm evil. That's what's upsetting me.'

'Hmm. Now, if you were evil, you wouldn't be saying that. You wouldn't be upset about your actions at all, even.'

'Does it make much of a difference?' I ask. 'Does it matter how I feel afterwards, if I've intentionally hurt someone?'

'Yes,' she says, fiddling with the tea label. 'Actually, it does matter. Of course, either way the hurt's been done, but you can choose to sit in your feelings and turn things around. What have you done, if you don't mind?'

Tears sting my eyes. 'I can't even begin to share it. I hurt a friend. I hurt a close friend.'

'Is there a chance to apologize? Have you tried?'

'No. I don't think so.'

'You're very self-aware, Sirad. I don't know many bad people who are self-aware. Be kinder to yourself.'

'No. No. Maxine, I love you, but there's no coming back from this. I made a choice, and it was the wrong one.'

Maxine starts laughing. 'You're twenty-three. You'll realize one day how ridiculous you sound. Do you know how many friendships I ruined at your age? There is such a thing as self-forgiveness, and I can't wait 'til you learn that.'

'I'm worried I'll always make the wrong decision.'

'And that's normal. That's actually very healthy. It's called growing up. We constantly question the kind of person we'll become. But you will disappoint people and you will also be disappointed. It's part of life. Let go of the need to be perfect.'

'So how do I let it go?'

'You learn to. Slowly. It never fully goes away, but it becomes easier. Stop all the worrying. It will make you sick.'

'So, what if I keep doing it?' I worry. 'When does a person who does the wrong thing simply become a bad person?'

The skin between Maxine's tattooed brows creases as she thinks carefully about her answer. 'Good lord, that's a good one. I guess I can't answer it for you. You're you and I am me. But I tell you what, you'll get to a point in life where things are less black and white. You'll mess up. Badly. And at that point, all that matters is that you can say, "You know what, this is me. I'm here. There is still time to change."'

After that, for a week straight, Maxine knocks on my door each morning. Nobody has told her that I am struggling to get out of bed and go to work. Nobody has told her that I am struggling to eat anything but the leftover dinner that sits atop the stove after everyone goes to sleep. At the weekend, she gets me out of the house and takes me for walks. She sits by me at home as I finish my dinner each night and reminisces on the past with my mother, both of them recalling memories that are so lovely, I can hardly believe them.

'*The Art of Starting Again*,' says Maxine, as we walk around Greenwich Park with Gail's blueberry and custard brioche bread and coffee. 'That's what I would call my memoir if I bothered to sit down and write one.'

'Why would you call it that?' I ask, impressed by the fact that she has even thought about writing a memoir.

'Because life requires you to know how to keep renewing yourself. Your intentions. Your reasons for living. You learn to start again, even when you weren't expecting to. Even when you think you know exactly who you are.'

'What about those who don't get to have what we have?' I ask. 'Who don't get to reinvent themselves? This is what holds me back. I can't imagine why I deserve to be here, right now, lapping up this coffee and this safety like it's a given. It holds me back.'

Maxine draws a deep breath. 'Well, you have to assert your presence first. You haven't yet arrived. You must arrive first. Only then can you make some room for others. I couldn't see myself here right now, working, *living*, because for much of my twenties I was homeless and squatting around the city with no claim to anything. I heard about the library job through someone at my church and I didn't tell anyone that I was going to apply. I prepared by borrowing my roommate's smart trousers and finding a white shirt in a charity shop. I felt like I had to act the part, even writing down the exact lies I would tell about my life if they asked. Did I grow up freely reading books? Not then, no. Not yet. I planned to say my mum would buy them for me, when in reality I had to hide my books under my bed growing up. There was only one role up for grabs and for the first time, I told myself that it would be mine. Everybody waiting to be interviewed chatted among themselves in the foyer and I couldn't even bring myself to look at them in case I caught a whiff of something that would make me want to give up and just go home.

'So, I got the job. Me! And God knows I paid it forward. I taught many kids how to read. I fed children during the breakfast club, something that took me years to get approval for, because everyone around here was afraid of the big Black woman with the locs. I just wanted to mind my business in the beginning and read books, but of course the kids who came in here wanted my help. Sometimes they wanted me to define a word or simply let them borrow a pen and some paper.' She shrugs as though pushing off a thought. 'My point is, when you accept the right opportunities, the effect is everlasting.'

'Wow, Maxine,' I whisper, awestruck. 'I wish I had known all this about you.'

'Well, now you know.'

'I've just never thought it was OK to be who I am.'

She tsks. 'It's more than OK, star. It's extraordinary to be you.'

*

Using the money from the UNCLASSIFIED project, I manage to discreetly pay off all our debts. The money plants seeds of stability that allow life to bloom over the summer.

The cleared debt has an instant effect on my mother and her mood. She can sleep soundly now. She goes on walks again. The brightness has returned to her eyes; I can't remember the last time I saw them twinkle. Seeing my mother so happy has also somewhat resolved my own internal battles. How could anyone's happiness matter more than hers?

On a warm morning in August, we're sat anxiously eating

leftover tiramisu in the kitchen while Ahmed is out picking up his GCSE results. He flew out of the door an hour earlier. He comes home as we finish the tiramisu, holding a brown envelope in his hands. His expression gives nothing away.

'Is this going to make me smile or cry?' asks my mother, giving him a stern side-eye. I'm standing over the sink washing the dishes. I immediately dry my hands on my pyjama trousers and rush over to Ahmed.

Ahmed opens the envelope: two As, four Bs and a C. I scream with joy for him. 'I can't believe it!' I cry. I pull him into a tight hug and pass the yellow letter to my mum.

She puts her hand over her mouth. 'You passed!'

'He didn't just pass, he did very, very well!'

My mother kisses Ahmed on the head. 'I'm so glad we never gave up on you.' She steps back and looks at the letter again. 'Maybe next time you can make them all As.'

Ahmed laughs. 'For my A-levels, I'll bring home nothing but As. I promise.'

'And then you'll go to university?'

'Sure. Whatever you want.'

Hooyo squeals with pride. 'I have to call everyone! Of course, I won't mention the C.' She winks at us and goes to find her phone.

Ahmed and I sit on the balcony to play a game of Ludo. We can hear Hooyo in her room talking about his results. She pops her head around the curtain.

'Come here. Let me take a picture to send to your uncles in Somalia.'

'Hooyo, please, no. I don't want to.'

'Come here. Put on a smart shirt and take a picture. Just a quick one.'

'OK,' he grumbles. 'But you can't post it on Facebook!' He follows her into the apartment.

Alone on the balcony with my thoughts, a wild realization courses through me. Not all has been lost. Here are the people that I need, alive and near, and life can be beautiful if I allow it to be.

The sun has almost set, leaving behind a soft purple haze.

Part II

'A Somali never tells a false proverb.'

Chapter Fourteen

'Only the water in your hands can satisfy your thirst.'

In a recurring nightmare I had for several months, I would find myself teetering on the edge of a building. Gripped by vertigo, I was afraid. I didn't know what had brought me there. The building was often a school or a museum or some kind of public establishment, and it was always completely empty of people. That was how my waking life often felt – like I was just waiting to be pushed off higher ground. In the nightmare I felt a pair of hands pressing at my back, unbalancing me. I never got to see whether I landed safely, because I would wake up before I hit the ground.

The dreams stopped the moment I moved out of the apartment I grew up in with Hooyo and Ahmed. For a long time I had a feeling that it was what I needed to do to make them stop. I went from doctor to doctor to discuss my sleep. They kept telling me I needed therapy. I'd never felt ready to actually go. It turned out my body had just been desperately seeking a change, and I had finally made it happen.

The cure was not just the change of scenery, but the fact that I eventually gave myself permission to become a new version of myself. I didn't take any of my old clothes or belongings with me into my new apartment. I decided that I had full agency to rewrite my identity if that was what it took to heal. To create this new identity, I alchemized the anger of my youth that I'd spent so long passively suffering from. I own my feelings, I told myself, so I can use them however I like. And I used them for good. I had been rising up the ranks at the magazine, and eventually Rita gave me the role of features editor. I found myself sitting in the writers' room writing about my experiences, and for the first time, I began to know myself. Others began to recognize how much I had developed my confidence. I came to believe inherently that my voice mattered and that I was indispensable. Writing gave me a sense of power and a way of self-soothing. Life wasn't perfect all of a sudden; nor was I living a fairy tale, not by any means. But I wrote and I wrote. I wrote my way out of one mode of existence and into another.

In the months before leaving my childhood home, I spent some time living there alone. That was around the time the nightmares started, but I look back on that time fondly, because it was when I experienced the biggest push to change my life. My family had already changed so much in the years leading up to that point. Ahmed had successfully finished his A-levels and graduated from university with a computer science degree. He found a remote software engineering job and spent most of his time travelling from country to country, feeding his love for photography. Our mother had struggled with her health until she found out that she had high blood pressure. She immersed herself in the lush, green land of Garowe, Somalia, with the rest of her siblings, resting and focusing on her health. When Aunt Najma's divorce was finalized, she moved to Garowe with her two daughters too.

In my first few weeks of living alone, I would come home after a long day at work to the quiet apartment and experience a kind of loneliness so raw and disarming that I would weep until I fell asleep. I'd lock my bedroom door, turn on the TV and fall asleep to the sound of people's voices in movies.

I remember those months clearly. In the evenings, I would sit on the balcony pretending to relax, but most of the time I was working. I was busy scanning the news for interesting things to bring up in morning meetings so that I could impress my colleagues. I was drafting, editing, taking online courses. After a series of redundancies at our magazine I was the youngest editor on the team, and I was desperate to level up and provide unique value.

I saw Rosie quite a bit in the years following her Rwanda trip. She spends most of her time in New York now, lecturing at a community college. I spent a summer there one year. She is married to her long-term boyfriend – they met in Rwanda – and they live in a charming loft with their two cats. We don't see each other so much now, but we have accepted that even if years pass, we will always gravitate back to one another.

Sometimes, in between those intense bouts of work in the old apartment, I would walk down as far as Salutation Road, wondering if there was still time for me to start again. The UNCLASSIFIED portacabins were long gone, but they had left behind an unmissable mark.

People I had gone to school with were starting to get married and have babies; some of them, mainly the ones from strictly religious families who had married very young, had already gone through divorce. I was envious of the varied experiences of other people my age. Then there I was, almost thirty and still sleeping in my childhood bedroom, still existing in the same square mile, still stuck on my past mistakes.

*

On my twenty-ninth birthday, I wake up in my own quiet apartment and tear off my bedsheets. I spend the first half of the day cleaning and decluttering. I booked a massage and a sweet afternoon tea for myself at the InterContinental Hotel, so I indulge in an afternoon of peaceful reading. I wear a turquoise satin wrap dress and an expensive chiffon scarf to the hotel. Some ladies admire it as I walk by, which almost makes me smile. I sit with my book, unperturbed, content even.

It has taken me some time, but I have begun to tolerate my loneliness. I make a promise to myself that no matter what happens in life, I will remember this feeling. This will be my baseline. I can return to it if I ever lose my way.

On my way home I pass one of my neighbour's young daughters in the estate car park. She's standing in the rain without a coat, holding a remote-controlled aeroplane in her hands. It is a very cold evening. Part of me wants to wrap her up in my coat or at least suggest that she go back inside, but instead I feel compelled to watch her. She inserts batteries into her toy with a look of euphoria lighting up her face. I don't know her family well, but I do know that her older brother was fatally stabbed a few years ago by a gang in North London.

The little girl is still wearing her school uniform despite it being almost eight o'clock. Her hair is pulled back off of her face with a pink headband. I watch her discreetly as I walk by, intrigued to know what it is about the new toy that has made her immune to the cold. It's been a long while since I've even seen a child play with an actual toy and not some kind of screen. Watching her brings on a surprising wave of nostalgia.

I'm always in awe of how children manage to find moments of joy amid the chaos. There is something so sacred about it. I am reminded of a time when I was gifted with a toy plane of my own, back in the nineties. I would have been around the same age as this little girl – seven or eight. I had begged my dad to buy it for me as a birthday gift after seeing an advert on TV: laughing children in brightly coloured clothes, a small white plane slaloming between the trees. I remember the moment I set it down on this same concrete ground in an ecstasy of expectation . . . only to see it take off, wilt against the wind, and then crash back down to earth.

I now walk past the girl without warning her about the inevitable crash. I don't tell her to wait for a less windy day, or to go to a park where there is soft grass for her plane to land on. I could tell her, at the very least, not to have so much hope; but maybe I want her to learn the same lesson I learned once.

The plane starts to take off as I hurry into my block. I hope that it will soar, but I hear it crash too soon after the thought occurs to me.

I think about this incident for days, until I'm not sure who has been more affected, me or the little girl. I don't know why, but it makes me think of Ubah. I haven't heard from her, or from Mama or Aabo. I don't know what life is like on the other side or whether we can ever meet again.

*

Six months later, I get married.

I meet my husband at the wedding of a family friend. He is outside making a phone call, and I am sitting on the steps of the wedding hall while the women dance to the drums of the buraanbur. A few minutes later, he walks up to me and introduces himself. Later, I will tease him about the manner of his approach, but I am secretly impressed by it. No frills. It says a lot.

We soon find ourselves deep in conversation, as if we have known each other for years. It starts to rain heavily, and instead of going back inside the hall to part ways at our respective sides of the gender-segregated wedding, we escape into a nearby dessert shop. We talk for the entire night, until it is time to go home. Speaking with him, I experience a warm and gratifying feeling in my chest. His presence makes me feel safe, and somehow I sense that he will be a part of my life for a long time.

We talk every day. I accidentally bump into him and his aunt while volunteering at a mosque charity event and we laugh at all the silly quirks we both know about him. He proposes pretty soon after that, and I ask for a week to labour over the question. He is taken aback by my request, but honours it patiently.

He is an orphan of the civil war who arrived in London as a ten-year-old. I know he has secrets, and I know that he knows I do, too. That's what draws me to him. Not once does he ask me to lay them out in front of him, and this, to me, is dearer than anything else anyone could ever do for me.

He makes me happy without threatening to take anything away from the life I have made for myself. Except maybe stress – he silently, unprompted, unpacks my load. He takes my worries on as his own, and my joys too.

Omar is his name. I am happiest when I see how perfectly and soundlessly this man has slotted himself into my life. He is consistently attentive. All of this scares me, in a way; I sometimes fear that if he left, everything would come crashing down like a failed game of Jenga.

I fall in love with Omar for many reasons, one of them being the fact that he remembers which days I am working from home so that he can order my lunch and have it delivered to me. Rosemary chips and a steak burger show up at my apartment at exactly noon; I peel my body away from my desk and half skip to the door. As I take the food from the delivery man's hands (having grown well acquainted with him over time), we talk about the weather, but really we are both talking about our respective loves. 'The rain clouds are gone. The sun has come back out. Have a beautiful day.'

It is all so dizzying to me at first – it's almost debilitating. It's like I am lying on a cloud, with no concept of tomorrow or yesterday. I walk slower, talk slower, take time with my work. Love makes you taste things differently. It's a steroid for the senses. I people-watch in the street, trying to spot those suffering the same symptoms.

On the day of the wedding, Ahmed, Hooyo and Aunt Najma come up to our room to say good morning and pray with me. I am tearful by the time we've finished. Hooyo holds me in her arms like a little girl while Aunt Najma pats my shoulder. Hooyo has had a white and gold dirac made for me in Somalia. She weeps when she sees me in my dress and takes endless photos. Eventually Omar comes into the room for our first look. He's speechless. I shake with nerves, but he holds me close and tells me that he won't leave my side the whole evening.

What is the rush? I wonder silently to myself. Why do we need to make such a big fuss, with a reception of three hundred people – most of whom are Omar's relatives or people related to our families only by clan? I'm anxious about all the people, the drama of it all, the traditional female poet who will sing praises about my lineage and the women who will skilfully dance to the drums, chanting and ululating. It will swallow me up whole.

At the end of the reception, Omar and I get undressed together. He tenderly helps me take off my gold and all the pins in my hair, but I ask him to excuse me while I finish undressing. I'm not comfortable with him seeing me. It is going to take some getting used to.

*

A year into the marriage, instead of rose petals on the marital bed, there are exam papers and exercise books, piles of them, from the three different maths classes Omar teaches. He comes home, potters around the house for half an hour and then leaves them there to get on with later while I sleep. We struggle to spend as much time together as we did in the early stages, but we're reassured by each other's efforts to try. I cross the T's and dot the I's on whatever piece I have been drafting on paper that day. The heating goes on at around seven. The lights are dimmed in the living room and we chomp on our dinner together, happily, in front of old episodes of *Law and Order*. He rests his head in my lap.

*

I cherish mornings sitting with Omar at our dining table before he goes to work, but this morning I'm stressed about our upcoming move.

'The estate agent has already called me twice today,' I say. 'And both times, I just let it ring. I can't handle the stress of this.'

We have been living in a tiny one-bedroom flat not too far from where I grew up. We've found somewhere better to move into at last, and it's a step we have worked hard to be able to take. Our moving day is drawing near. The final nuts and bolts are being hammered into the walls as we speak.

Omar rolls up his sleeves. 'Don't worry,' he says. 'I'll get back to him.' He eats his toast in three bites. 'I've packed everything I can, but there's stuff spilling out of every corner of this place – argh!' He has spilt some tea on the table. He begins wiping it up with a paper towel.

The opportunity has come at the right time; Omar is about to begin a new role as deputy head of the school where he works, a private school in East Greenwich for children with special educational needs. He is a hero to those children. He does find it a little awkward that a few of them live near our block and bump into him on his morning jogs, but he wouldn't consider moving away and finding work elsewhere. To many of the children, he's not just a teacher but a counsellor, a father figure, another one of the boys. 'They're an extension of me now,' he says. 'I can't just leave.' This is partly why it has taken us so long to find a new place. Thankfully, we've found a home in Blackheath, so Omar can remain at the school.

'You know, I've never lived in a house with a garden,' I say, taking our plates.

'Neither have I,' says Omar. 'I can't wait a second longer.'

Moving day comes faster than I expected. We spend the weekend dividing our lives into neat cardboard boxes picked up from Save the Children and Omar's school store cupboards. Our voices echo in the empty rooms.

My work is unaffected. I work from home for the most part, but I still like to go to the office from time to time for team meetings or to show off my new shoes, desperate not to fade into the background. I listen to true crime podcasts as I work. Omar doesn't understand what they do for me, but it's just the right kind of background noise.

'The forever home,' I call it, as we're having our last meal before waiting for the removal van to arrive. Omar starts laughing. He finds the term endearing. He likes to make fun of me for my idealism. I'm secretly often frustrated by his nihilism.

'Are we in a Disney movie?' he asks, laughing playfully.

'Yep. Small blue birds come to make the bed in the morning. People whistle tunes as they trim their hedges.'

'I can't wait for us to get settled in.'

'There's not a single Somali in that area, not that I'm aware of. Makes for a huge change, doesn't it? I've always felt like we are being secretly watched by the ones in our block.'

'Nah, I think you're just paranoid, love.'

'Oh, come on. You know what I mean,' I say. 'We're a gossipy lot, Somalis. I know that well enough.'

I pace up and down the hallway in anticipation of the movers. 'I'm going to check the rooms again to make sure we've got everything. How long are they going to be?'

He takes his phone out of his pocket. 'They said they'd be here at half past. They should be here by now. Let me call them.'

Standing in our living room, I call out 'Hello,' just to hear my voice echo and bounce off the walls. I notice that I've forgotten something. One last box, just a small and mostly empty one. It has my old bedside lamp inside, one with roses on that I picked up from the old junkyard on Salutation Road so many years ago.

I begin to feel cold and uneasy. I leave the box by the balcony door and look out through the glass. Over the past couple of years, the area around Salutation Road has been under construction. Cranes now jut out into the sky. The abandoned Royal Mail van is gone and the Spice Girls billboard has been taken down.

The removal men eventually appear and distract me from my thoughts.

'Any last bits you want to check before we pull away?' asks one of them.

'Nothing at all. We're good to go.'

We get into our car. Omar rubs my shoulder, and I can finally relax. We back out of the driveway, following the removal van to our new home.

A forever home. *Forever* sounds like a nice word. It's tender, light on the tongue, the syllables rolling seamlessly into each other. I tell myself that one day, when we are old, Omar and I will look back on this afternoon and it'll bring back warm feelings. I search for another word to describe it. I rack my brain in both English and Somali, failing to find it in either one. There must be a word for that feeling of experiencing something in the present and wondering what bits of it will remain in your memory when it all becomes a part of the past.

Chapter Fifteen

'Your woman should be in the house or in the grave.'

Our new house is nestled in a cluster of meandering hills over the green common in Blackheath, making the ground below look like soft, fat rolls. I recall watching the sunsets here with Rosie back in secondary school. Every so often I bump into her parents taking a stroll through Blackheath Village and we stop to exchange pleasantries. Whenever Rosie is in the city, we have coffee together and traipse through the farmer's market. Though we haven't moved very far from the Greenwich Peninsula, it feels as if we are a world apart from my childhood home. There is so much green space here that it doesn't even feel like we're in London any more. In this sleepy suburb, the moon goes to sleep in our garden and the sun gives us the very first rays of its light. Birds hide in the trees outside our window, singing their ballads of spring in the winter. Our new garden is planted with rosebushes, carrots, tomatoes and a variety of vegetables. We know our neighbours on a first-name basis; they are a pair of empty-nesters who are both artists and art dealers. They own their four-bedroom home and a holiday home in Cornwall. For once, that kind of life seems within reach.

Omar makes simple interior design choices for the house: white walls and plenty of natural light, a quiet corner for a study, dark wood flooring all the way through. Over time I begin to decorate the living room, bit by bit, in hues of red, burnt orange and terracotta, until it resembles a beating heart in the centre of our home. Our lives start to intertwine harmoniously, unlike before. Omar likes to eat a fuss-free breakfast in the kitchen before a long shift of marking books and planning homework in his study. I, on the other hand, like to enjoy my breakfast at my laptop before starting edits and going through new pitches from writers in my inbox. Neither of us likes to admit that we're workaholics, afraid of stopping in case everything is suddenly pulled out from under our feet.

Nevertheless, we rest purposefully from time to time. We organize a barbecue for both Eid celebrations in the summer, hosting over eighty friends, family and community members. We've already planned the next one. I begin to notice the power that our new house has over our lives, but I also notice what it hasn't changed within me. In more ways than one, I have been acting out a character that I know I am not. Sometimes I feel like I'm watching my life from behind a low wall, with my knees in the mud, afraid that someone will discover me.

When things are good, they often seem too good. It worries me whenever anything feels too easy because I believe that somehow, sooner or later, I will pay the price. I know I've worked hard to be where I am, but I don't often feel like I deserve it. I know why I feel that way, and I make sure no one else ever does.

Omar thinks I'm too hard on myself. It upsets him to hear how I talk to myself whenever anything goes wrong. Although he isn't aware of the full extent of this inner battle, it's clear to him that I'm completely at ease with who I am. I keep joking about wanting to quit everything and move to Garowe, to be near Hooyo and live on the farm with a new name and a new identity.

'Why change your name?' he questions, whenever I describe this fantasy. He has no idea what crime I've committed in my own name and in the name of greed. I pray he never finds out.

Whenever I start talking like this, Omar thinks I'm going through depression. Maybe he's right. I find it hard to simply go from one day to the next. I forget to eat and I have to be told when to get out of bed, to shower and to change my clothes. I remember the days when Hooyo was like this and I would have to baby her from one day to the next. I hate that I put Omar in that position.

Omar believes the sickness stems from constantly questioning life. Life shouldn't be questioned so much. Fate is in God's hands, so we'll never understand it.

'You can feel your feelings, but to question the path you're on is the root of all your pain.' I let him speak his mind and respond with enlightened nods. It makes him feel good to think he has the answers.

It's one of those days. I'm struggling to get out of bed, and this makes Omar especially emotional. 'Just know you're doing amazing, no matter how this day goes,' he says, rubbing my arm. His dark brown eyes are swimming with pride and strength. 'Even if you decide to just stay here, in bed, that's OK. I'll bring you everything you need. But please pray. Don't give up on prayer.'

When my anxiety is at its worst, Omar's reassuring words feel suffocating, too unnaturally positive, to the point that I feel stifled with my sadness. I never dare to express this to him. I know better. I just keep my distance and try to do as many things alone as I can until I feel lighter again. Long walks, lonesome train journeys with a bag full of books, a table for one by the window at a restaurant. He understands why it's important for me to do this from time to time. That, I remind myself, is why I married him.

On a frosty December day, we're walking through Winter Wonderland in Hyde Park when we spot a little girl, not much older than three or four, toddling around on her own, evidently lost. We take her to the information desk and wait with her until her parents arrive, fear and gratitude plastered across their faces. Omar is upset by this incident. He can't stop talking about it. It has triggered something within him, something very painful.

Children seem to be all around us these days, crawling and toddling their way into our path wherever we go. They coo and laugh with us in the line at the supermarket, at the post office and in the mosque. I can't escape Hooyo's desire for grandchildren. Imagining myself as a parent is a big, scary mental leap to make.

I do not yet feel my womb twitch at the sight of a baby's cute, tiny feet or at the thought of being pregnant. I am happy enough as it is with Omar. Just the two of us. Adding to what we have could spoil it all. Besides, I still keep secrets from him. He doesn't know about Ubah and what I did to her. I can't imagine the weight of a baby growing in my body – my secret is heavy enough.

In the summer, Hooyo visits us for a few weeks. She sees how Omar takes care of me and says, 'You're going to make a great father, Omar.' We have only been married a year. I feel like it is still too early in our marriage to plan for children, but Hooyo makes us feel like we have waited too long already. Whenever she says this kind of thing, Omar tries to change the subject. I can tell he loves talking about children, but even he knows how overbearing Hooyo can get with this. Omar is like another son to Hooyo. She looks at him with pride. She thinks my reluctance to have children is some kind of oppression of him.

'You don't want to wait too long,' she warns me while he's in the bathroom. 'You're past thirty. You're not going to be able to keep up with a child if you wait too long.'

'Please, let's discuss this another time,' I suggest.

'Omar is an orphan. I bet he really longs for a child, a son especially.'

'Am I supposed to fill that void for him?' I ask.

'Well, who else will?'

'I never once told him I wanted children,' I say, obstinance setting in.

'He didn't ask you?'

'No, not really.'

'Well, isn't that strange?' asks my mum, raising her eyebrows.

Maybe it is strange, I think. Or maybe he just understands me on a deeper level and knows that it isn't the time to have this discussion. Or perhaps he shares the same feelings.

Omar is a deeply ambitious but private person. When we first met, he talked to me about himself as if sharing a secret. He only revealed things about himself in stages, but it was never anything bad or shocking. I suppose I preferred getting to know him that way. It was more interesting, and it increased my attraction to him.

Sometimes he speaks in half sentences, never quite finishing them. But I don't ever require him to. I don't place much importance on the things people say about themselves; it's how they treat me that's more important. He was a quiet boy growing up, the youngest out of all six of his cousins on his mother's side. He grew up on one of South-East London's toughest council estates, where one of his friends was murdered in front of him. Yet somehow it didn't leave him jaded in the way one would expect. He worked hard to make something of the lack of stability in his life. That's the same space we occupy and that's how we were able to connect.

*

One afternoon Omar leaves the house, only to return shortly afterwards with a rather cute ginger cat in a carrier hanging off his hand as naturally as if it was an umbrella.

'She's called Honey. Bit too late to change the name, because she answers to it. Don't you?' He opens the carrier and reaches in to scratch the cat between her ears. I can hear her loud purrs.

'Huh? Omar, what is this all about?'

He places the cat on the fourth step of the stairs and stands back to look at her. The cat begins to lick her paws and groom herself, then lies on her side and meows, as if calling Omar.

'I got her from a colleague who's moving to Australia.' He says this as if it's a piece of furniture he's talking about, not an animal that will need food, toys and expensive veterinary care. He doesn't appear to understand why he should have told me beforehand.

'I thought you liked cats,' he says.

I am extremely annoyed, but try hard not to show it. 'Yes, but I've never said I want to take care of one. I appreciate what you're trying to do, but it's hardly a gift, is it? It's a responsibility.'

'Don't make a big deal out of it. They're not hard work, cats. I'll assume most of the responsibility if it helps. Just go with the flow, please.'

I bring it up that same night when we are in bed. I am furious inside, and this time I want it to show.

'You know, the way you dumped that cat on me really rubbed me up the wrong way. It's not a toy. It's a living soul. There is so much to be careful about when you're taking care of a soul.'

'What are you saying, Sirad?' He sits up and turns on the bedside light.

'I'm saying you should have asked me what I thought. You never ask me what I think before you decide things. What's that about?'

'Sorry. I got too excited about it and didn't stop to think.'

'Don't apologize!' I say. 'That's not what I'm looking for. I'm just saying, I'm not ready to take care of something else just yet. I'm not saying I never will be. Just not right now.'

Omar knows exactly what I'm talking about. He knows this isn't just about cats. But he doesn't take the bait. He looks away and turns off the light.

*

I spend the better part of a day with Omar's aunt, Asmaa, the woman who raised him. Like my mother, she is excited for us to one day have a child, but she never takes much interest in our lives beyond that. She is robotic and sits on the very edge of the sofa in our house as if in a hospital waiting room, never quite relaxed, always braced for something. Sometimes she comes with gifts, like cookbooks and kitchen appliances, but it is all a formality. By the third ceramic dish, I understand that she only wants to bring the tools that she thinks I need to be the perfect wife for her nephew.

I ask as many questions as I can about Omar's bachelorhood whenever she comes around. I want to know things that Omar has never spoken about – the silly details, the things he is too embarrassed to share. She once revealed to me that he used to be deeply in love with a girl whose parents were so staunchly tribalist that they wouldn't allow her to marry him. He saved for a ring, bought himself a new suit and went to her father's house to ask for her hand. After he was turned away, Omar changed. The funny, sociable young man grew introverted, more interested in his work, and found solace in religion. He never fully returned to his old self. Hearing that devastated me, but I understood that Asmaa was probably embellishing the story to get a reaction out of me.

Today I ask, 'Has he always been this restless? He seems so worried all the time. Is he afraid of failing at something?'

'It's just the way he is. The poor boy has been through a lot.' She pours herself some more tea.

'So, what can I do?' I press. 'How can I make him easier-going?'

She swirls her tea around in her cup anti-clockwise and smirks as if remembering something amusing. I can sense her configuring exactly the kind of response that will get on my nerves.

'A baby will do that for a man like Omar. He is ready to be a father.' She tips the tea down her throat in one swift movement, like a shot of alcohol, and places the cup on the wooden floor beside her feet.

In the following months, Omar's aunt visits less frequently. If she does come over, it's always when she knows Omar is working. I get the sense that she is curious to know whether I'm pregnant yet and whether her advice has had any effect. She never asks me directly, but when she asks about my health, I know what she is hinting at. This is the thing that makes me distance myself from her as much as I can. When she realizes I'm no longer keen on having a particularly special relationship with her, she stops inviting herself over.

Omar's cousins are mostly younger than him but somehow

light years ahead of us in terms of what they have achieved out of life. Some of them are already on their second or third child. Some of them have already lived abroad together or have purchased their first home, like me and Omar. They're also open books. They talk about everything from what their children are eating to their on-again, off-again diets. I realize that Omar certainly wasn't raised to be so closed off. His aunt is probably right. Something that happened much later made him this way.

Sometimes we have dinner with his cousins and their spouses and I can spot the tension between the couples. I am sensitive to this kind of thing, obsessive even. I want to know whether or not they, with their children, are happier than we are. I am always interested in seeing how Omar and I compare on the normality scale.

The cousins and their spouses are preoccupied with life events that are somewhat agreed upon as important milestones. Having more children, buying expensive appliances, starting a business, travelling around the world. Aside from the babies, they have these milestones to work towards together. Omar and I don't have those kinds of plans. We just exist together – peacefully, but certainly not in a strategic kind of way. We are fused together in an entirely different way that I am not yet able to clearly define. There is a deeper reason why we have washed up on the shores of each other's lives and taken each other in.

*

Every Friday evening, Omar and I pause whatever we are doing and go out for our weekly movie night and dinner. We fill my bag with supermarket snacks to sneak in and laugh like children as we push the boundaries of what we can get away with. A tub of discounted strawberry ice cream, chips, a box of chicken wings, a huge birthday cake. Sometimes, like a pair of teens, we used to creep down the corridor after the film was over to watch another one without paying. Every so often, one of us would spot a member of staff at the door and we would make ourselves small in our seats, hugging our knees to our chests, choking with laughter. We did it just for the thrill of it. It was always just for the thrill of it.

One warm Friday evening in May, we are sitting on a busy bus on the way to the cinema while a couple beside us try their best to quiet their crying baby. The father rocks the baby girl in his arms as the mum attempts to place a dummy between the baby's irritated, red gums. The couple look around apologetically at their fellow passengers. The baby is wearing a thick pink cardigan. I begin to go through a list of all the possible reasons she might be crying so hard: hunger, tiredness, boredom. The list grows longer and longer. Without much warning, I begin to panic inside. I look over at Omar until he returns my gaze.

'I don't know if I could ever do that,' I say in Somali, so that no one else can understand. 'Each time they shriek it can mean a million different things. They get hot and they cry – they get hungry and they cry. Either way, it always ends up in tears. How do they know?'

'They just know,' says Omar sadly. He has a far-away expression on his face.

'Would you know?' I ask. I'm desperate to reach him.

'I think so,' he says. 'I think I would.' He takes my hand in his. 'But we don't have to worry about that right now.'

He rubs his thumb over my knuckles. It's the word *now* strung at the end of his sentence; the weight of it, what it foreshadows. No, Omar, I want to say, I don't want to deal with that kind of thing *ever*.

I reach for his hand as we walk into the cinema. We stand in the queue to get our tickets. I hide the bursting bag of food under my jacket, realizing it resembles a deformed baby bump.

When the film starts, I rest my head on Omar's shoulder and he rests his head back on mine. When the film is over and the credits roll, I plead with him to watch another, even though he has to be up early the next day. He gives in and we go into the screen next door, this time after paying. Time seems to stop for us as we watch the film. I don't want to go back home. I want to move from room to room and keep watching films. I don't want to hear a word Omar says. Sitting in the dark, being held by him, is enough.

Chapter Sixteen

'Where there are no women, there is no home.'

For a long time, I try to persuade Hooyo to move back to London and in with Omar and me, now that we have more space to accommodate her comfortably. I've been needing her these days; I miss her presence more than ever. When I suggest the idea, she wonders if I'm struggling to cope with the demands of married life. But there is nothing difficult in particular that life is demanding of me. I speak to her several times a day, always interested to know what she is up to on the farm with my Aunt Najma. Growing food and looking after animals has brought her soul back to life. She lights up whenever she speaks about the intricacies of the crops and the rainy season. I give up asking her to join us after a while, accepting that she is happier in her hometown, where, as an adult, she can have the childhood she would have wanted. She has found her purpose and is thriving in it. That is all that matters

One night I am woken by the sound of the cat wailing outside the front door. We are used to being disrupted by her racing through the house in the early hours of the morning, but tonight it's the high pitch of her mewing that unsettles me. We find her scratching the front door almost as if she is begging to be let in.

I look through the peephole. There is my mum standing on our dimly lit front lawn, having arrived without a warning.

Omar and I rush to welcome her in. Omar begins unloading her bags from the taxi. For as long as I can remember, my mother has never taken a taxi alone. The driver lights a cigarette and smokes it out of an open window as Omar goes to get some cash from the house. I stand there in the cold, eye to eye with my mum, both furious and bursting with love. She's dressed in varying shades of purple from head to toe: a lilac jilbaab down to her knees, a lighter oyster-shell purple chiffon draped loosely around her head. She hugs me and kisses me on the cheek.

'Hooyo, what happened?' I usher her in and show her where to place her shoes in the closet under the stairs.

She thanks Omar for carrying her bags and follows him into the house.

'Let me get you something to eat and drink.' He begins to fuss over her. She removes her jilbaab and sits on a high stool, her small sock-covered feet dangling.

'No, no, no. If you could just get me some water, please.'

'Why didn't you call and say you had booked a flight? Why didn't you at least call me before you left for the airport?' I ask.

'Sirad,' she says, between loud gulps of water, 'are you not happy to see me? It was a last-minute decision.'

'Of course I am! I've been begging you to visit again! But you should let us know when you're travelling. Anything can happen.'

I guide her through the corridor, where I almost expect her to vanish under the bright lights. As she walks, she observes every surface, running her hands over the wallpaper and then stopping to look up at the high ceiling. She has lost a noticeable amount of weight since the last time I saw her and her skin is radiant. It takes me a while to recover from the surprise of seeing her there at our door.

'I would have called,' she reiterates, 'but I wanted it to be a surprise. Don't you like surprises? Is everything OK?'

'Everything is fine,' I reassure her. 'Have you met our cat? Her name is Honey.'

'Preparing for motherhood?' She grins at me. I look back at her, annoyed. 'I'm just playing with you.'

The spare room smells faintly of sawdust and wallpaper adhesive. My mum opens the window.

'If I had known you were coming, I would have done a better job of decorating this room,' I say. The only things in the room are a bed and a rug.

'It's just right.' She rubs the bedcover between her fingers. 'I don't need much.'

'Are you still taking sleeping pills?' I watch her pull out a small packet of tablets from her bag.

'This is a herbal supplement.' She tosses two into her mouth. 'I only need it when I come back to London. I sleep very well in Garowe.'

'It's OK. You must be very tired. There are towels in the drawer under the bed for you to use. You might not like to be woken up by the sound of the children from the nearby playground, so tell me if you would like me to move the bed away from the window tomorrow. In this neighbourhood people don't like to use curtains for whatever reason, so always draw them completely shut in the morning, otherwise they'll be able to see you from across the street. About a carpet – I know it's summer, but I can always ask Omar to bring one down from the attic if you would prefer? Or is it fine as it is? Personally, we like the wood—'

'Stop babbling.' She playfully pinches my cheek. 'I need the bathroom.' She traces her fingers in the grooves in the wooden door frame as she leaves the room to go to the bathroom opposite. She turns on the bathroom light and scrunches up her eyes. 'Ahh! Too bright!'

I sigh. 'I'll change it for you tomorrow.'

A long time passes while she uses the bathroom. After a while, I knock gently on the door.

'OK, Hooyo, I'll get some sleep and go back to my bed. I'll see you in the morning.'

'Wait.' She comes out of the bathroom with her hair tucked into two plaits. 'The dawn has already broken. Won't you pray?'

I stutter. The prayers I offer on time are largely due to Omar's reminders. I can't remember the last time I willingly put my head on the ground. It has been weeks, maybe even longer.

'Since you are here, why don't we pray together?' I suggest.

She dries her face with a corner of her baati and turns off the light, leaving only a lamp on. She waits for me to use the bathroom and wash. Then she asks me to set the prayer mat to face Mecca.

The prayer is short, but we kneel up on the mat in silence for a long time. Foxes screech in the back garden. My mum puts her hands together and raises them towards the window before wiping them over her face.

'*Allahu Akbar.* God is great.'

'He is.'

'Do you feel blessed with everything that you have now? Remember when you wanted all of this?'

'Very blessed.'

'So tell that to your Lord. Tell him every day,' she says. 'Know that as long as you still have your spirit in you, you have another chance to be better. God's mercy is abundant.'

'How are things going with the farm? How is Aunt Najma?'

'Ah. Aunt Najma really loves it there. Life is sweet. Maybe it's just how I've been feeling lately.'

'How?'

'I've just felt like I need to be around you more. I don't know why I feel so worried about you.'

'You're here now, Hooyo. Just relax. There is nothing to be afraid of.'

'I felt so strongly within myself that I should be here and be near you. Ahmed is in his own world, travelling and living life like he's in some sort of movie. And here you are living the same day on repeat, it seems.'

'But I'm OK. Everything is fine as it is. I don't want a big change.'

'How are things with you and Omar?' she whispers.

'They're good. You know, he's always working so hard. But I'm proud of him.'

'I won't stay for very long. You know what this country does to me. My blood pressure will rise again.'

'How come?' I ask. 'What is it about this place that makes your body react so strongly?'

'I don't know. It's something I've been trying to understand.'

I feel like crawling into her lap and just lying there, so I do. Her presence is comforting, but it also slightly worries me. It feels as if, without knowing it, she is here to prepare me to deal with something completely out of the ordinary.

'When I first got married, my mother had passed away. I was dealing with so much at once, both grief and those early stages of love. There was a lot of outside pressure to be this happy, charming wife, but also to grieve openly. I was feeling so many tense emotions and I wasn't resilient enough. I had no one to talk to about it. I sometimes wonder if you're feeling the same way.'

'All the time,' I say, looking up at her from her lap. 'I feel that way all the time. Do you ever think about visiting Mogadishu?'

'Not that often any more. I don't think I can still relate to that past version of me.'

I think about Mama and wonder if Hooyo would feel differently if they met. Yes, they are different, but it's clear they have the same soul. They would find a lot to talk about.

'My greatest fear,' says Hooyo, 'is spending so much time away from my country that I can't find any place in it to call home. Garowe is home. It's where I was born and grew up. I made a mistake when I didn't visit for all those years. I can't forgive myself for the lost time.'

'If Mogadishu isn't home for you, and neither is London, then it doesn't make sense for me to see these places as home either,' I say. 'Maybe home is another place I haven't visited yet.'

'A home to us all is heaven. And you can only get there by being a good person. Go back to sleep,' she says. 'You need it.'

I lift my head off her lap. She moves back to the prayer mat.

*

My mum stays with us for three months. Having her there makes an instant difference to the quality of our days. She brings with her a kind of warmth that was missing from my life and our home, one that can only come from a mother. She sees us through the winter with her dinners and desserts, and her presence brings us frequent visitors from her side of the family, even some that I would have naturally lost touch with if it wasn't for my mum's ways of keeping everyone together. My mum's visit is a pleasant reminder of how much Omar loves her and sees her as his own parent. He drives her around the city on her long errands, shopping trips and visits to friends whom she hasn't seen since she left.

Seeing how Omar is with my mother also makes me feel sad. I can tell that he truly suffered after the deaths of his parents. He interacts with my mum as if searching for the essence of the mother he lost. He draws nearer to me through her and through the way he has memorized my habits and quirks. He is always there to make sure her day is going as smoothly as possible.

'Look at how he takes care of you,' says my mum one day when Omar has not yet come home from work. 'He could only be more gentle and doting on a child of his own. That is what his heart yearns for.' I am in the conservatory, catching up with my laundry for the week. She has followed me there with glasses of cold milk and dates. I continue folding the freshly tumble-dried clothes and try to think of a change of subject.

'I know,' I reply after some time. 'But still, we're not ready.'

'*You're* not ready. He is. I can sense it in him.'

My mother holds the view that bloodlines are supposed to go on and on until the end of time. To her, new children are a chance for each generation to better themselves and right the wrongs of the previous ones. Over the three months she stays, we speak about it a few more times. She's more enthusiastic about it than she has been about anything else I can remember.

'I only have two children,' she often says. 'One of them is too busy running around the world to find himself a wife, and the other one wants to remain a little girl for as long as possible. What will I do when I become old and the only thing I can do is talk and talk? Who will I tell stories to?'

I try to brush off her comments.

'None of you raised in this generation will be able to tell those stories unless you learn them from your elders. And even then, it won't sound the same. Stories die if they are not passed on.'

I know that I can't have a child just to keep my mother happy. There has to be a deeper, more intentional reason. Nevertheless, I like the idea of passing down stories. In a world full of harmful narratives, there is something so powerful about that.

My mother has a strict routine. She starts her day before dawn, praying and reading the Quran. After breakfast, she gets on the phone to Aunt Najma and they catch up about the farm and family matters. Despite my mother's rigid structure and ritual, I can tell that she isn't completely happy. I see the effort that it takes her, some days, to get through the day. Sometimes she is disengaged and struggles to relax and enjoy her time with Omar and me. We invite her on our regular cinema outings and each time she declines. She has never visited a cinema since we came to the UK. The last time she sat down to watch a movie in a cinema was in Somalia before the war, and before Ahmed and I were born.

One morning I visit the guest bedroom. 'Hooyo,' I whisper to her, intending to wake her up for the dawn prayer. I find she has dozed off while sitting on her prayer mat, her fingers loosely wrapped around her prayer beads. It is just before sunrise. I can hear Omar getting ready to pray in the next room. I like sitting with her at these times and just talking about anything that comes to mind.

'What do you think about when you remember my father?' I ask.

She replies with her eyes still closed. 'I remember his slow, low laugh and his sense of humour.'

'Tell me, is he the real reason you haven't been able to go back to Mogadishu?'

My mother scrunches up her eyes and then opens them. 'No. Not at all. I've told you the reason why.'

'Then how come we've never visited since?'

'You're really asking me that?' She's annoyed. 'It is dangerous and expensive to get to.'

There were two separate things, I think, that broke my mother's heart. Those things were deeply entwined. The first was my father leaving, and the second was when she realized that her Somalia was never going to be the same again. It was gone. The essence of what Mogadishu had once been could never return. Even the happiest of memories, and the places in them, can become spoilt for us at some point in life. We have to learn to be at peace with that.

Chapter Seventeen

'A childless old woman dreams of seashells.'

At the start of the school Easter holidays, Omar and I rent a two-bedroom villa in the mountains of Italy, a scenic drive from the Amalfi Coast. I float in the private pool, feeling the sun on my skin, my hair and my eyelids. Omar sits inside sneakily catching up on emails. He has promised that he won't use his laptop for work while we are away, but he's inseparable from it. If he isn't responding to school queries on the laptop, he is doing it on his phone.

I call him angrily from the pool.

'We're in Italy! If you don't put that thing away right now, I'll chuck it over the cliff!' I half mean it. He quickly appears at the doors of the garden, watching me float in the water on my back, my white kaftan spread out in the pool like the wings of a dove.

'All right, all right, I've put it away.' He stretches himself out on the deckchair. 'This place is unreal.'

We are both completely stunned by the beauty of the place. He gets up and stands on the balcony in his new sunglasses, surveying the coast and the hundreds of microscopic umbrellas on the silver sand below. We are high up, so high that the sun looks like it's setting below us. When the entire coast is enveloped in the rose-gold light of dusk, we get changed and walk hand in hand towards the centre of the beauty.

The coast is embossed by the light of the setting sun, outlining the edges of the white flowers on the stone roofs, the church steeples, the little legs of the laughing children making sandcastles on the seashore. In every corner of the maze-like cobbled streets, there are people strolling slowly, climbing the steps up and down twice and thrice over to examine the wonders of this town.

Inside the sea-view restaurant, we are hit by the smell of fresh lemons. Omar breathes in deeply and takes my hand. He twirls me under his arm, causing the pleats in my pastel-blue skirt to fan out. I point to a table by the window, wanting to watch how the sun still holds onto the tide.

Omar's eyes are lit by the candles on our table in red glass tealight holders. He cracks his knuckles slowly, one by one, trying to get a reaction out of me. We eat in comfortable silence. Occasionally we swap bits of food from our plates, commenting on how it tastes and then falling silent again as we continue eating. The quiet contentment between us is reassuring. Distant music wafts in from the square.

*

We spend each morning in our villa high up in the cliffs. I take a book to the pool to read in my deckchair as Omar swims before breakfast. The salty sea air blows into our lives, tasting like newness. The constant exposure to the sun in our secluded garden has given my hair and skin a deep russet quality.

One evening, after we have tired ourselves out with all the walking and exploring, Omar lays his head in my lap. We are on the balcony. His chest rises and falls softly and steadily until he falls asleep. I watch him go further and further into deep slumber until he eventually opens his eyes.

'You're so beautiful, do you even know that?' he says, touching the fleshy part under my chin. 'Never known anyone to look this good from their chin up.'

'You look like a well-rested baby,' I say.

'I want us to have a baby.'

'You do? Why?' I am alarmed at the curtness of my voice.

'Why not?' he asks, wounded. He waits for me to say something. I hold my lips apart, making a strange sound at the back of my throat, the sound of restrained words. 'We love each other, don't we? So, we should let something be made out of this love.'

'What about the other ingredients?' I ask.

'What about them? What's missing? I want to raise a child with you.'

It is now completely dark outside. The only thing I can see clearly besides Omar's head on my lap are the stars, hundreds of them spread out as far as I can see. Below are the lights from the boats, like a mirror reflection of the stars above. The sea melts into the sky, leaving no trace of a seam. I'm completely disoriented, unsure of what's up or down.

I feel dizzy, like I could hurl myself over the balcony at any minute, right into the void. I feel the back of Omar's hair with my fingers. I can't trust anything but the weight of his shoulders and head in my lap to anchor me to my seat. I look down at his face, blinking slow and hard. Without a word, he stands up and carries me inside.

*

The next morning is our last full day in Italy. Instead of going to swim with Omar and sit on the balcony as I have done every morning we've been here, I stay inside, reading a book on the bed. I'm worried we made a baby last night. If I end up pregnant, it will be my fault. I haven't been taking my birth control.

'Come on, get dressed and let's go and get some breakfast,' says Omar, putting on his belt.

'We've done that every day this week. Can't we just order something and stay in today?' I am irritated by Omar's ceaseless energy.

'Don't be boring. We didn't come all this way to sit inside. Let's do something fun.' He jumps on the bed exaggeratedly. I throw a pillow at him.

We take the Sita bus to Positano, joining the sea of happy holidaymakers flocking out of the buses towards the cliffs. Omar swings his arms as we walk. I hold his left arm tightly. My shoes are beginning to rub the back of my sweaty feet and all I want to do is just stop, but it's too hot to stand anywhere for longer than a few seconds.

If only we could just be, I think. Just the two of us, walking for ever. How wonderful it would be to see more of the world with Omar. I don't mind the fact that no one but me is wearing a headscarf here. I don't mind the heat, or feeling like we're just living from one moment to the next, without anyone expecting anything of us. But if there really was a child growing in me, then it would be one more wandering soul in the world. I would have to teach him or her how to be happy and content being just that.

Omar uses his thumb to wipe a bit of cappuccino froth from the corner of my mouth. I stare at his bent hitchhiker's thumb and then at my long, straight one. I wonder which kind our child would have. Which eyes, nose, heart and soul.

*

There is a lot of waiting in Italy. Waiting for buses, taxis, meals in restaurants. Everything happens according to some non-existent timetable, so it's no surprise that our flight back to London is also delayed.

By the time we land in London, it is already late at night. Omar and I are cold in our summer clothes, me in my airy kimono and him in his linen shorts. I rest my legs over his on the Stansted Express to Liverpool Street. My knees are sore from the uncomfortable flight.

I package the memories we made in Italy in pretty red tissue paper like keepsakes. The rosy light, the cliffs, the coloured houses, the stars. When the train pulls into Liverpool Street and we exit the station, I am strangely relieved to be back. We pick up food from Leon before calling a cab home.

We have a long lie-in the next morning. Our suitcases, bags and shoes are left at the bottom of the stairs from the previous night. A cold, grey morning greets me through the garden doors as I make breakfast. Spring has not yet fully arrived. I pour water and milk into a small pot and begin to make tea with cardamom, cloves, ginger and cinnamon. As I wait for the milk to froth, I look through the pictures we took on Omar's camera. Not wanting to lose them like we once lost holiday pictures before, I quickly go and save them on his hard drive.

The curtains in our tiny study are thick and brown, refusing to let in any light. The room is an organized mess, with books stacked up in every corner in categories. Politics, economics, the philosophy of light, space and time, old tattered copies of the *Guinness Book of World Records* Omar has been collecting since he was young.

I open the curtains and the window. Blotchy, damp spots stain the inner panes. Fine droplets of water, first appearing as raindrops and later registering as condensation, gather on the glass. The light from the hard drive blinks from under a pile of paper.

Omar's screensaver is the view from Primrose Hill where we had a stroll after dinner on the night he asked me to be his wife. I open the file of photos on the camera. Omar is usually good at clearing the camera of old pictures, but this time there are many taken before our trip to Italy.

A series of images catch my eye. There is a woman in each one. A smiling, pretty Somali woman with a slender, pixie-like face. In all the photos she is holding the hand of a little girl. I close my eyes, squeeze them, then open them again as if trying to reboot my vision. A sudden current of hot flushes passes through my body.

I close my eyes again and squeeze them shut, this time longer and harder. The pictures are still there when I open them again. I select each picture at random. Omar himself is the main focus of the first image. In the second, he is standing beside the woman and the girl, about a metre away. I have never seen the girl or the woman before. Omar's face is lit with joy and a hint of surprise. In the next photo, tugging his hand, is the little girl. Her hair is long and tousled by the wind.

My mouth becomes dry and I can taste sharp metal. I feel sick as I realize exactly where he is. In the background of the photo are the faint outlines of the old lighthouse on the coast of Mogadishu. I check the date of the pictures. They were taken just days before we left for Italy. Omar definitely didn't take a flight to Somalia by himself. The images certainly don't look edited. I take a second look through his camera. Just before these photos are some from our last trip to Amsterdam.

I take a seat amid the mess on the desk. The realization hits me with such force, I almost scream out loud. The only way

Omar could have gone to Somalia without me knowing is if he was part of the UNCLASSIFIED project.

I put my hand over my mouth in disbelief. I can hear Omar walking around the house. I put the camera charger back into the bag and zip it up as quickly as I can, my fingers trembling. 'Sirad? Your tea's getting cold,' calls Omar from the corridor. I hurry back out.

At breakfast, I move a piece of fried egg around on my plate as Omar talks at me without realizing that I'm not responding and barely looking at him. 'It's my good friend Ilyas's wedding tomorrow. You remember Ilyas, don't you?'

I don't respond.

'Well, he found someone and he is finally settling down. It doesn't feel real. I'm not sure if he's marrying for the right reasons.'

'Really?' I say, huffing emphatically.

'So do you want to go?' he asks.

'Where?'

'To the wedding . . .' He notices my mood is off.

'Why are you telling me now?' I ask. He is taken aback by my bluntness. 'You think I can just go to a wedding, just like that, without finding a dress and getting my hair done? Look at my nails, for God's sake!'

'Sorry, it slipped my mind. It's OK. You don't have to go. It's short notice anyway.'

'Slipped your mind, did it? What else manages to slip your mind?'

He goes quiet. I'm not even thinking about what I am saying. My mind has become frighteningly jumbled with those images on rotation, the face of the little girl.

'Sirad, I said you don't have to go.'

'So you're going to go without me?'

'I have to. I already accepted the invitation.'

I get up and leave the table, afraid that I might smash every glass. It takes an unimaginable amount of strength not to say anything to him. I know I have to be a lot more strategic.

Omar stands up too and begins to clear the table. 'Anyway, it was just a suggestion. I don't know what has gotten into you today. Do you want to come on a walk with me? Get some fresh air?'

'I think I'm going to lie down for a bit,' I say.

I still haven't looked at his face properly. Just a few days ago I believed he was the most constant thing in my world. I'm not sure if I am angrier at him or at myself. All along I have known that there has to be more to his story. *Get lost*, I want to scream. *Get out of my life.*

Chapter Eighteen

'You lend a false ear to false words.'

It has taken weeks of strategizing to decide on my next move. For days on end, I unlock Omar's laptop when he's out at the gym and scroll through hundreds of emails, until one day I find exactly what I'm looking for. This is it, I think. It's the frequent use of the word 'crossing' across numerous emails that catches my eye: *'I'm crossing next week, with the stuff you needed.' 'I'm crossing early today.'*

I am surprised to find that these journeys have something to do with his job as a teacher. He mentions classes and books quite often in the emails, but nothing is very clear. Perhaps it's all in code, I wonder.

Every so often, I go back into the camera and look at those pictures again. I can't stop torturing myself with them. It's clear that Omar has crossed back and forth to the other side numerous times. The only thing that cools my anger is the realization that we have both been hiding the same secret, both of us afraid that the other won't understand. If I allow myself to fly at him in all my anger and disappointment, I will only be a hypocrite.

I don't find out more about the woman and the child from

Omar's camera, but I come across the name of a man called Nabil in several emails. He has sent Omar an address somewhere in East London and his phone number. I put the address into my phone, and it turns out to be a warehouse in West Silvertown. One quiet Saturday morning while Omar is out visiting his aunt, I set out to locate it.

Driving through the Blackwall Tunnel in my car, I am afraid of what I'll find. I can't imagine what business a deputy teacher could have in a warehouse in East London.

When I arrive, I spend some time sitting in the car observing my surroundings. The area is dull and lifeless; I can't see anything beyond the warehouses and factories.

Eventually I step out of the car. I've considered calling this Nabil person and speaking to him on the phone first to let him know I'm coming, but I quickly realized that this would be a foolish idea. I want to see the raw truth. I want to know what is really going on.

Omar's not a bad person, I tell myself as I wander around the factories and storage units alone. He has never done anything immoral in his life. He's not bad, he's not bad. I repeat this to myself until I get tired. But he lied, says another part of me. I'm married to a man who is lying to me, day in and day out. Maybe we deserve each other.

I call Nabil and ask him to meet me where I parked my car. To my surprise, he comes promptly. He takes long strides as he walks up to me. Strangely, he reminds me of a Quran teacher that used to come to teach us at home when we were little. He had the same untamed beard, the same expression that looked like he was in a state of permanent disappointment.

He is extremely tall. He wears trousers that stop just above his ankle. For a moment we don't know what to say to each other.

'Are you lost?' he begins.

I shake my head. 'No. No, I'm not lost. I know this is random, and you don't know who I am, but I need to talk to you.'

'Sure. About what?' He is cautious.

'I want to know what my husband does here.'

'I beg your pardon? Who is your husband?'

'Omar,' I say.

He narrows his gaze and takes a deep breath. 'Right. Omar.' He says the name slowly, as if choosing his next words. He turns his eyes away from me and looks towards the grey horizon. 'Does he know you're here?'

'Look, I read the emails you sent each other. I saw some photos on his camera. I just want to know the truth. I'm not here to start any trouble.'

'Omar and I work together. We have a business. Why don't you talk to him? He's your husband, isn't he? I can't come between you.'

I'm getting annoyed. 'He's obviously hiding this part of his life from me. Do you think that's OK?'

'No, actually. I don't. But it's none of my business.'

With the tip of my boot, I squash down a stray dandelion that is growing out of the concrete. 'Please, just tell me what you know. I promise I won't tell anyone else. I'm married to a man that I evidently don't know. Help me.'

'Listen.' He lowers his voice. 'I hear your frustration, but I have to go now. Please come and find me on Friday.'

'Friday? *Why?* I came all the way here just to talk to you.'

'I know, but I can't give this conversation the time it needs. I promise. I will share everything properly on Friday. Don't call me. Just come straight here.'

'OK. What time should I get here?'

'Early. Nine a.m., if you can.'

'OK. Fine. But just tell me before I go. Should I be worried about him?'

'No. You shouldn't.'

'OK,' I respond, although I don't feel reassured. 'I'll see you on Friday. Thank you.' I turn on my heel and get back into my car.

For the rest of the day, I try to act as normal as I can around Omar. He makes lasagne for dinner and puts on a movie, but I can't hold the food down. Just before the film ends, I run to the toilet and throw up violently. Omar doesn't seem to notice anything different about me. He busies himself with some school policy documents for the rest of the evening.

I consider the possibility that he knows what I know. But it makes no sense. Either way, it angers me how soundly he sleeps at night, how easily he mills around the house as if everything is fine. Sometimes I feel a disgusting urge to keep going through his things. He hides nothing. His camera remains in plain sight. His laptop is still unlocked and always left on the living-room sofa. To me, it is a sign that he doesn't care. He's in too deep. There is nothing left for me to do but maintain an artificial sense of calm, at least until Friday.

I throw myself into my work for the rest of the week, taking on extra projects in an effort to silence my mind. I am praised by colleagues for going above and beyond. They are always in awe of me. I hold an unspoken reputation for being the most dedicated to the job. But the good feedback no longer lands how it used to. Their words take on a new, mocking quality in my ears. This is what I get for going above and beyond. A lying, secretive husband. A marriage that evidently lacks true mutual understanding. A stranger in my house who, it turns out, I don't know much about. Even worse, he doesn't seem to know much about me.

I arrange to take Friday off, transferring my pending workload to a pair of new interns.

I come to meet Nabil prepared for anything. I take Omar's Swiss army knife with me, just in case. Never, in all my years of living in London, have I imagined myself carrying a knife through the streets. I brace myself for possible danger. After all, I don't know Nabil or what his true intentions are.

Nabil is waiting outside the warehouse at 9 a.m. with his arms crossed. I'm surprised that he's punctual. I was worried that he wasn't going to show up. Hardly saying a word, he ushers me along the back streets to a small cafe tucked away among the factories.

I'm relieved to find there is hardly anyone in there, especially not anyone Somali. The last thing I need is the implication of a local scandal.

I never knew this cafe even existed. I take in the simple interior and sit opposite Nabil, in the corner by the window. He pulls out my chair and takes off his coat. I, however, keep my coat on. I don't want to give him the impression that I am here for a cosy chat. I mirror his grave, almost angry expression.

'So, you want to know what Omar does here.' There is a glint in his eyes as he says this. I can tell he feels powerful because of this knowledge, but he is trying to hide it. He takes a long pause.

'Yes. Exactly,' I respond curtly.

'Tell me, why does it seem like you expect me to say something bad?'

'When did I say that?'

The waitress comes over with black coffee for Nabil and a bottle of water for me. We wait until she sets down the tray before we resume talking. I can tell by the way Nabil looks at me that he is enjoying this uncomfortable exchange. I ball my fists and put my elbows up on the table defensively.

'It just seems that women always—' He catches himself. 'People always expect the worst. From what I know about Omar, he's an honest man. He wouldn't like it if he knew you were suspicious. Or this.' He motions at the drinks between us with his index finger.

'Like what? The fact that I'm speaking to you?'

'Yes. I think he would much prefer it if you asked him directly.'

I am far too tired and too determined to let this man derail the conversation. I don't want him to see me get riled up or back away. In my mind, I have every right to know what is going on.

'I found pictures.' I choose my words carefully. 'Of Omar, in Mogadishu, with people I don't know. Looking like he's lived a whole life there simultaneously with the life we share as husband and wife. I found a picture of a woman and a child. He has never told me about them or why he even has these pictures. I don't know if you heard of the UNCLASSIFIED story years ago . . .'

'Of course. Everybody has.'

'Does it have anything to do with that?'

'You could say that. But let me be clear. Omar is a teacher. He's not a criminal or a liar or a cheat.'

'So what is he doing working with you, if he's a teacher?'

'No, I mean, his role in my business is that he teaches children from the other side. He runs a supplementary school.'

'What?' I am in shock. 'A school?'

Nabil laughs. 'Do you feel silly now?' He scratches his head and yawns. 'He joined us a few months ago. He really cares about what he does and there is nothing sinister about it.'

'So why hasn't he told me about it? I'm his wife.'

'I don't know. Maybe he's protecting you. It's a dangerous job. If the authorities found out, he could be in a lot of trouble. But I guess you know him. You're his wife.'

'What about the woman and the child in the pictures I found? Who are they?'

'Probably one of his students. I don't know. Look, he really cares about these children, more than anyone I've ever met. It's not just a job for him. He cares about everything they go through. Their families, their health, their dreams.'

'How often does he teach?'

'Twice a week.'

I realize that Omar has probably been using the time he's been telling me he spends at the gym.

'We take school supplies: books, pens, used laptops, paper. He gives children his time, knowledge and advice. That's all he's been doing, I'm sure you're glad to know.'

I hesitate. 'But that's not what I'm worried about,' I say. 'Why is he hiding it? Why is he doing it this way? If he cares about kids in Somalia, he can get on a flight and help them.' I pause, swallowing hard.

'Can he, though? Can he do that and still have his regular job and come home to you every night? Everyone has their reasons for being involved in this business. It's personal. I can't speak for him.'

'So you think what he's doing is right?' I ask.

'Like I said, I can't speak for him. What do you want me to do in this situation?'

'Nothing. Thank you for your time, but I'm done talking to you.' I stand up and refasten the belt on my coat.

Nabil scoffs. 'Why do I feel like you're more involved than you're letting on?'

'Hmm. I think you're just being suspicious,' I say. I grab my bag and walk off.

Back at the car, I put my face in my hands. I've seen Omar before in situations that have sparked fleeting, insecure feelings within me. I've seen him be incredibly kind and smiley with waitresses or the mothers of his students. He never means anything bad by it, but it still makes me feel uneasy. The pictures on his camera made me seethe with jealousy. If he was just teaching children, what was he doing with that woman on the beach? Why was he smiling like that with her? It could be the case that he is just teaching, but there could also be more to it than Nabil knows.

I snap out of my thoughts when I realize exactly what I need to do. I need to cross over to the other side myself; I need to find Ubah.

I go running back to the cafe. Nabil is just getting up when I approach him. I stop in my tracks.

'There's something else I need, actually.' I pull out my phone. 'Can you get me on that bus?'

He is amused to see me back. 'I can. But it's going to cost you about £200.'

'You charge?'

'For my time.'

He bursts out laughing at the look on my face. 'I'll let you go for free. But I'll only take you once. I want you to do something in return.'

'What is it?'

'I want you to forgive Omar.'

'That's got nothing to do with you.'

'Keep it in mind, at least.'

'Can I go tomorrow?' I ask.

'I'll get someone to pick you up,' says Nabil. 'I'll call you. But please, don't say a word to him.'

As I head back towards my car, I realize the gravity of what I'm planning to do. I don't know if I'm ready to see Ubah again, or if I will even be successful in finding her. I have no desired outcome in mind, but I know that I need to apologize to her. I want to do that even more than I want to understand what Omar has been doing.

The guilt of what I did to Ubah has gnawed away at my heart for years. It has made me, in many ways, a lesser person. It stops me from being able to respect myself. Discovering Omar's secret has felt like the past coming back to bite me.

Around me, people scurry along the street carrying children or shopping, bundled in coats and scarves. The past is calling me. I can't ignore it. I know that redemption isn't guaranteed, but perhaps the only way I can move forward is to go back one more time.

Chapter Nineteen

'The youth who taught their mother to give birth.'

I retch in the bus as we're crossing over. A bead of sweat slips down my temple. I don't remember feeling sick last time; I wonder why it's different now.

'Are you nervous?' asks the driver, staring me down. 'If it's your first time crossing or you haven't done it in a long while, it can be a shock to the system.'

The bus's windows are so dusty I can barely see out of them. Every seat is covered in piles of things: books, paper, newspapers, cardboard boxes, empty packets of food.

I look out through the front windows as I sit doubled over, clutching my stomach. The driver has urged me to close my window as we pass through the tunnel.

'Head between your knees!' he reminds me. 'Please don't vomit all over my seats.'

I want to throw up on him to shut him up. He switches between BBC Somali and old qaraami songs I recognize from my childhood.

'So you're Ubah's double, right?' asks the man, looking back.
'How do you know?' I ask him.
'Everyone knows Ubah and what she did.' The driver drums

his fingers against the wheel as if what he's just said was nothing important at all. He moves his shoulders awkwardly to the music.

'What is her story?' I ask, gesturing at him to turn down the music.

'She ran away from her husband years ago, and her respectable family, all to run a brothel disguised as a salon.'

'How do you know that's true? Do you know her husband?'

'Well, I don't know for sure . . . but there have been stories. We're part of the same clan.'

The driver is careful not to exceed the speed limit at any point. The lights in the tunnel flash white, completely engulfing the horizon. I shut my eyes tight. Nausea begins to bubble up in my stomach.

'Not long now,' says the driver. 'Hang in there.'

The bus goes faster. We alternate in and out of complete darkness and bright lights for what feels like ages. The city of Mogadishu stretches before us. I'm moved to tears by nostalgia at the distant tangy smell of the ocean. We pass street vendors buzzing with life. There is not a single cloud in the sky. Memories of seeing Ubah and being with Mama and Aabo come rushing back. I gather myself in the minibus, checking I have everything with me. Unlike the first time I travelled, on the UNCLASSIFIED bus, the bus stop is relatively quiet, and the driver seems to pass through fairly inconspicuously. Money changes hands in a smooth movement between the driver and one of the soldiers.

The driver takes a long drink of water from a plastic bottle before offering me one. I take it and glug the cool liquid down quickly.

Women linger along the streets, selling gold jewellery and

skincare from stalls. Children run around, their laughter ringing further than their little legs can take them.

I pull a longer scarf over my regular scarf. I'm afraid of being discovered by the wrong people, so I cover my face with some of the fabric from my scarf, creating a makeshift veil.

A lot has changed since I last visited this alternate version of Mogadishu. There aren't as many soldiers now. The few that stop us at the checkpoint don't scare me as they once did. 'Come back as soon as you're finished,' says the driver as he hands me a piece of paper with some rough directions. 'Don't go looking for anyone else.'

A woman walks up to the minibus holding a box of bananas. She pleads with us to buy one. The driver hands her a few coins and takes a banana, but says to me, 'Don't buy anything or try to help anyone. Not even an innocent old lady or a child. Lay as low as you can.'

He points me towards the colourful streets of Xamar Weyne. I walk through the side streets of the ancient district, clutching the directions in my hand.

People walk around in a lull, as though waiting for something to happen. The whole time I walk, the city looks as though it could crumble into dust at any moment, taking along with it the intricate ancient doorways and big drooping trees. On one corner, the glory of Mogadishu before the war has just died before my eyes; on another corner, it is just being born.

Following the driver's scribbled map, I reach the street where Ubah has her salon. UBAH NURA, the sign says in bold red italics. Seeing her name on the door, proud and pronounced, I feel a glimmer of pride in my heart.

A woman in a veil stops just short of the entrance, watches me for a moment and then walks on. Neatly dressed women come out of the salon in dresses and shoes that match their bags. I stand outside for longer than I intend to, trying to get a feel for the mood inside the salon by observing the women who emerge. There are no windows to see in.

After a few minutes, I muster up the courage to go inside. There are about ten women in the salon. A strong, citrussy fragrance pervades the room. Some of the women are having their hair done and some are being decorated in intricate black henna. In a far corner, a woman is having a thick white substance applied to her face.

I sit down on a comfy chair in the waiting area and wait patiently to be seen as a Turkish drama dubbed in Somali plays on a small TV. The women seem to pay me no mind. They laugh and sing as they work, chattering just like any other hairdressers.

A stylishly dressed girl with unnaturally bright skin comes over to me. She greets me without a smile and stares at me blankly, as if waiting for me to speak first.

'Is Ubah working today?' I ask.

'Did you book something with her, habibti?' She yawns, covering her mouth.

'No. I just wanted to pay her a visit.'

'Does she know you're coming?'

The other women in the room are staring. They're analysing me. A couple of them begin to whisper.

'Yes,' I lie. I refuse to waste this trip. The girl's eyes scan me once more. She reminds me of a cousin from my dad's side who lived in Northampton who once came to stay with us for a few days when I was young. She shrugs. 'She should be here any moment now. Can I get you some water, habibti?'

'No thank you. I'm OK.'

The girl sighs and walks away. Some of the women in the

waiting area continue to stare, completely unbothered by how blatantly uncomfortable I am.

Every so often a woman walks in through the front doors and they stare her down too. The air has become thick with tension. I can't take it. I decide to step outside and take in some fresh air to clear my head.

I stand up and rearrange my makeshift veil, drawing deep breaths. I worry that Ubah isn't going to want to talk to me. Someone has turned on the air conditioner, and the sweat beads on my neck instantly dry up. A cat wanders into the salon.

Stepping outside, I see a woman climbing out of a white Toyota some distance away. She holds up the hem of her dress to expose the delicate straps of her red sandals and the red henna patterns on her feet. She walks with a slow determination, as though the whole street will stop for her.

'Ubah!' I yell.

She maintains her pace, staring right at me. I jump up and down, waving my arms like a maniac. Of course, with all but my eyes covered, she doesn't recognize me. I can barely conjure a full sentence. She is a lot slimmer than I remember. She looks much older, I realize as she approaches. Her made-up eyes stand out on her artificially lightened skin, the thick kohl bleeding into the tiny creases around them. The wind scatters a pile of empty plastic bottles across the street, making a clattering noise.

'I'm sorry, are you waiting to be seen?' she asks.

I lift up my veil. Ubah does a double take. An expression that I can only make out to be anger flashes across her face.

'Who sent you?' she demands.

'Nobody. I wanted to come. To speak to you.'

'Get away from me,' she huffs. The anger turns into deep,

visceral pain. 'I'm here, minding my business. I didn't ask for you and I don't think about you. What do you want from me?'

'I want to apologize and I want to explain myself.'

'I'm busy,' she says, walking away. She circles around the building. I follow her, dodging the stray cats and dogs. 'My life doesn't stop for you.'

She steps into a laundromat a few doors down from the salon. 'Number 578,' she says, reading her receipt to the attendant. She collects her washed and dried clothes in a bag and hefts it over one shoulder.

'I know I did a horrible thing. I was young and stupid. I thought I was doing the right thing.'

Ubah barely stops to look at me. She walks down the alleyway with the bag and stops in front of a door which she skilfully unlocks with one hand. Inside there are three sets of bunk beds, a small dining table, a gas stove and a sink. She gestures at me to come in.

'Is this where you live?' I ask.

'No,' she retorts sarcastically. 'I just unlocked the door to a random person's home and asked you to come in.'

'Do you stay here alone?'

'I share with a few friends. We work together. We take care of each other . . .' She gazes out of the window. Her gold tooth glitters in the sunlight.

'I'm so sorry. It sounds like things haven't been easy for you.'

Ubah puts her feet up on the table, loosening her scarf and the straps of her shoes. I am hypnotized by her henna.

'I heard some rumours,' I say, embarrassed even to mention it. 'I don't want to go into them. But are they true? Are you also running a brothel?'

'You know, the things people come up with about my life are always so much more interesting than the truth.'

'I think they're just jealous. You have a great business and they're not happy about that.'

Ubah shrugs. 'Why did you betray me like that? I trusted you and you didn't even think twice about breaking my trust.'

'I'm so sorry. I know they sound like empty words. Whatever difficulty you have endured since London is entirely my fault. I didn't know what to do and I was under so much pressure.'

Ubah's eyes turn glassy. She closes them for a moment, then opens them again, managing to keep tears at bay. 'This is a pointless conversation. I forgot you a long time ago anyway. What is an apology going to do for me? Do you think I sit around thinking about whether or not you're sorry? Do you know how many years have passed now?'

'You have every right to have forgotten me, but I haven't forgotten you. I came to do what's right, no matter how much time has passed. I feel awful about it all the time.'

Ubah laughs. It takes me by surprise. She swings her legs off the table in one smooth movement and sits up. 'Who cares what it makes you *feel*? What has that ever changed in my life? In all those years, what has it changed for me?'

I am too stunned to respond.

'This is the problem I have with people like you. This is why I didn't even want to meet you in the first place! You come here searching for the missing piece to your story or whatever you're told you'll find here. You bring us your emptiness and you expect us to do something about it. Didn't I warn you in the first place?' Her voice is hoarse. 'What was my role in all of this? Was I supposed to be your equal? Or was I just supposed to give you what you want: an exciting story, some claim to personal growth? Aren't I done serving you yet?'

'That's not what I mean—'

'You chose this story. Now play your part. *Mean* it. That's what I have to do every single day. I don't get to spend a second telling anyone about how I feel.'

I am silent for a few seconds. 'It's complicated. You're right. I did choose to hurt you under those circumstances. At that time. I made a mistake – I was twenty-three! With a struggling mother and all of these responsibilities. I won't defend myself. I may never forgive myself either.'

Ubah nods her head and smiles. 'I didn't expect any less from you back then.'

The cat I saw earlier strolls into the room. She hops up onto the table and nestles herself between us. Then she begins to groom herself under a ray of sunlight.

There is a dull pain in my stomach. I wish I could disintegrate right here. I can't believe how much I have hurt another person. I deserve all the consequences.

'Honestly, I hope you got what you wanted, at the very least,' says Ubah.

I think about the pictures on Omar's camera. 'I got what I deserved, I guess.'

Ubah smiles sadly. 'One way or another, we all get what we deserve.'

I want to open up to her about Omar. I want to tell her that he is a teacher who cares for children, that he did everything right. I want to tell her about the photos, about not knowing how to confront him. I want to tell her that I just want to run away.

We both sit, staring out of the window or at the ceiling. Ubah eventually speaks again. 'I had a child and ran away from her. I left her with her father. I couldn't be what she wanted. How could I subject that soul to a life like this? I succumbed and gave her to her father, who, in a short space of time, managed to make a lot of money. He was able to give her everything a little girl should have.' On the surface, her voice is void of emotion, but I can tell that underneath it is a whole mountain of pain. 'I hope that has satisfied your curiosity.'

'But Ubah,' I start. 'I don't mean to judge or anything, but you could have given her so much more. Nobody can love her more than you can.'

'In my situation, you would have done the same.'

I take the opportunity to stand up for myself. 'Actually, you couldn't be more wrong,' I say. 'I would have stayed.'

She laughs drily. 'Then what the hell are you doing here? Go back to where you came from and have your babies. Leave me alone and let me work.'

She charges towards the door and opens it wide. 'Out, out, OUT!'

*

I arrive back at the bus drenched in sweat. I'm panting, but the driver doesn't seem to notice or care. He is parked up under a tree, smoking a cigarette out of the window.

'What took you so long?' he asks. 'Did you get into any trouble?'

'No, no. I'm fine.' Adrenaline pumps through my body. My face is hot. 'Do you have any more water?'

He hands me another of the small bottles and waits until I've finished drinking it before he starts the engine.

He plays the same four songs on a loop for the entire journey. We barely speak, both of us hypnotized by our own thoughts. Then, out of the blue, he says, 'You know, I wanted to ask you something earlier.'

'What is it?' I ask. I am almost falling asleep from exhaustion.

'It's about a girl who used to work with Ubah. Her name is Aisha.'

'What about her?'

'She crossed over and married a man in London. She had two kids with him the last time I heard anything. She's doing all right now, although she had a rough start. We grew up together. I used to love her. I'm ashamed to say it, but I still really love her.'

There is so much sadness in his voice — I am startled by it. I know that nothing in his heart has changed, only life, only his circumstances. It dawns on me just then that the true violence of the UNCLASSIFIED project was deeper than I have ever imagined.

'I'm sorry,' I say. 'I can tell you really care about her.' I don't know what else to say.

'What I wanted to ask you is, does this kind of love ever just give up? I want to forget her.'

'I wish I knew,' I offer. 'I hope it does.'

Chapter Twenty

'The best bed that a man can sleep on is peace.'

The ease with which I pack a suitcase and leave Omar stuns me. A wicked and intuitive force moves me around the house in the dark hours of the morning as he lies sleeping. It is too early for me to think clearly, but I move with the precision and confidence of someone who has done this before many times. I am on tiptoe. I pull down the suitcase from the top shelf of the storage unit and gently lay it down without a sound. I step over squeaky floorboards and pull open doors at just the right angle to avoid creaking. This feels innate. This feels like it comes from somewhere deep.

I think of people in films who leave notes in places they will be found: 'Gone to do some thinking,' or something along those lines. I want to write that on the notepad on Omar's desk but decide against it at the last moment. I think about just writing 'I love you,' but dismiss that idea too. Omar doesn't need to read that from a notepad. If he doesn't know I love him from the ways I have shown him over the years — from how I've lived my life beside him, around him, for him — he ought not to know at all.

I'm leaving because I love you, I imagine myself saying to him if he were to suddenly wake up and catch me. What does that even mean? I'm not sure. It just sounds good. He would fight with me until his voice was hoarse. Then he would help me with my suitcase and it would break me. I'm so glad that he's asleep.

There must be a genetic predisposition for being able to leave a loved one like this without missing a step. I think my father has passed it down to me through his blood. He showed me, all those years ago, how easy it would be to just pack my things and walk away.

Over the years I've saved some money in a second bank account to pay for somewhere warm and clean to stay in case a war suddenly broke out, or a natural disaster that meant we had nowhere to go. I got that from my mother. To her, we were always on the brink of needing to escape. We kept all of our important documents, passports, photos and her gold, in one bag in a safe under her bed. She could just grab our things from one place in no time at all. She knew what it was like not to have papers, to have to wait for them for months on end while her children barely ate – she would be damned if she found herself in that state again. I took from her philosophy.

I transfer money from my secret getaway account into my main account. I gather my important documents into one file. I've made copies of everything, just in case: my passport, driver's licence, old letters from my GP, bank statements, letters from my job.

I drive up to a petrol station a few streets away and open the window, letting in the early morning breeze.

My mind begins to wander back to the years I was forced to fill in the blanks as to what might have happened on the other side of the front door as my father walked away. Maybe frankincense still haunts him too. Maybe he also had a reason. Maybe it was just something small and mundane that he had noticed on his way out of the estate car park that he now replays in his mind for no God-given reason, like seeing a pigeon rooting through an empty crisp packet.

I wonder how often Ubah thought about leaving everything and going back for her child. There was nothing behind her eyes when she spoke about her baby, but one could argue that she did what she thought was best with the information that she had. I told her I could never have done what she did, that I would have stayed. But now, creeping away from the husband I love to death in the middle of the night, I doubt myself.

One night when I was eleven, the evening before a big school trip to Wales, I saw my parents' fear of not being able to protect me, and it stayed with me for years. My mum had helped me pack my things as my dad smoked on the balcony, one cigarette after another, until he realized what we were doing. He came back inside. He looked down at me and my mum as we knelt on the living room carpet together and rolled my T-shirts and jeans.

'Laa,' he said, shaking his head. He often said *no* in Arabic; I think he thought it sounded more emphatic. 'She's not going any more. I have changed my mind.' I looked to my mother, my eyes about to burst from their sockets in disbelief. Very calmly, she continued to pack my things into my rucksack.

'But why?' I cried. 'I'm already packed and you've already paid!'

'Well, unpack then. I've changed my mind.'

I don't remember if my mum said anything to him. All I recall is her continuing to pack my clothes into my bag, quickly and calmly, until he exploded at her in a verbal rage. I was told to go to bed.

'Is it because I'm a girl?!' I asked, first thing in the morning, shouting directly at my dad for the first time. The school coach would be setting off in about forty minutes. My cereal remained untouched. If he would just hurry up and come around, I could make it there on time.

'No,' he said. 'It's not you. You have done nothing wrong. It's just that anything can happen to you while you're there. We don't know – maybe good, maybe bad. And what would we do then? We'll be here, totally powerless while you're in Wales. *Totally* powerless.'

I felt like throwing things. I couldn't calm my anger.

I was still expected to go to school while my entire class were in Wales. I spent most of those empty days in the school library, reading. Books, outlandish fictional stories, were my only defence against a real world that did not make sense.

Where is my father now? I think. How come he stopped caring about what fate might do to me? Back then I was in year seven, the first of four years in secondary school. An awkward and equally defining year. I was the only girl out of all five form groups who didn't go to Wales. The trip was even fully funded for the girls from low incomes who couldn't afford it. For four years, I had to listen to my friends reminisce about that trip. It was one of the most alienating experiences in my early life.

I'm fascinated by the beautiful femmes fatale in films who check into fancy hotel rooms for no reason other than to enjoy a comfortable night's sleep and an adventure. I want to be one of them, even if just for a few days. I think of the days I spent alone at home before I met Omar. That was a sacred era. I check into a small hotel in West Greenwich and immediately unpack my things to make the room look and feel as much like my own place as possible; then I collapse into the soft sheets and pillows.

After I order some pizza, I take a long shower, change into a silky nightgown and put my phone on silent. I already have twenty missed calls from Omar. At some point he will probably call Hooyo and Ahmed.

The next morning I awake to calls from Ahmed, Hooyo and Omar. I message them all separately and let them know that I am safe and will be back soon.

Outside is a sombre, bluish dawn. Maybe I should have gone to Wales, I think. I could run around in the open air and be everything I never got to be. I could walk up the mountain until my legs ache and then just stay there, until I feel better again, until I feel clean. My poor beloved Omar. He isn't the only villain. I have run away not because I don't want him but because I can't bring myself to ask him what I think I know. About the pictures, about crossing over. I can't give him a chance to show me he doesn't want me. I fall back into a deep sleep.

It's almost noon when I wake again. I order a large breakfast. That second round of sleep has left me feeling a little more refreshed. I deserve to be at peace, I tell myself in the mirror as I make up my face. I won't let anything or anyone take that away from me. A young man delivers croissants and coffee to my door. 'Good morning, Madam,' he says in a slightly phoney way. I am sickened by his facial expression. I take my food and slam the door shut.

I spend all afternoon and evening in the room. That night, I wake with the savage remnants of a nightmare. I rise from my pillow with a loud gasp and stare right ahead at the mirror on the opposite side of the wall.

The nightmare was about Omar. I saw him coming home after a long day at work. A woman appeared in our home as if from thin air. The woman's face wasn't clear. First she gave him a hug, then she pointed at her stomach. A few seconds later, a baby materialized in her arms. As the baby began to cry, I woke up from the nightmare.

I stare into the mirror. I've always heard that you're not supposed to do that in the middle of the night, but I can't resist. My reflection has some sort of magnetic pull. There is something so uncanny about it. I scream.

A few minutes later, one of the hotel employees is knocking at my door. 'Is everything OK?' she asks. 'Some of the guests heard a scream.'

'Yes. No – I'm fine. Sorry.'

The next day I decide to go outside. I should go and find a busy cafe, I think to myself. I can't bear the isolation.

I settle on a new coffee shop within a few minutes' walk of the hotel. It is a family-run cafe serving strawberry matcha. I've never had one before. I order one and sit by the window.

My phone rings. It's my mother. She is livid.

'Do you realize what you're doing?' She is screaming down the line. I lower the volume on my phone, afraid someone else will hear her. 'This is no way to go about a marital dispute!'

'We didn't have a dispute,' I reply. 'Nothing happened. I just felt overwhelmed, and . . .' I stop midway through the sentence. I don't even know why I am giving an explanation. It isn't going to make her calm down.

'You're ridiculous. At your age, you're still acting on impulse and you don't consider anyone else's feelings but your own. Listen to me. I want you to put an end to this behaviour right now. Are you in any danger? Where are you?'

'I'm not in any danger. I'm in the area.'

'Don't you *ever* scare me like that again!'

'Hooyo, please. I'm safe. I love you.'

She cuts the line.

I sip my drink, and after a while I start to feel a lot calmer. There is no one to bother me and no one to be obligated towards for the day. I can eat wherever I want, go back to my hotel room at the end of the night and wrap myself in the fresh bedsheets.

Halfway through my drink, a man comes and sits in the chair next to me. I instantly have my guard up. I pull my bag close to me.

'You're staying at the same hotel as I am, aren't you?'

'I – I think you've got the wrong person,' I stutter. My heart is racing inside my chest. I scan the room. Everyone seems to be in their own little world, reading a book or scrolling away on a phone.

'Are you waiting for someone?' the man asks.

There is something boyish about his stance. He must be in his forties but he holds himself like a teenager.

'Yes,' I say, flashing him the gold ring on my finger. 'And he'll be here soon, so you'd better disappear.'

He backs away. 'I just wanted to tell you that you're beautiful. That's all.'

'Go away!' I raise my voice in an attempt to sound authoritative. Some people in the cafe look up, then go back to what they're doing.

I succeed in getting him to walk out of the cafe, but am close to tears anyway. I make the decision almost instantly to change hotels. It is time to relocate somewhere else.

An hour later, as I take my suitcase down to the lobby to check out, all I can think about is Omar.

*

I check into a new hotel in Canary Wharf. I have chosen this, I remind myself. I have chosen to be here and made my way with my own two feet.

At the new hotel, it occurs to me that the only person I can talk to who won't make my situation more complicated is Maxine. With Maxine near, I can ignore the fact that life is changing. She has been there for me in that way ever since I was a little girl. I can cling to her during the stormiest moments of my life. Sometimes she will email me and I will forget to email her back, and other days I will email her and she will forget to email me back. We come and go in each other's lives as freely as possible. Such is the ebb and flow of our friendship.

Chapter Twenty-One

'A sealed mouth is gold.'

'What do you do when something's playing on your mind and won't go away?' I ask Maxine during our day out. She is eating her 99p Flake ice cream with the enjoyment of an innocent child. It melts and drips onto her black T-shirt. She wipes the drips away with a piece of tissue.

'I go for a walk. And I just keep walking. By the end of it, I've either resolved my issue or I'm so tired of having it on my mind that I just let it go.'

We are walking through Greenwich Park on a bright and unusually mild day. Instead of her usual monochrome, polished look, Maxine is dressed casually in a pair of white plimsolls, light blue jeans and a cream linen shirt. Her hair is wrapped up in a pink satin scarf. A few pieces of grey hair poke out from the sides. I'm wearing a long-sleeved white dress with small blue flowers, a pair of white sandals and a pink scarf too, but in a slightly lighter shade than Maxine's. She walks much more slowly and is much shorter than me, so I take shorter strides. I try to make sure she can't tell that I'm slowing down for her.

We notice a small crowd forming in the middle of the park. Someone has hung colourful pieces of cloth from a tree, perhaps some kind of art installation. We shade our eyes from the bright sun as we approached them. On each piece of cloth is the face of a child or teenager embroidered with a name, age and date. A description of the project is displayed on a large easel: it's called *The Day I Learned to Fly*. On a board, I read that a cohort of twenty children from a Syrian refugee resettlement made these pieces and hung them from the dainty branches. Seeing the passion of the children and their smiling faces warms my heart, but some of the faces on the cloths look very sad. I notice Maxine looking at one of the smallest ones. She shakes her head and holds her cheek. 'Come on, star. Let's keep walking.'

We move on, walking slowly up the concrete path, dodging rollerblading teens and dogs running wild. The wind begins to pick up. In her pink headwrap, Maxine looks like she could be my grandmother. I wonder if passers-by think we are related. Can they tell that we're two very different people who have chosen each other as friends?

'How are things at the library?' I ask. We sit down, cross-legged, on a small slope of the hill facing the museum. Maxine fiddles with blades of grass. I wonder with amazement at her persistence in fighting so hard for the library over so many years, when the forces working to close it down are so great.

'So much is changing. We're running out of equipment and we can't afford to do repairs or update the computers. But we're still standing.'

'What makes you want to fight so hard?' I ask. 'Where do you find the strength?'

'I don't know, dear. I really don't know how I do it any more. It's been my life for so long. I don't know anything else. I've written reams of letters, I've invited MPs to the library, I've run fundraisers and coffee mornings. I've done it all now, star.'

'And you're going to win,' I say. 'Because you're so determined.'

'I hope so,' Maxine says. 'I can't bear to think of the library being no more.'

She gives me a sweet smile and begins to make a daisy chain with the few little daisies around us. The trees shimmy in the gentle breeze, one after another. I'm so glad I have Maxine in my life, I think to myself. 'Not as many people care about it any more,' she adds, looking out towards the museum at the bottom of the grassy bank.

'Why?'

'They're over it. It's inevitable, they say. What can we do? It's just me and four others who are still organizing.'

'But the locals still care, don't they?' I ask.

'Much less so. Greenwich has changed. All the young people that used to live here, the ones who made the library their second home, have been forced to move on. Who can bloody afford to live in Greenwich now? That was their *home*. Sure, we get a few locals every now and then who offer to support the campaign with their skills and knowledge, but we're not fighting for the same thing. I'm fighting for the one thing that belonged to us; for them, it's just politics. Something to align themselves with. The library is ours. It is always going to be ours.'

'You know, growing up, I didn't appreciate it as much as I could have. You're right. It was like a second home. I don't know many places where I can just walk in and feel like I belong. School never did that for me,' I confess.

'I say to almost every young person I meet at the library that where there are stories, there is a home for everyone. A lot of the boys that come to the library every single day have been excluded from their schools. They're in between institutions and are feeling hopeless because of it. There are also many children whose parents can't speak English, who come to the library for extra help that isn't offered at their school. When I think of the library closing, I think of children like this. They won't have anywhere else to go.' Maxine's eyes are amber in the sun.

'Let's walk around for a little longer,' I suggest, standing up and straightening my dress. I pull Maxine to her feet after me. 'I need to tell you something.'

She dusts off her jeans and pauses, looking at me with a serious expression. 'Don't scare me, star. What's happened?'

'Don't be scared. It's OK. I think . . .'

She raises her eyebrows.

'I left Omar.'

Maxine grabs my hand in shock. 'You didn't!'

'I did. It hasn't really sunk in. It's still fresh. I don't know what to do now or where I'll go from here.'

'Oh Sirad! Why?'

'I'm terrible, aren't I? Tell me I'm a bad person for doing this. It's a long story. I learned some things about him that I didn't know before – I got scared and left.'

Maxine shakes her head at the ground as she walks. 'You *are* a good person, Sirad, and you deserve good things. You deserve to love and to trust. I'm just in shock. You seemed so happy.'

'I was. I am. I miss him. I love him with all my heart. But I'm afraid of getting hurt, and I feel like I'm about to be hurt in the worst way.'

'Do you need to talk to a professional?'

'Maybe I will soon. For now, I just need to make sense of things, alone.'

I watch Maxine moving across the grass, so carefully, as if she is afraid of hurting the earth.

'Try to stay together if you can, Sirad. Forgiveness is a

powerful thing. You'll realize that one day when you're old like me.' I always get the sense that Maxine has made peace with everything she is missing in life. Eventually she tells me she has some important calls to make, which marks the end of our walk.

'Have a good evening, darling,' she says as we walk to her bus stop. My heart sinks at the realization that our day together is over, and that I'll have to go back to the hotel alone. I know that deep in my heart, I love Maxine. I want to know if she loves me too, and more importantly, if she truly believes I am capable of overcoming everything that lies ahead. If only I could get her to say that to me once more – that she believes that I am good.

'OK,' I say weakly. 'I'll see you again soon?'

We part ways, waving until she gets onto the bus. I find myself alone again, back in the choppy waves of life, bobbing along with the current.

Chapter Twenty-Two

'Rise to the one who finds you sitting.'

Maxine dies a few days after our last encounter.
   In a state of shock, I attend her funeral, which has been organized by her sisters and a few library patrons and activists with whom she was very close. They asked me to help organize it with them, but I couldn't do it. I couldn't bear to be part of the process, because then I would have to accept that she was truly gone from the world. Saying goodbye to Maxine, even in the most sincere and heartfelt way, is too much for me to handle.

At the funeral, a man named Joe finds me sitting alone at the back and strikes up a conversation. He says that he went to school with Maxine and they remained good friends for decades. He believes she was too involved in the politics of the library for her own good, that her health deteriorated because of it, and that she should have retired years ago. I feel uneasy listening to him speak about her work in this way; I think Maxine was honoured to keep fighting. Her purpose was far greater than anyone at this funeral will ever realize. I think she saved that for herself.

It wasn't the campaigning that killed her. It was her

heartbreak when she realized that things weren't getting any better. It was the fact that she hid her suffering. No one knew she was battling cancer, not even her relatives. The results of the library's fate came down on her like a sledgehammer. Her job was gone. Her youthful spirit and vitality gone with it. In the days before she passed away, I left her many calls, and she didn't return a single one. I had a bad feeling that day in the park, but I didn't stop to explore it further.

Maxine died of loneliness, too. Few things are as poisonous as loneliness is on the body.

'She'll be with the angels,' says Joe at the end of the service. Everyone is already preparing to eat. I can't bear the thought of eating. Finding myself completely disarmed, I begin to cry. No words can capture the essence of Maxine's inimitable soul.

While in tears and desperate for a piece of tissue to clean up my face, it occurs to me that I can't find my bag. A few people attempt to search for it with me. As they look around, I begin to wonder if I showed up with a bag at all, and get angry at myself for somehow managing to make this about me.

I lag behind at the end and manage to find my bag hanging on the coat-rack by the door. I have no recollection of how I even entered the building in the first place. It's as though I floated straight from my nightmares to this room with its rotting wooden beams.

*

A few days later I find myself climbing up all the twenty-three flights of stairs up to my childhood home. The lift is broken. It has been over a year since I was last here. After the first few flights, I can feel the acid burning in my legs, so I stop and pause every so often. I must really be ageing, I think to myself, remembering how easy it used to be to fly up the stairs and home. Through the wide windows all the way up the staircase, I watch the ground disappear as I rise higher and higher.

Every now and then, no matter how I try to resist it, nostalgia rears one of its many heads. This time, it is the deceitful kind that makes even the hardest times seem like the best times of my life. Suddenly I'm craving my old bed and its poky mattress. I want to drink a cup of my mother's shaah and eat endless hot pieces of malowax with Ahmed while playing Ludo. In those days, peace and quiet, time to think – solitude – was a luxury. I crave the hard-earned moments when I'd lie down in bed and squeeze in a short nap. What's cruel about nostalgia is that there's often not much truth to it.

The closer I get to the twenty-third floor, the more I start to second-guess myself, not sure I'm ready to go inside. Fear and longing mix together. I open the front door and see the shimmery green curtains with the gold flecks, the ripped computer chair, the worn sofa covers and our dust-covered TV. The thick, stuffy smell in the room carries both a beauty and a suffocating sadness.

I find my bedroom exactly how I left it. The pastel-blue sheets are neatly folded on the end of the bed, the vases are empty, the bookshelf still holds the Judy Blume and Anne Fine books of my pre-teens. The walls are still a periwinkle blue, the paint not quite meeting the white door.

Down the corridor, through the living room and onto the balcony, the seasons of my life seem to flash before me. The chair on the balcony is now splattered with bird poo. Down below, the view has dramatically changed. No longer is there a barren stretch of land with weeds overtaking the concrete; instead there are brand new roads with neat hedges. Sleek new apartment blocks have sprung up, and I even spot a new cafe and spa. I can see people now, walking home in their work wear or gym clothes.

I gasp at the fact that I can now see the river. They have cleared the warehouses and trees to make space for the spectacular view. My eyes become hot with tears. How different life might have been if I could have gazed out to the river from my balcony over the years. With the muddy brown rocks on its bank and the scattered planks of wood. I'm convinced I would be a different person.

For the first time, I no longer feel like I am looking down on the edge of the world. The world has come to us.

With a large bin bag, I go through some of my old belongings to see what I can salvage. Old books, chipped mugs I received or bought as souvenirs, half-full bottles of perfume and skincare remain exactly where I left them. How naive I was, thinking I could escape this place.

I fill a glass with tap water and go to sit in the living room. Music comes through the walls from next door, but not the upbeat party music our neighbours used to play. This melody is a soulful, slow ballad I have never heard before. Maybe the old neighbours have moved too, I think. How can things change so much and yet still remain the same?

My tears feel corrosive. As a child, I thought tears came from the heart, filling it like a vase and only dripping from the eyes when they overflowed.

After crying, my eyes are blurry. I try to rub them but each swipe worsens my vision like a thickening mist. The grey light of the living room is changing colour, becoming purple as the sun begins to set. I have a warm feeling in my heart. A purple sunset stands for renewal; it stands for a long-awaited, weary victory. It also casts an enchanting iridescent light over everything in the living room. The music from next door stops abruptly and there is a knock on the front door. I sit still, pretending I haven't heard it. It's the wind, I reason.

There is a long gap before the knocking comes again. It is firm and intentional. I put my glass of water on the floor and stand up. Ahmed is working abroad and Hooyo on her farm in Somalia. No one else has visited us at this address in years.

Frozen to the spot, I hear the sound of the door opening and the whistle of the wind flowing through. I look down at my body. Maybe if I curl into a tight ball on the floor, I can protect myself. I don't have a single cell left in my body willing to fight.

A male figure stands in the dark corridor. For a moment, I almost call out for my father. The realization whips me across my heart – it's Omar. I jump at the sight of him, my heart lurching up to my throat.

'I've been calling you for days,' he says softly. 'I thought you might be here.' He moves towards me, but I don't get any closer. 'I called and I called, and you never picked up. I called your family and then I called Maxine. I'm embarrassed!'

'Maxine died!' My hysterical voice catches us both off guard. 'She's never coming back!' I cry into my hands.

Omar charges across the room, taking my shaking body into his arms. He picks me up effortlessly and sits us down on the sofa, still holding me in a tight embrace.

'I'm really sorry,' he says. 'Why didn't you answer my calls? Even just once?'

I shake my head. 'Omar, I couldn't face you. I don't know what to say to you.'

'What do you mean? You're still my wife and I love you. Just come back home and we can forget this ever happened.'

'I found the pictures on your camera. Of the girl and the woman. Who are they, Omar?'

His eyebrows seem to twist into a knot. 'I had a feeling you knew something, but I was afraid to ask.'

'I know about the UNCLASSIFIED project and the buses. I know it very well. I just want to know who the woman is.'

He draws in a sharp breath. 'How do you know about it?'

'I was once invited. Years ago.'

'So you understand it, then? You know how it feels? How someone can get caught up in that stuff and want to hide it . . .'

'I know, I know.' I cut him off. 'It's not just that, though. It's *everything*. It's the woman on your camera. Who is she?'

'That's my sister, Sirad. I promise, I'll share everything. Just, please, come home . . .'

'What's the point? We failed each other. *So miserably*, Omar. We've both kept big secrets from each other.'

Even in the fading light, the hurt is clear on his face. 'You say the craziest things, Sirad, and you expect me to just follow along. What do you even mean? We've failed according to what?' I feel him take a gulp of air. 'There's always a chance for us to be more honest and try again. I'm asking you to take that chance with me.'

'She's really your sister?'

'Yes. It turns out that my parents had a daughter who was raised by my grandmother. I didn't know until I crossed over.'

'Why didn't you tell me you were crossing over in the first place?'

'I assume for the same reason you've never told me. Where do you even start with sharing something like that? Do you think I ever wanted to risk you seeing me as some kind of freak?'

'I don't know,' I moan, like a caricature of a sorry child. 'I don't know what I want from you.'

I push myself up from Omar's arms and turn away from him, somewhat embarrassed. The last of the purple sunlight is slowly shrinking from the room.

'Don't overthink it,' he says, putting a hand against my back. 'Let's stop overthinking. It's already destroyed us.'

Turning to face him, I look intently at his smile, his eyes, the curve of his perfect nose. In no time at all, he hugs me tight. His eyes are slightly wider than normal, as if he has been in a prolonged state of shock. The sense of abandonment in them strikes me. I want him to squeeze me against his chest until I disappear into it. I want to fill the void in him, whatever it is void of, with my entire being.

'Years ago, before I met you, I went to see my double,' I tell him. 'Her name is Ubah. After that, she tried to cross over and figure things out here, but it didn't work for her. And it was because of me. I was greedy and stupid. I snitched on her and I have never forgiven myself.'

'I'm sure you were only doing what you thought was right.'

'I went to see her again recently. After I saw the photos on your phone. She hasn't forgiven me.'

'You did what? You crossed over?!' Omar's voice rises in disbelief. 'Don't you know how dangerous that is?'

'You would know! You do it all the time!'

'You know what? I'm done with all of it. I'll quit the teaching job,' says Omar firmly.

'Why?' I reply haltingly. 'It's your passion!'

'It's also dangerous. I don't want to lose you. I don't want us to sneak around any more. Let's both put it behind us.'

'How can I? I can't get Ubah out of my mind. After seeing her in that state . . .'

'Aha. That makes sense. I feel like I finally understand why you won't just let yourself be happy. If what happened to Ubah makes you feel like you don't deserve to be at peace, I'm letting you know that you deserve it anyway. You deserve it more than you know.'

I'm shocked into silence by Omar's words. In a matter of

moments, they have freed me from a force that has held me hostage for years.

I am silent for a long time, and Omar's body becomes completely still against mine. Eventually, I realize he has fallen asleep. The sound of his soft snores slowly sends me to sleep after him.

We awake on the sofa a few hours later. Omar stands up, quietly lifting his coat over his shoulders.

'Where are you going?' I ask sleepily.

'I'm going to sit in my car, turn on the radio and just listen to the seven o'clock news. And I'm going to leave you here. But I'm going to give you a choice. If, by the time I've finished listening to the radio, you've joined me in the car, then we'll drive home together. And if not, if you decide to stay here, I'll leave on my own and we can call this the end.'

I pull myself up and rub at my eyes. He walks over to me and kisses me carefully on the forehead, his tenderness sending a shiver down my spine. Then he walks away, along the corridor and out of the front door.

I don't get up to follow him. Instead, I think back to the wedding hall the night that I met Omar. In my mind's eye, I watch myself sitting there, waiting. At the time, I couldn't figure out what I was waiting for, but somehow, I was sure that it was going to find me. It was one of the few times in my life that I had given in to believing that things were going to be OK, a kind of intuition. I just had to sit there, and soon enough it would be OK.

I never fully realized the role that the rain had played that night. How I was forced by nature to get up and run back inside the wedding hall as I felt the raindrops fall. It was by chance that I was thrust into Omar's arms. I recall how I decided, with uncharacteristic confidence, to slide under his umbrella, and how he let me; how we dodged the judging eyes. He introduced himself as if he had been rehearsing the lines his whole life.

As we talked, he didn't ask why I had my eyes closed; instead he just kept talking, as if we had known each other for years. For some reason I found the entire situation so funny that I started laughing. He joined in, his laughter much louder than mine and full of heart. Each time I snorted, his roars of laughter echoed down the empty road.

We walked together and despite the cold, wet weather, he insisted on us getting ice cream. And that was that.

Eventually, pulling myself from my daze, I begin to clean the flat. I scrub the floors on my hands and knees. I change all the dusty bedding and open the windows. I'm in desperate need of a change of clothing. I have taken for granted the idea that life plays out in the same way it begins. Here I am, back in my childhood home, scrubbing the toilets as if it's a Sunday morning.

I get myself a glass of water. My mother's room is the last one I clean. Then I hoist myself up onto the window sill and look down at the parking area. There, in the spot where my father's car used to sit, is Omar's car. In that car is a man who once offered me ice cream in the rain. I am astonished that he's still there. It has been hours. I smell bad – I can't go anywhere like this, I think. I need to take a shower. I need to scrub myself anew. But perhaps it's too late.

The outcome of my actions no longer matters as I surrender to the life that lies before me, whatever it may be. When I finish my shower, I find myself hurrying through the door. I run down all twenty-three flights. Someone is starting up their car engine. Maybe it's Omar. Or maybe it's somebody else. The closer I get to the bottom, the less afraid I feel. I'm ready to go home. I'm ready to give myself to the unknown current of fate with my eyes closed.

Acknowledgements

This book is the culmination of years of dreams, doubts and vision that demanded patience and courage. I am profoundly grateful to everyone who helped me bring it to life.

I want to say a special thank you to my agent, John Baker. Your 'yes' changed my life. Your acceptance and effortless understanding of what I was trying to achieve with my book was incredibly affirming. I want to thank the judges at the Future Worlds Prize for seeing something special in those first three chapters. I had a good feeling that walking into that awards night, after years of waiting and painful rejection, would lead to something worthwhile.

Thank you to the stellar team at Mantle and Pan Macmillan for making this such a fun and easy experience. To my editor, Kinza Azira, who just gets me, page after page. To Kim for her warmth and support; to Maria, Charlotte, Jodie, Carol-Anne and all the rest of the team who delved into my story in earnest – you don't know much that means to me. As I write this, I know my proof edits are well overdue. Thank you to Rosa Watmough for your incredible patience and understanding. Editing can be excruciating, but working with you has been a dream.

Acknowledgements

I want to thank the community who uplifted me through the years of writing and trying to find my way. Those Sunday afternoons surrounded by fellow writers at Literary Natives events were precious, and I often feel my soul trying to crawl back. Nothing beats the connection made between people who share the same joy and struggle. Thank you to my friends who spoke life into me, especially Hafza Yusuf. As an artist and as a Somali woman, you knew my journey intimately.

I want to thank my parents, to whom this book is dedicated. You taught me how to stand apart from everyone around me and be an individual. Without that, I wouldn't have become a writer. You nourished me physically and spiritually. To the rest of my siblings and family, I did this for you all.

And finally, to my husband. Your unwavering support has been my anchor through the long days of editing. Your boundless love and care make me believe that I can do anything.